DELILAH MARVELLE

Forever a Lady

D1019741

H HARLEQUIN®

entertain, enrich, inspire™

Recycling programs
for this product may
not exist in your area.

ISBN-13: 978-0-373-77646-7

FOREVER A LADY

Copyright © 2012 by Delilah Marvelle

www.Harlequin.com

Printed in U.S.A.

Dear Reader,

Everyone deserves a second chance at life. Especially when at the core of who and what they are, they define all things good. Sometimes, life cheats us out of opportunities we deserve. But even then, we have the right to dream and to be more than what everyone expects from us. Such is the story of Matthew Joseph Milton. Educated, dashing and a true gentleman at heart, he finds that being a good man simply isn't enough to survive in a world looking to take everything away from you. So what do you do in an effort to fight back? You redefine yourself, even at the cost of yourself. In that, Matthew and Bernadette are the same (without knowing it). They both had to redefine themselves, only to discover that they buried far too much. *Forever a Lady* is my twisted version of *Newsies*. Only, I'm going with buff, older men toting pistols, instead of boys toting newspapers. It is my hope you will enjoy the searing passion Matthew and Bernadette learn to share not only for each other but for life as they return to who and what they really are. I feel blessed enough to speak from experience when I say, there is no better happily-ever-after than finding yourself *and* the love of your life.

Much love,

Delilah Marvelle

To my sister, Yvonne.
In honor of Once Upon a Time.

PROLOGUE

Survival, gentlemen. Life is all about survival.
> —*The Truth Teller, a New York Newspaper for
> Gentlemen*

*June 1822
New York City—Orange Street*

When it had been uncovered that their bookkeeper and longtime friend, Mr. Richard Rawson, was actually a money-pilfering son of a mudsill, Matthew and his father had sent the authorities straight to Rawson's house to make an arrest. Rawson, realizing he was about to hang, saddled a horse and galloped off, leaving behind a clutter of furniture and foppish clothing worth a sliver of nothing. The rest of the money taken from coffers of the Milton newspaper—two thousand dollars of it—Rawson had long since squandered on gambling and countless whores, whose extravagant tastes included every imaginable trinket known to please female humanity.

When armed marshals had finally cornered that bastard just off Broadway and Bowling Green Park, it was there, before all of New York City, Rawson's own horse heroically intervened by rearing up on its hind legs. Rawson's neck snapped from the toss and the man was pronounced dead, right along with the once-thriving Milton newspaper, *The Truth Teller,* which had sunk into bankruptcy.

If only such men could die twice. Perhaps then Matthew Joseph Milton would have felt some sense of justice knowing that he and his father, who both had once owned said newspaper and been worth a good three hundred a year, were now worth only eight dollars and forty-two cents.

Lingering beside his father on the street curb of their new neighborhood, Matthew tightened his fingers on the rough wool of the sacks weighing each shoulder. He stared up at that looming unpainted building, the acrid stench of piss lacing the heat-ridden air.

Could the good Lord truly be this cruel?

Oh, yes. Yes, He could be, and yes, He was.

The sweltering heat of the afternoon sun pierced Matthew's furrowed brow, beading lines of moisture down his temples. Shirtless men lounged with dirt-crusted bare feet on the sills of open windows, some guzzling bottles of old Irish whiskey, while others leisurely smoked half-cut cigars. It was as if these bingo boys all thought they were on a blanket on the grassy plains of a lake. One of the bearded men in the window directly above him menacingly held his gaze, leaned over and loudly spat. A large pool of thick brown saliva slapped the pavement half a foot away.

The man had been aiming for him.

Matthew glanced toward his father, who still held a crate of newspapers from the print shop. "Was, uh, this the best your associate could do for us? I would think a much bigger discount would have been in order."

His father, Raymond Charles Milton, slowly shook his head, those silvering strands of chestnut-colored hair swaying as he, too, surveyed the building. It was obvious his father was no more prepared to enter the building than he was.

One of them had to be optimistic. Matthew nudged the man with whatever assurance he could muster. "It could be worse. We could be sitting in debtors' prison."

His father gave him a withering look.

Matthew paused as a boy of about six or seven, whose brown matted hair hung into his eyes, wandered past in billowing clothing and large boots. The boy shuffle-shuffle-shuffled in an effort to keep those boots on his small feet.

Upon seeing Matthew, the child jerked to a halt, that oversized linen shirt that came down to his trouser-clad knees swaying against his lanky frame. The boy lingered before them, those large brown eyes quietly scanning Matthew's cravat and embroidered vest as if assessing their worth.

One day, Matthew knew he'd have a house full of children just like this one. One day. Though he certainly hoped that by that day, he could afford to dress his children a bit better than this child was dressed. Matthew couldn't help but smile. "And how are you today, sir? Good?"

The boy's eyes widened. He edged back and back and then sprinted past and across the street, stumbling several times in those oversized boots.

His father bumped Matthew with the crate. "What did you do?"

"Nothing. All I did was ask how he was. He mustn't be used to people being...friendly."

They fell into silence.

The clopping and clacking of carts and the occasional profanity and shouts of men from down the street reminded them that they weren't on Barclay Street anymore. No more vast treed square, no more pristine lacquered carriages or elegant men and women of the merchant classes. Only this.

"I should have never entrusted Rawson," his father confided in a strained tone. "Because of me, you have nothing. Not even a prospect of marriage. If it weren't for me, you would have been married to Miss Drake by now."

Matthew whipped both sacks to the pavement at hearing that woman's name. "I can do with the poverty, Da. I can do with the stench and everything that goes with it, but what I can't do with is listening to you blather as if this was your goddamn fault. To hell with Miss bloody Drake. If she had loved me, as I had stupidly loved her, she would have followed me here. Like I had asked her to."

His father paused and eyed him. "Would *you* have followed yourself here?"

Matthew hissed out a breath, trying not to let it hurt knowing he had meant so little to her. "I'm only twenty,

Da. I have my whole life ahead of me. One day, I'll find myself a good woman capable of respecting me, no matter my financial worth."

His father dug into his vest pocket, balancing the crate on his hip. "God bless you, Matthew, for always making the best out of even the worst." He tossed him a quarter. "Buy us something to eat. And try to ration it. We have yet to find jobs. I'll go settle us in. Hand up those sacks, will you?"

Matthew snatched both up from the pavement and stacked them atop the crate. His father tucked the upper wool sack beneath his chin and strode through the open doorway, angling himself up the narrow stairwell.

Puffing out a breath, Matthew swung toward the dirt road, scanning the wide street of squat buildings plastered with crooked wooden plaques. Unevenly stacked crates of browning fruit and half-rotten vegetables sat unattended alongside open doors. A floating swarm of insects hovered in unison over one crate of food before darting to the next. It was as if the insects themselves were questioning the quality at hand.

He already missed their cook.

A strangled sob made his gaze jerk toward a commotion just across the street. A russet-haired gent in a frayed shirt and patched trousers held a boy roughly by the hair, shaking him.

Matthew drew in a breath. It was the boy with the oversized boots.

As a coal cart trudged past, the unshaven giant leaned down, shaking the boy by the hair again and again, saying something. The boy sobbed with each violent agitation, stumbling in an effort to remain upright.

Matthew fisted the quarter his father had given him. He'd never formally boxed, but he sure as hell wasn't about to stand by and watch this. Tucking the quarter into his inner vest pocket, Matthew dodged past women carrying woven baskets and dashed across the unpaved street toward them.

"Tell your whore of a mother," the man seethed, "that I want me money and I want it now. She owes me fifteen cents. *Fifteen!*"

"She don't have it!" the boy wailed, grabbing at his head.

Matthew jerked to a halt beside them, his pulse roaring. He tried to remain calm, lest this turn into a brawl the child didn't need to see. "Let him go. I'll pay whatever his mother owes."

A sweat-sleeked, sunburned round face jerked toward him. The stench of rotting cabbage penetrated the stagnant air. The man shoved the boy away and stepped toward him, that rather well-fed thick frame towering a head over Matthew's own. "She owes me twenty cents."

The bastard. "I heard fifteen." Matthew dug into his waistcoat pocket. "But here is what I'll do." Matthew held up the quarter his father had given him. "I'll give you an extra ten cents to leave off this boy from here on out. You do that, and this is yours."

The man hesitated, then reached out a calloused hand. Grabbing the quarter, he shoved it into his own pocket. "That be fine with me. He's got nothing I want. His hag of a mother be the problem."

"Then I suggest you take it up with her. Not him." Matthew veered toward the child, bent down toward him and nudged up that small chin. "Ey. Are you all right?"

The boy pedaled back, tears still clinging to those flushed cheeks. He nodded, touching his small hands to his head.

The man grabbed Matthew's arm and pulled him back toward himself. With a smirk, he fluffed Matthew's white linen cravat. "Rather fancy and all, aren't you? I know I've always wanted me one of these."

Matthew jerked back, out of reach, and narrowed his gaze. "I suggest you leave."

The man lowered his unshaven chin and tightened his own penetrating gaze, those fuzzy red brows creeping together. Raising a thick hand, the man now tilted a sharp blade toward Matthew's face, the metal glinting against the sun. He leaned in and tapped its smooth edge on Matthew's cheek. "Are you going to take it off? Or would you rather I slice it off?"

It was unbelievable. Barely twenty minutes in these parts and he was being robbed for assisting a child. Fisting both hands, lest he jump and get sliced, Matthew offered in a low, even tone, "Put away the knife and we'll talk."

A full-knuckled fist slammed into his head. Matthew gasped in disbelief against the teetering impact.

The man casually tossed the blade to his other thick hand, announcing that the worst was yet to come. "I say what goes. Now take it off, lest the boy sees something he oughtn't."

Shifting his jaw, Matthew grudgingly unraveled the linen. He wasn't stupid. Sliding it off, he wordlessly held it out.

The man snatched it away, wrapping it smugly around his own thick neck, and stepped back, tucking away his blade. "Next time, do as I say."

As if he was going to wait for a next time. Knowing the blade was out of the game, Matthew gritted his teeth and jumped forward, throwing out a straight-faced punch.

The giant grabbed his fist in midair, causing Matthew's arm to pop back from the swift contact of his large palm.

That gaze threatened. "You're dead." A blow hit Matthew's skull, jaw, nose and eye in such rapid fire, his leather boots skidded against the pavement with each teeth-jarring wallop.

Matthew jumped forward again, viciously swinging back at the bastard, but only decked air as the giant dodged.

The boy beside them swung his own small fists in the air, stumbling left and right and shouted up at Matthew, "*Come on!* Pound the dickey dazzler. *Pound him!*"

A brick of an unexpected whack to his left eye not only made Matthew rear back, but made everything in sight fade to a hazy white. Jesus Christ. He caught himself against a lamppost, his bare hands sliding against the sun-warmed iron.

"Enough!" a man boomed, stilling the boy's shouts. No blows followed.

Drawing in shaky, ragged breaths, Matthew squinted to see past the sweltering pain pulsing through his face and skull.

A broad figure with long black hair tied in a queue, garbed in a patched great coat, held a pistol to the side of Matthew's assailant's head. "Give this respectable man his cravat, James," the man casually offered in an educated New York accent that was laced with a bit of European sophistication. "And while you're at it, give him your blade."

The russet-haired oaf froze against the barrel of that pistol set against his head. His grubby hand patted and pulled out the blade, extending it *and* the cravat to Matthew.

Pushing away from the lamppost, Matthew tugged his morning coat back into place, trying to focus beyond the heaviness and blur that clouded his one eye. He reached out, his arm seemingly floating and slid the scrap of linen toward himself.

"Take the blade," the man with the pistol ordered.

Matthew didn't want the blade, but he also didn't want to argue with a man holding a pistol. In his opinion, they were all mad. He blinked, trying to refocus. Though he could see where the men stood in proximity to him, an eerie dense shadow lingered, making him feel as if he were seeing the world on an angle. Matthew took the blade.

Pressing the pistol harder against his assailant's temple, the man gritted out, "If you touch either of them again, James, we go knuckle to knuckle over at the docks until one of us is dead. *Now, brass off.*"

James darted, shoving past others, and disappeared.

The man jerked toward the child. "Away with you, Ronan. And for God's sake, stay out of trouble."

The boy hesitated. Meeting Matthew's gaze, he grinned crookedly, his brown eyes brightening. "I owe you a quarter." Still grinning, he swung away and thudded down the street in those oversized boots.

Matthew huffed out a breath in exasperation. At least he got the boy to smile, because he doubted he'd ever see that quarter again.

Lowering the pistol and methodically uncocking it, the man before him adjusted his billowing great coat. Piercing ice-blue eyes held his. "Where the hell did you learn how to mill? At a female boarding school?"

Matthew self-consciously stuffed the cravat into his coat pocket, his hand trembling at the realization that the dense shadow in his eye remained. "Where I come from, boxing isn't really a requirement." He fingered the wooden handle of the blade still weighing his hand. "I appreciate your assistance."

"I'm certain you do." The man waved the pistol toward Matthew's embroidered vest. "Nice waistcoat. Sell it. Because fancy won't matter for shite when you're in a grave, and I'm telling you right now, it's only a matter of time before you get robbed of it. Now, go. Off with you."

Matthew hesitated, sensing this man wasn't like the rest of these rumpots. He held out a quick hand. The one that wasn't holding the blade. "The name is Matthew Joseph Milton."

The man shoved his pistol into the leather belt attached to his hips. "I didn't ask for your name. I told you to go."

Matthew still held it out. "I'm trying to be friendly."

"I don't do friendly, and in case you haven't noticed, no one else here does, either."

Matthew awkwardly dropped his hand to his side. "Is there anything I can do for you? Given what you just did for me? I insist."

"You insist?" That dark brow lifted. "Well. I could use a meal and whiskey, seeing I'm between matches."

"Done." Matthew paused. "Matches? You box?"

The man shrugged. "Bare-knuckle prizefighting." He patted the leather belt and pistol. "This isn't me being lazy. It ensures I don't injure myself during training. An injury means I don't box. And if I don't box, I don't eat."

"Ah. Isn't bare-knuckle prizefighting...*illegal?*"

The man stared him down. "I'll have you know the bastards who publicly go about condemning my fights are usually the same ones merrily throwing big money at it. I've already had three politicians and two marshals try to buy me out for a win. So, no. It isn't illegal. Not whilst they're doing it."

Knowing a professional boxer in these parts would be a good thing. A *very* good thing. "And what is your name, sir?"

The man shifted his stubbled jaw. "I have several names. Which one do you want?"

How nice. It appeared this man was involved in all sorts of illegal activities. "Give me the one that I won't get arrested for knowing."

"Coleman. Edward Coleman. Not to be confused with the *other* Edward Coleman running about these parts, who by the by, is murder waiting to happen. Stay away from that imp of Satan."

"Uh...I will. Thank you."

Coleman pointed at him. "I suggest you learn the rules of the ward. Especially given that you appear to be a do-gooder. 'Tis simple really—don't overdress, and always carry a weapon."

"I will heed that." Matthew held out the blade weighing his hand. "Except the weapon bit. Here. I'm not about to—"

Grabbing his wrist, Coleman yanked it forcefully upward, jerking the sharp tip of that steel toward Matthew's face.

Matthew froze, his gaze snapping to those ice-blue eyes.

The smell of leather penetrated the air between them.

Coleman smirked and let the blade playfully scrape the skin on the curve of Matthew's chin. "You ought to keep it. You never know when you'll need it to slice... *vegetables.*" He released his hold, allowing Matthew to lower the dagger. "I'll teach you how to use a blade, how to box and do a few other fancy things in exchange for meals."

Matthew self-consciously tightened his grip on the

blade. "I know how to use a blade. One simply points and—"

Coleman jumped toward him. With a quick hard hit to the wrist and a jab and twist, the blade clanged to the pavement. Coleman kicked the blade away with his whitened leather boot and eyed him. "Lessons for food."

Food wasn't going to be all that useful if he was dead. "Agreed."

ONE MOMENT MATTHEW WAS silently and miserably eating cold, mucky stew at a splinter-infested table with his father and Coleman, and the next, the left side of his world edged into piercing darkness.

Matthew's spoon slid from his fingers and clattered past the table, dropping against the uneven wooden floorboards. Oh, God. His throat tightened as he blinked rapidly, glancing about in disbelief. His peripheral was...*gone*. Black!

His father lowered his wooden spoon. "What is it?"

Coleman ceased eating midchew.

"I can't see." Matthew scrambled out of his chair and stumbled. He fell back against the doorless cupboard behind him with a thud. "I can't see from my left eye!" He scanned the small, barren tenement, only able to make out the uneven plastered walls to his right.

His father jumped toward him. "Matthew, look at me." Grabbing his shoulders, his father firmly angled him closer. "Are you certain? That eye is still swollen."

Matthew placed trembling fingertips against it. He

could feel his fingers grazing and touching the lashes of his open eye, but dearest God, he couldn't see them. "Everything to the left is black. Why? Why is it…" He dragged in uneven breaths, unable to say anything more. Nor could he think.

Coleman slowly rose to his booted feet. "Christ. It's from the blows."

Matthew turned his head to better see Coleman. "What do you mean, it's from the blows? That doesn't make any sense. How can a few—"

"I've seen it in boxing, Milton. One man I knew took so many hits in one match, he went blind within a week."

Matthew's breaths now came in gasps. It had been a week.

Shaking his head, Coleman grabbed his great coat from the back of the chair. "I'm hunting that prick down."

Despite his panic of being half-blind, Matthew choked out, "Hunting him down isn't going to change anything."

"This isn't about changing anything." Coleman stalked toward him. "It's about sending a message on what is and isn't acceptable."

His father pushed and guided Matthew toward the door. "If this is what you say it is, Coleman, the first thing we need is a surgeon. *Now!*"

"There is one over on Hudson." Coleman wedged past them and yanked open the paneled door leading to the corridor. "Though, I really don't know what the man will be able to do."

THE LAST OF THEIR MONEY was gone. And so was the vision in Matthew's left eye. He fingered the leather patch that had been tied over his unseeing eye by the surgeon who had pronounced it permanently blind. The surgeon agreed with Coleman, stating that the blows he'd sustained had something to do with it, which meant he, Matthew Joseph Milton, was going to be a one-eyed, poverty-stricken freak for the rest of his days.

Gritting his teeth, Matthew jumped up from the crate of newspapers he'd been sitting on, whipped around and slammed a knuckled fist into the wall. He kept slamming and slamming and slamming his fist until he had not only punched his way through the plaster and the wooden lattice buried beneath, but felt his knuckles getting soft.

"Matthew!" His father jumped toward him, jerking back his arm, and yanked him away from the wall.

Matthew couldn't breathe as he met his father's gaze.

His father rigidly held up the hand, making Matthew look at the swelling welts, scrapes and blood now slathering it. "Don't let vile anger overtake the heart within. *Don't.*"

Matthew pulled his hand away, which now throbbed in agony. He swallowed, trying to compose himself, and glanced toward Coleman, who still hadn't said a word since he'd been pronounced blind by the surgeon.

Coleman eventually said, "I'm sorry for all of this." Pushing away from the wall he'd been leaning against, he continued in a dark tone, "Assault, as well as murder, rape and everything else imaginable, is so commonplace here, not even the marshals can keep up with it. Which is why, even with my boxing skills, I *always* carry a pistol. These bastards don't bow to anything else."

Matthew shook his head in disbelief. "If the marshals can't keep up with it, it means there isn't enough muscle to go around. It's obvious some sort of watch has to be put together using local men."

Coleman puffed out a breath. "Most of these men don't even know how to read, let alone think properly enough to do the right thing. It would be like inviting a herd of unbroken stallions into your stable and asking them to line up for a saddle. Believe me, I've tried to round up men. They only want to fend for themselves."

"Then we will find better men." Matthew flexed his hand, trying to push away the throbbing and angst writhing within him. "Though, I should probably invest in a pistol first. How much does a pistol cost anyway?"

"Matthew." His father set a hand on his arm. "You cannot be taking justice into your hands like this. 'Tis an idea that will see you arrested or, worse yet, *killed.*"

Matthew edged toward his father. "In my opinion, I'm already in manacles. And if I die, it will be on my terms, Da, not theirs. I don't know what the hell needs to be done here, but I'm not doing it sitting on a crate filled with whatever is left of your goddamn newspaper."

Those taut features sagged. His father released his arm with a half nod, and quietly rounded him, leaving the room.

Realizing he'd been stupid and harsh, Matthew called out after him. "I'm sorry, Da. I didn't mean that."

"I deserve it," his father called back. "I do."

"No, you—" Matthew swiped his face and paused, his fingers grazing the leather patch. God. His life was a mess.

"A good pistol costs ten to fifteen dollars," Coleman provided. "Not including the lead you'd need."

Matthew winced. "Gut me already. I can't afford that."

"I never bought mine."

Matthew angled his head to better see him. "What do you mean? Where did you get it?"

Coleman quirked a dark brow. "Are you really that naive?"

Matthew stared and then rasped, "You mean, you stole it?"

Coleman strode toward him, set a hand on his shoulder and leaned in. "It's only stealing, Milton, if you do it for your own gain or if you never give it back. Do you know how many people I've saved with this here pistol? Countless. I doubt God is going to be punishing me anytime soon. If you want a pistol, we'll go get you one. A good one."

Matthew held that gaze. Mad though it was, this man was on to something momentous. Something that, Matthew knew, was about to change not only his life but the lives of others.

CHAPTER ONE

The city inspector reports the death of 118 persons
during this ending week. 31 men, 24 women and
63 children.
>   —*The Truth Teller, a New York Newspaper for*
>   *Gentlemen*

Eight years later
New York City—Squeeze Gut Alley, evening

THE SOUND OF HOOVES thudding against the dirt road in
the far distance beyond the dim, gaslit street made Matthew snap up a hand to signal his men, who all quietly
lurked across the street. The five he'd chosen out of his
group of forty, strategically spread apart, one by one,
backing into the shadows of narrow doorways.

Still watching the street, Matthew yanked out both
pistols from his leather belts. Setting his jaw, he edged
back into the shadows beside Coleman before whispering in riled annoyance, "Where the hell is Royce?"

Coleman leaned toward him and whispered back,

"You know damn well that bastard only follows his own orders."

"Yes, well, we're about to show that no-name marshal how to do his job. *Again.*"

"Now, now, don't get ahead of yourself, Milton. We've got nothing yet. We're all standing outside a brothel that appears to be out of business, and most of our informants are worth less than shite."

"Thank you for always pointing out the obvious, Coleman."

They fell into silence.

A blurred movement approached and a wooden cart with two barrels rolled up to the curb, pulled by a single ragged-looking horse. A large-boned man sat on the dilapidated seat of the cart, his head covered with a wool sack whose eyes had been crudely cut out. The man hopped down from the cart, adjusting the sack on his head. Glancing around, he pulled out a butcher knife and hurried toward the back of the cart.

Justice was about to pierce Five Points. Because if this didn't look nefarious enough to jump on, Matthew didn't know what nefarious was anymore. Pointing both pistols at the man's head, Matthew strode out of the shadows and into the street toward him. "You. Drop the knife. Do it. *Now.*"

The man froze as Coleman, Andrews, Cassidy, Kerner, Bryson and Plunkett all stepped out of the shadows and also pointed pistols, surrounding him.

The wool-masked man swung toward Matthew, tossing his knife toward the pavement with a clatter and held up both ungloved hands. "I'm delivering oats.

You can't shoot me for that." His clipped, gruff accent reeked of all things British.

Cassidy rounded the cart, his scarred face appearing in the glow from the gaslight before disappearing into the shadows again as his giant physique stalked toward the man. "Oats, my arse. You Brits seem to always think you're above the law. Much like the Brit who had the gall to slit me face." Cassidy paused before the man. He yanked the wool sack off that head and whipped it aside, revealing beady eyes and a balding head. Cassidy cocked his pistol with a metal click and growled out, "I say we kill this feck and send England a message."

Matthew bit back the need to jump forward and backhand Cassidy. This was exactly what happened when an Irishman had too much justice boiling his blood. He fought against *everyone*. And woe to the man who also happened to be British. If it weren't for the fact that Cassidy was dedicated to the cause and would fight with his own teeth to the end for it, Matthew would have booted him long ago.

Veering closer to Cassidy, Matthew hardened his voice. "This has nothing to do with England or your face. So calm the hell down. We don't need dead bodies or the marshals on our arses."

Cassidy hissed out a breath but otherwise said nothing.

"Check the barrels," Matthew called out to Coleman.

Tucking away both pistols, Coleman jogged over to the cart and, with a swing of his long legs, jumped up onto the back of it. Angling toward the two wooden barrels, Coleman pried each one open, tossing aside both lids with a clatter. He glanced up, his chiseled grim face dimly lit by the gas lamp beyond. "They're both here."

A breath escaped Matthew.

Bending over each barrel, Coleman dug his hands in and hefted out a young girl of no more than eight, gagged and roped, along with another young girl of about equal age. He set each onto bare feet. Using a razor, Coleman sliced off the ropes and removed their gags.

Choked sobs escaped the girls as they jumped toward each other, clinging. The lopsided wool gowns they wore were crudely stitched and most likely not what they had been wearing when they had been taken from the orphanage.

Matthew's throat tightened. He knew that if not for the interference of him and his men, these two girls, who had disappeared from the orphanage all but earlier that week, would have been sold to a brothel. Shoving his pistols into his leather belt, Matthew gestured toward the balding man. "Rope this prick up before I do."

The man shoved past Kerner and Plunkett, and darted, running down the street.

Shite! All of Matthew's muscles instinctively reacted as he sprinted after the man, leveling his limited vision.

"I told you we should have killed him!" Cassidy boomed after him. "What good are pistols if we never use them?"

"Everyone *move!*" Matthew yelled back, running faster. "Spread out! Coleman, stay with the girls!"

Matthew refocused on the shadowed figure who was already halfway down the street, those thick legs splashing through muddy puddles as his cloak flapped against the wind blowing in.

Matthew pumped his legs and arms faster and sped into the darkness. Through the sparse light of the moon and passing lampposts, Matthew could see the man repeatedly glancing back, his self-assured run turning into a jogging stagger as the balding man huffed and puffed in an effort to keep moving.

The man wasn't used to running.

The man was used to the cart.

And this was where he, Matthew, who did nothing but run for a damn living, brought an end to the bastard's grand delusions of escape. Closing the remaining distance between them, and just before a narrow alleyway between two buildings, Matthew reached out and grabbed the man hard by the collar of his cloak.

Gritting his teeth, Matthew flung his body against that hefty frame, knocking them both down and into the mud with a skidding halt, spraying water and thick sludge everywhere.

As they rolled, Matthew used his weight to stay on top, shoving the man back down. The bastard punched up at him, hurling frantic blows that rammed Matthew's shoulders and chest.

Holding the man down with a rigid forearm that trembled against that resisting body, Matthew swung down a clenched fist, thwacking him in the head, sending his balding head bouncing against the mud beneath. "Stand down, you son of a bitch! Stand down before I—"

"We got him!" Bryson yelled, pushing in and setting a quick knee against the man's throat.

In between ragged breaths, Matthew scrambled up to his booted feet. He staggered back, feeling mud sloughing off his arms and trouser-clad thighs.

Cassidy skidded in, spraying more mud and shoved aside Bryson's knee. "I'll bloody show you how things are done over in Ireland."

Effortlessly jerking the man up and out of the mud, Cassidy swung a vicious arm around his throat, causing the man to gag and stagger. Bryson scrambled over with the rope.

Once the man's arms were tightly roped against his sides, Kerner jumped forward and, with a growl, delivered a swinging fist into the man's gut. "*That's* for every girl you ever touched, you feck!" He swung back his arm and delivered another blow, causing the man to gasp and stagger against the ropes. "You think you can—" Kerner jumped forward again and punched that face, a pop resounding through the night air.

"*Kerner!*" Matthew boomed.

Kerner stumbled back and swung away, his chest heaving.

Matthew swallowed, trying to calm the chaotic beat of his own heart. Despite the reprimand, Matthew knew all too well that Kerner, who had lost his twelve-year-old daughter to a brutal rape and murder just down this very street six years earlier, was relatively calm given the situation.

Sadly, a deeply rooted need to right the wrongs that had been committed against them was what had brought each and every one of them together. Their grief had become his own grief. They all struggled with anger. "I know this isn't easy for you. Breathe."

Kerner swiped at his bearded face with a trembling hand. "Aye. I'm sorry." As if lurching out of a trance, he said, "Tend to those girls. Coleman is probably scaring the piss out of them."

"Ah, leave off the man. He's not as rough as he lets on." Matthew flung off whatever mud he could from his hands and jogged his way back down the street until he reached the cart. "We got him," he called out to Coleman, who was bent over the cart, waiting for the verdict.

Coleman huffed out a breath. "Good."

Heading toward the back of the cart, Matthew leaned against the uneven planks of wood. Neither barefooted girl was crying anymore—thank God—but both were still tucked against the barrels they'd been removed from, huddling against each other.

Coleman gestured toward the two. "You should probably take over. They don't seem to like me. Or my stories."

Hopefully the man hadn't been sharing the wrong sort of stories. Swiping his muddied hands against his linen shirt, Matthew held out both hands toward them and gently urged, "All of us are here to help. My name is Matthew and this gent beside you is Edward. Now. I want you both to be brave and ignore the mud and the scary eye patch. Can you be brave enough to trust me? Just this once?"

They stared, still clinging to each other.

Matthew lowered his hands and smiled in an effort to win them over. "Tell me what you want me to do and I'll do it. Do you want me to act like a monkey? One-eyed monkeys are my forte, you know. Just ask anyone." He scratched his head with his fingers and softly offered, "Ooh, ooh, eee, eee, aah, aah."

Coleman leaned down toward them. "I can do a better monkey than he can. Watch this." Coleman swung his long, muscled arms in the air and garbled toward them.

The girls darted away from Coleman. Their dark braids swayed as they scrambled toward Matthew in clinging unison, as if deciding that Matthew was a better choice than Coleman.

Matthew bit back a smile. Good old Coleman. He could always depend on the man to scare *anyone* into cooperation. Matthew held out both hands. "There's no need to be frightened. He's merely being silly. Now come. Give me your hands."

The girls paused before him, each slowly taking his outstretched hands, though they still clung to each other. Those small, cold fingers trembled against his own.

Matthew gently tightened his hold on them, trying to transmit warmth and support. He leaned toward them and whispered, "Thank you for being so brave. I know how hard that was. Are you ready to go back to Sister Catherine? She's been very worried."

To his astonishment, both girls flung themselves at his throat, bumping their heads against his shoulders. They sobbed against him.

Matthew gathered them, sadly unsurprised as to how little they weighed, and draped each girl around a hip, ensuring his pistols were out of the way.

The thudding of a single horse's hooves echoed in the distance. The girls tightened their hold against him as he turned toward the sound.

The lamppost beyond resembled a golden halo eerily floating in the bleak distance. The steady beating of hooves against the trembling ground drew closer as the silhouette of a man in full military attire with a sword at his side, pushed his horse toward them.

Marshal Royce. The bastard. *Now* he arrived.

Matthew glanced at each girl and chided, "This here man was supposed to assist, but the mayor wouldn't let him out of the house in time to play. The mayor is his mother, you see. And neither do enough for this city. Make sure you remember that when women are finally given the right to vote."

The horse whinnied as it came to a stop beside them. "I heard that," Royce snapped from above, his rugged face shadowed. "Why don't you also tell these girls how I always look the other way when you're doing something illegal?"

Matthew glared up at him. "Why don't you offer up your horse so I can take them back?"

Royce wagged gloved hands and commanded, "I've had a long night that included almost getting my throat slit. Why the hell do you think I'm late? Hand them up. I'll return them myself."

Their arms tightened around Matthew and sobs escaped them.

Matthew stepped back, adjusting his hold on them. "You know, Royce, I don't know if you care enough to even notice, but these girls have been through enough and don't need to hear about throat slitting. So tone down that voice and get off the horse. I'm taking them back. All right?"

Royce hesitated, then blew out a breath. With the swing of a long, booted leg, he jumped down and off the horse with a thud. Digging into his pocket, he held out a five-dollar bank note. "Take it to pay your bills," he grudgingly offered. "I heard you up and stole another shipment of pistols. Just know the next time you do something like that on my watch, I'll ensure you and your Forty Thieves end up in Sing Sing Prison. And believe me, men don't sing sing there."

The bastard was fortunate Matthew was holding two girls. "I don't need your money. Give it to the orphanage. They need locks on their goddamn doors."

"You won't take money from me and yet you have no qualms stealing." Royce shook his head from side to side, lowering the money he held. "Your pride is going to hang you one of these days."

"Yes, well, it hasn't yet."

CHAPTER TWO

All that you hear, believe not.
>—*The Truth Teller, a New York Newspaper for*
>*Gentlemen*

July 22, 1830
Manhattan Square, late evening

"BRING HER OUT!" a man yelled in a riled American tone that drifted from beneath the floorboards of her music room. *"Bring that woman out before I damn well dig her out!"*

Bernadette Marie let out an exasperated groan and dashed her hands against the ivory keys of the piano she'd been playing. She really needed to lay out more rules for these American men. Not even the hour was sacred anymore.

Heaving out a breath, she gathered her full skirts from around her slippered feet, abandoning her Clementi piano, and hurried out of the candlelit music room. Rounding a corner, past countless gilded paintings and marble sculptures, she veered toward and down the sweeping set of stairs that led to the dimly lit entrance hall below.

She paused midway down.

Hook-nosed, beady-eyed, old Mr. Astor glanced up at her from the entrance hall. "Ah!" He tugged on his evening coat and strode around the sputtering butler. "There she is."

Mr. Astor was not the man she had expected to see, given the late hour, but the endearing, quirky huff of a man had long earned her trust. He was one of the few to have welcomed her into the upper American circle, which had been most hesitant about accepting her due to the fact that she was British. He had also become the ever-guiding father she'd never had. Of sorts.

She hurried down the remaining stairs. "Mr. Astor." She alighted to a halt on the bottom stair and smiled. "What a pleasant surprise. Emerson, you may go."

Her butler, whom she had dragged all the way over from London—much to the poor man's dismay— hesitated as if wishing to point out that the hour was anything but respectable.

Mr. Astor snapped out his hat to the man. "Take it and go, you Philadelphia lawyer. I'm not here to kick up her skirts."

Bernadette cringed. The mannerisms of New Yorkers, even ones as privileged as Mr. Astor, was something she hadn't quite gotten used to. She had watched in unending astonishment all but two weeks ago as, after a meal, the man had wiped his greased hands on a woman's dress at a dinner party. Prankster that he was, he thought it was funny. And it was, in a son-of-a-butcher sort of way. But the woman whose gown was ruined didn't care for his humor at all, even though he had offered to buy her four new gowns.

Not that Bernadette was complaining about the company she was keeping these days. No, no, no. He and all of New York were refreshingly, gaspingly glorious in comparison to the boring, overly orchestrated life she'd left behind. "Emerson, go. You know full well Mr. Astor deserves late entry."

Emerson sniffed, grudgingly took the hat and disappeared into the adjoining room, silently announcing that the British were by far the superior race.

If only it were true.

Mr. Astor swung toward her, patting frizzy white hair back into place with a gloved hand. Dark eyes glinted with unspoken mischief. "I'm here to collect on a debt, *Lady Burton*."

Bernadette stiffened at being addressed by a name she had never hoped to hear again. 'Twas a name only a select few in New York knew of, given she now publicly went by the name of Mrs. Shelton. And coming from Mr. Astor, it was especially troubling, be he jesting or not. "Is there a reason you are addressing me as such?"

He clasped his gloved hands together, bringing them smugly against his gray silk embroidered vest. "I'm a man of business first, dear. That is how this son of a German butcher came to trade and buy every last fur from New Orleans to Canada, making me the wealthiest man in this here United States of our Americas. Because when an opportunity presents itself, a man has to set aside being nice for a small while and lunge on said opportunity. So I suggest you do the favor I'm about to ask, *Your Highness*."

She rolled her eyes, sensing he knew she wasn't about to cooperate. Their viewpoints were never the same despite their bond. "I am not the queen. Please do not address me as such."

"Ah, but you're related to the woman."

"My husband was related to the woman. Not I."

"Are you telling me I can't depend on you for anything? What sort of friend are you? Is this how you British get on?"

Drat him. She knew it would come to this. New York, after all, hadn't really been her original destination when she had left London with a deranged twinkle in her eye. She had actually planned on staying permanently in New Orleans to better explore the history of privateering—and its men—until she was robbed right down to her petticoats during a less-than-reputable street masking ball. She had wanted to know what it would be like to frolic with the locals and found they didn't frolic fair at all.

If it weren't for Mr. Astor and his grandson, who at the time were all but strangers when they had heroically come to her assistance that night on the street, she might have been robbed of a lot more than just her reticule and gown. After that night, they had all become not only good friends, but old Mr. Astor had also brilliantly proposed she abandon New Orleans and accompany him and his grandson back to New York City under an alias to stave off all the newspapers who sought to exploit her after what had become known as "The Petticoat Incident."

It was good to be plain old Mrs. Shelton, living in New York City, entertaining good-looking men whenever she had a fancy for it, as opposed to being Lady Burton gone wild, who had made United States gossip history by being included in every American newspaper from New Orleans to Nantucket. She had no doubt whatsoever that London had also long heard of it by now. Right along with her father. Gad.

She drew in a ragged breath and let it out. "I am forever indebted to you and your grandson, Mr. Astor. You know that."

"Then do as I say, will you? Because my grandson is actually the one who stands to benefit from this. We are talking about squeezing ourselves into British aristocracy and making those prissy, tea-sipping bastards acknowledge that money is what makes power. Not a name smeared with drips of blood."

Her brows rose. "You wish to…*squeeze* yourself into British aristocracy? I see. And what is it that you believe I would be able to do for you in that regard?"

He shifted toward her, his aged features taking on the sort of mock severity he reserved only for business associates. "You would be able to help us open doors, is what. How? By overseeing the *first* American marry into aristocracy. 'Tis a nugget of an opportunity. What I need is for you to assist this American girl along. Georgia Emily Milton is her name. Though, we'll have to change it. 'Tis overly Irish and plain and needs tinsel. You see, there is an aristo this girl seeks to wed—a Lord Yardley who is next in line to become the Duke of Wentworth—who is already willing and waiting. What *you* need to do is make her palatable to British society, for her sake and his. It would involve teaching her everything you know about the *ton,* then guiding her through a Season over in London next year. The duke and I will ensure you have infinite resources to guards. No man will touch you whilst you're in London. No man. Unless you want him to."

An astonished laugh escaped her. Oh, now, this was humor at its finest. "Whilst the idea is most amusing, and I have no qualms about assisting this girl if that is truly your bidding, I am *not* going back to London. It would be an even bigger mess than the one I left behind and I will admit that I am infinitely fond of my new life. None of the men here in New York know who the bonnet I am and I can skylark all I want without getting dashed for it. Unlike back in London, where I was getting dashed for even breathing."

He stared at her for a long moment. "You owe me."

Bernadette let out an exasperated laugh. "I do not owe you hanging myself. I am *not* crossing an ocean for that."

He gestured grudgingly toward the adjoining parlor. "Would you rather my favor involve a piano and a parlor full of naked men? Is that it? Would that be more to your devil-may-care liking?"

Oh dear God. Americans. No wonder the British finally relented on letting them go. Bernadette lifted a brow, knowing that, as always, the man was merely being crass for crass's sake. It was time he realize that she was no longer the same girl he and his grandson had to rescue on the streets of New Orleans. She knew how to rescue herself and she was *not* about to touch a toe to London by exposing herself to vicious gossip-mongers who knew nothing about a woman's right to a life or privacy. "The last time I was in London, Mr. Astor, I had a man break into my home, intent on *proving* to me that he could beget me with his child in the hopes of beguiling me into matrimony. And he was the friendliest of my money-salivating suitors.

"Sadly, my inheritance has only served to encumber my happiness thus far, and I am *trying* to create a relatively pleasant life for myself. Going back to London would only impede that. For heaven's sake, I have yet to do a sliver of all my plans. In fact, I'm about to negotiate a two-year trip to Jamaica."

"Two years?" He pulled in his chin. "What for? Last I knew, all they had in Jamaica was water and sand."

"Port Royal and Kingston happen to be known for their extensive privateering history. I also hear that the men there dress down because of the heat." She smirked. "That alone would be well worth traveling for. And unlike New Orleans, I intend on hiring a guard to accompany me everywhere I go. So you see, Mr. Astor, *that* is what is next for me. Not London rain and pasty pale men, but Port Royal and sun-bronzed pirates."

He stepped toward her. "You know I would not normally ask this of you, but my grandson stands a chance to follow in the footsteps of this girl if we do this right. He stands to marry into aristocracy. 'Tis something he and I have talked about for years. Hell, I would have gladly married him off to you to ensure that title, but for some reason, you won't have him."

Bernadette lowered her chin. "The boy is twenty."

"And all the more virile for it! Unlike your old William, he'll ensure you have twenty sons in twenty minutes."

She cringed at the thought. "Mr. Astor, really. Jacob, whilst very lovely, is fifteen years younger than myself. I wouldn't even know what to do with him."

"Lovely? Did you just call him lovely? Don't ever call him that." He sighed. "I need you. My grandson's entire livelihood needs you. Don't make me kneel for this."

"Why would you ever want that poor boy to be part of the aristocracy? 'Tis a queernab existence I have spent my entire life trying to escape. Besides, with your vast fortune, you and Jacob already *have* everything."

"Everything *but* that." He hissed out a breath. Eyeing her, he went down on a grudging, wobbly knee, grazing the hem of her gown, and slowly spread both arms wide, giving sight to everything known as Mr. Astor. "The dreams of a mere butcher's son is something you would never understand. You, who were born unto a rare breed few touch. Do this for me. Seven months of training this girl here in New York, a little over a month of continuing to train her during travels abroad and one month in London. *One.* That is all I ask. My wife will be the one playing chaperone. Not you. So you needn't worry in that. I tell you, this girl is going to establish a taste for all things American if we do this right. 'Twill be a sky-brightening storm that will *finally* see that my grandson wed into his dreams. I beg of you. Take pity upon his dreams and mine. Have you never had a dream?"

Too many. She had once dreamed of sweeping, heart-pounding adventures, true love meant to make one sigh and unadulterated passion that no music from her piano could ever evoke. All of that had drowned rather quick, however, when her father married her off at eighteen to an old man whose idea of love, passion and adventure was a carriage ride through Hyde Park and a pat on the hand.

She'd been trying to make up for it ever since.

Sensing that the man wasn't about to relent, Bernadette sighed. She did have unfinished business in London with her father after she'd packed up old William's estate and sailed into the night without a word to anyone. She supposed she owed her father one last visit. Bastard. "So be it. I will take on this girl as it means so much to you. But I am *not* staying in London beyond a month. Is that understood?"

His face brightened as he scrambled up onto booted feet. He grabbed her hands in both of his and shook them. "'Tis a pleasure doing business with you, dear, as always."

"Yes, yes, and you are most welcome. In truth, this idea of introducing an American into London society would be rather gratifying. Those self-righteous bastards, who dare act like gods thinking their blood is pure, deserve to have their blood tainted."

"I knew you were the woman to oversee this." He tapped at her hands one last time before releasing them.

"Though I will say, my dear, after London, I highly recommend you settle down before you set fire to those skirts. You've broken enough hearts. You ought to remarry."

Bernadette almost snorted. "I prefer to say yes to life and no to the altar."

He tsked. "Don't be taking off to Madrid and riding bulls next. You can do that *after* we get this girl into London." He paused. "My hat." Glancing about, he bellowed, "Where the hell is my hat, Emerson? You aren't pissing in it, are you? Bring it out already. Now!"

Bernadette blinked. Maybe time in London would be a good thing. Because sometimes, just sometimes, and rare though it was, she did miss the, uh…*culture*.

Seven months later
New York City—the Five Points

LINGERING BEFORE THE LOPSIDED, cracked mirror hanging on the barren wall of his tenement, Matthew affixed the leather patch over his left eye. It was annoyingly fitting that the only image he ever saw of himself every morning after shaving and dressing was splintered in half.

Turning, he grabbed up his wool great coat from the chair stacked with his father's old newspapers.

He paused, leaned down and touched a heavy hand to those papers. "Morning, Da," he whispered.

He drew in a ragged breath and let it out, fighting the sting in his eyes he could never get past, knowing this was all that remained of his father. *This.* An old stack of papers that personified his father's life. Though at least that life had amounted to something.

Matthew patted that stack one last time.

Draping on his great coat and buttoning it into place, he swung away, opened the door leading out of his tenement and slammed it behind himself. After bolting the door, he trudged down the narrow stairwell and out into the skin-biting, snow-ridden streets of Mulberry.

Matthew paused, glimpsing his negro friend heading toward him. Apparently, knuckles were about to get bloody. Smock only ever called on his tenement when there was a problem.

Matthew briskly made his way through the snow that unevenly crusted the pavement, his worn leather boots crunching against the ice layering it. The bright glint of the sun did nothing to warm the frigid air that peered over slanted rooftops. He squinted to block out the glare in his eye and stalked toward his friend. "Don't tell me one of our own is dead."

Smock veered toward him, large boots also crunching against the snow. He puffed out dark cheeks before entirely deflating them. "Worse."

"Worse?" Matthew jerked to a halt, scanning that unshaven, sweat-beaded black face. It was winter. Why was he sweating? "Have you been running? What the hell is going on?"

Smock lingered, his expression wary. He scrubbed his thick, wiry hair. "Coleman called a meetin' an' put Kerner in command."

Matthew's eyes widened. "What? Why? He can't do that."

"He already done did."

"But I own half the group!"

Smock shrugged. "He's leavin' an' yer goin' with him. To London, says he. What? Dat not true?"

"*London?* I'd rather swallow my own shite than go to—" He paused, thinking of his father's widow, Georgia. Last time he'd seen or heard from his "stepmother," was all but seven months ago, when the woman had ditched the Five Points in the hopes of creating a new life for herself in the name of some Brit. He only hoped to God her life hadn't sunken into mud. "Is this about Georgia? Shouldn't she be in London about now? Is that not working out?"

Smock threw up both hands. "Don't know. Don't care. All I know is—" He tapped a long finger to his temple. "Coleman's not himself."

"Where is he?"

"Don't know."

Bloody hell.

UNLATCHING THE DOOR COLEMAN never locked, Matthew stepped inside. The acrid smell of leather and metal wafted through the air. Matthew scanned the vast, high-ceilinged storage room that Coleman leased from an iron monger. Bags of sand nailed against dented, dingy walls lined one side and a straw mattress laid on crates with a dilapidated leather trunk full of clothes lined the other. Like him, Coleman had always been a man of little means, but sometimes, he sensed Coleman purposefully tortured himself into living like this a bit too much.

Matthew wrinkled his nose and muttered aloud, "Don't you ever air this place out, man?" Kicking aside wooden crates that cluttered the dirty planks of the floor, he jogged across the echoing expanse of the room, holding his pistols against his leather belts to keep them from jumping out.

Unlatching the back door, he shoved it open. Afternoon sunlight spilled in, illuminating the uneven wood floor, as a cold breeze whirled in from the alley with a dancing twirl of snow. Adjusting his great coat about his frame, he slowly strode toward the center of the room with a sense of pride. He had primed his first pistol here.

Shouts and the skidding of boots crunching against ice-hardened snow caused him to jerk toward the open door. A lanky youth dressed in a billowy coat and an oversized wool cap sprinted into and across the room, darting past Matthew so fast he barely made out a blurred face.

Was that— *"Ronan?"* he echoed.

"Can't talk! Two men. *I owe you!"* The youth dove headfirst into a stack of large, empty crates and out of sight.

Matthew's brows shot up as two thugs in stained wool trousers and yellowing linen shirts burst in from the alley. One gripped a piece of timber embedded with nails and the other a brick.

"Show him up, Milton," the man with the brick yelled. "That runt owes us money."

How was it everyone knew his name even when he didn't know theirs? Matthew widened his stance. "With this attitude of brick and timber, gents, the way I see it, the boy owes you nothing."

The oaf with the timber glanced at his burly companion. The two advanced in stalk-unison, their unshaven faces hardening as thick knuckles gripped makeshift weapons.

Matthew crossed his forearms over his midsection and gripped the rosewood handles of his pistols. Whipping out both from his belts, he pointed a muzzle at each head. "He'll give you the money by the end of the day."

They scrambled back. They raised their hands above those oily heads, those weapons going up with them.

Matthew advanced, cocking both pistols with the flick of his thumbs. "Given you both know who I am, it means you also know that my jurisdiction runs between here and Little Water. So get the hell out of my ward. *Now.*"

The men sprinted through the open door and out of sight.

He released the springs on the pistols and shoved them back into his leather belt. With the heel of his worn boot, he slammed the alley door shut. Turning, he strode over to the pile of crates. "I feel like all I'm ever good for is giving you money and getting you out of trouble, Ronan. It's been that way ever since I first saw you shuffling along in those oversized boots."

Several wood crates were frantically pushed out of the way by two bare hands. They clattered to the floor as Ronan crawled out. Still on fours, the youth peered up from beyond a lopsided cap, strands of unevenly sheared brown hair pasted to his brow. "If it had been one man, I would have taken care of it."

Taking a knee, Matthew smirked. "Thank goodness there were two. So. How much do you owe those cafflers? I'll pay it. As always."

Ronan hesitated, then blurted, "Two dollars."

He choked. "Two! What, did they introduce you to God?"

Ronan winced. "It was for this girl over on Anthony Street. She said it was free. *It wasn't my fault!*"

"You're fourteen, you—" Matthew flicked that cheek hard with the tip of his finger and rigidly pointed at him before jumping onto booted feet. "What the hell were you doing over at Squeeze Gut Alley? You could have been killed."

Ronan scrambled up, adjusting his brown coat. "She was worth it. She not only knew what she was doing, but had tits the size of jugs."

Matthew stared him down. "They could have been the size of Ireland and it still wouldn't have been worth two dollars *or* your life. Did you at least sheathe yourself?"

Ronan blinked. "What do you mean?"

Matthew groaned. "You need a father."

"What? You offering? Do I get to live with you, too?"

Matthew snorted, knowing the boy *would* move in with him. "I need a wife first."

"Go find one then. I ain't going anywhere."

Knowing his days of having a family were fading fast, given he'd be thirty in less than a year, Matthew grouched, "Not to disappoint you or myself, but all the good women in these parts are either dead or taken."

Ronan snickered. "Ain't that the truth. And the dead ones are the lucky ones, I say. So. I got a message from Coleman. You want it?"

Matthew paused. "Yes, I want it. What's this business of him overriding me?"

Ronan eyed the closed door and lowered his voice. "There's talk of another swipe on your life. Only, this time, it involves seventeen men from a neighboring ward, hence why Coleman up and put Kerner in charge. Coleman says he's got business abroad he's been putting off, so he bought two tickets on a packet ship to Liverpool and wants you on it with him tomorrow at noon. That way, you dodge the swipe, until these boyos are taken off the street by marshals, whilst Coleman ties up strings in London."

Matthew set a heavy hand against his neck, pinching the skin on it. Another swipe. God. He should have been dead years ago.

Dropping his hand, Matthew dug into the inner pocket of his patched waistcoat, and pulled out all the money he had on him—three dollars. He held it out. "Here. Pay off the debt and keep the rest for yourself and out of your mother's hands, lest she drink it. And next time, if you want a girl, Ronan, do the respectable thing and marry one."

Ronan searched his face. "Thanks for... *Thanks*." He took the money and tucked it deep into his pocket. He cleared his throat and adjusted his cap and trousers, trying to appear manly. "So, um…what should I tell Coleman? He's got business over at the docks."

"Tell him he's a son of a bitch for caring."

"Which means you'll be on that boat."

"Exactly."

Ronan sighed, grudgingly turned and made his way to the door, flinging it open. "I'll tell him." Ronan glanced back. "You're coming back, right? You're not leaving me?"

Matthew hesitated, knowing the boy depended on him for far, far more than money. "I'll be back once I get word from the marshals that the swipe is over. I promise. In the meantime, take my tenement whilst I'm gone. I'll give you the key in the morning. The rent has already been paid for to the end of the year."

"I'll take it." Ronan's face tightened. "I'm done cleaning up whiskey and tossing men out on the hour. No matter what I say and despite all the times you've gone over there to talk to her, nothing ever changes. I hate her. I do."

Matthew swallowed and nodded. Ronan's mother, who had once been a successful stage actress in Boston when the boy was two, was nothing but a drunk and a penniless whore, who now brought all of her cliental home, whether Ronan was there to see it or not. "She's still your mother and you're all the woman has. She needs you."

"More than I need her," Ronan muttered, disappearing.

Matthew threw back his head, exhausted. London? Why did he have this feeling Coleman was saving him from one mess, only to drag him into another?

CHAPTER THREE

All that you see, judge not.
> —*The Truth Teller, a New York Newspaper for*
> *Gentlemen*

The opening of the Season in London—Rotten Row

WHY, OH WHY, DID SHE feel like Caesar about to be stabbed by Brutus? Directing her horse alongside the stunning redhead who Mr. Astor was ardently gambling on, Bernadette Marie fixed her gaze on the remaining path leading through the rest of the park. She tightened her gloved hands on the leather reins, endlessly grateful not to have been ambushed or stoned. Yet.

Glancing over at Georgia, Bernadette withheld a sigh. She really was going to miss the girl. The idea of handing her off to London society made her cringe. Georgia was so much bigger in character and in spirit than these stupid fops around them, and after ten months of the girl's eye rolling and giggling and huffing whilst Bernadette attempted to mold her into perfection, Bernadette realized that she was about to lose a friend. Something she really didn't have. For whilst men flocked to her in the name of money, women never flocked to her at all. They only ever saw her as competition or a threat to their reputation.

Georgia groaned. "I hate London."

Bernadette tried not to smirk. "This is probably where I should remind you that you have come to Town to wed and stay in it."

"Oh, yes. That." Georgia's green eyes brightened as her arched rust-colored brows rose. "I wonder what Robinson will think of me when he sees me."

Ah, to be twelve years younger and still think men were worth more than their trousers. "He will most likely faint."

And Bernadette meant it. After the astounding transformation Georgia had undergone from street girl to American heiress, not even her waiting Lord Yardley was going to recognize her.

As Bernadette scanned the path before them, wondering if they were done showcasing Georgia for the afternoon, two imposing gents on black stallions made her pause. She lowered her chin against the silk sash of her riding bonnet.

Both well-framed men wore ragged great coats, edge-whitened black leather boots and no hats or gloves. In fact, their horses and saddles looked better kept than they did. The two clearly thought they had every right to be on this here path. One man had silvering black hair that was in dire need of shearing, and the other—

She blinked as her startled gaze settled on wind-blown, sunlit, chestnut-colored hair, a bronzed rugged face set with a taut jaw, and a worn leather patch that had been tied over his left eye as if he were some sort of...*Pirate King.*

She drew in an astonished soft breath. *Oh, my, and imagine that.* It was like meeting a phantom from her own mind. Ever since she was eight, she'd always dreamily wanted to meet a real privateer, like Captain Lafitte out of New Orleans, whom she'd read about in the gazettes she'd steal from the servants. She would dash herself out toward the Thames each and every morning with her governess in tow and rebelliously stand on the docks, watching the ships pass, whilst praying said privateer would spot her from deck, point and make her quartermaster of his ship.

Everywhere she went, be it the square, the country or sweeping the keys of her piano, she had waited and waited to be seized by pirates and dragged out of London. She had even envisioned one of them to be rougher and gruffer than the rest, bearing a leather patch over an eye he'd lost in a fight. She even gave him a name—the Pirate King. The Pirate King was supposed to introduce her to the span of the sea not set by female etiquette but by the wild adventures outside everything known as London. A life far, far away from her stern, penny-pinching papa, who had expected her to marry a crusty old man by the name of Lord Burton when she turned a walk-the-plank eighteen.

But this Pirate King was seventeen years and a marriage too late. And though, yes, pirates were considered criminals, and this one looked like one himself, she had learned at an early age that all men were criminals in one form or another, be they breaking the rules of the land or the rules of the heart. Oh, yes. She had no doubt whatsoever that this one probably broke *all* the rules. Even the ones that had yet to be written.

As he and his black stallion rode steadily closer alongside his other bandit of a friend, and the distance of the riding path between them diminished, he leveled his shaven jaw against that frayed linen cravat and stared at her with a penetrating coal-black gaze. His visible eyes methodically dropped from her face to her shoulders to her breasts and back up again with the lofty ease of a captain surveying a ship he was about to board.

An unexpected fluttering overtook her stomach. She squelched it, knowing that the man was probably just calculating the worth of her Pomona Green velvet riding gown.

Determined to trudge through whatever ridiculous attraction she had for the ruffian, Bernadette couldn't help but cheekily drawl aloud to Georgia, "Well, well, well. It appears the row is more rotten than usual today. I love it. For the sake of your reputation, my dear, ignore these two men approaching on horseback. Heaven only knows who they are and what they want." Because ruffians weren't supposed to be on this path. It was the unspoken rule of aristocratic society.

Georgia, who had grown unusually quiet, and perhaps a little too eager to follow Bernadette's orders, yanked the rim of her riding hat as far down as it would

go, until all of her strawberry-red hair and nose disappeared. She then frantically gathered the white trailing veil of her riding habit, pulling it up and over her
face, burying herself farther in it.

Bernadette veered her own horse closer. What was
she doing? Preparing for an ambush? "The veil *never*
goes over your face. 'Tis meant for decorative pur-
poses only."

"Not today it isn't." Georgia lowered her voice. "I
know those two. They're from New York. And of all
things, they're from my part of town."

"Are they?" Heavens, he was a *landlocked* pirate.
Even good old Captain Lafitte from New Orleans
wouldn't have been able to hold up his fists against a
New York Five Pointer. Why did that intrigue her? It
would seem her taste in men was fading quickly into
the pits of all things unknown. "Might I ask who the
man with the patch is? He looks rough enough to be
fun."

Georgia glanced at her through her drawn hat and
veil. "He's the last person you want to ever involve
yourself with. He's a thief."

Bernadette tossed out a laugh, pleased to know she
was being reprimanded. "All men are. Now, quiet. Here
they come." As she eased her horse to a mere walk, to
demonstrate she was not in any way ruffled, Georgia
altogether brought her horse to full trot and passed.

Slowing his horse with the tug of a wrist on the
reins, the man's dark brows came together, that patch
shifting against his cheekbone as he glanced toward
Georgia, who rudely barreled past, veil flying.

He paused and eyed Bernadette, as if expecting her to barrel by next. When she didn't—for she wasn't about to be *that* rude—he curtly inclined his head in greeting. The stiff set of those broad shoulders hinted that he didn't expect her to acknowledge him at all.

That alone deserved acknowledgment.

Bernadette politely inclined her head toward him, her pulse annoyingly trotting along with the feet of her horse.

A low whistle escaped his teeth. "Apparently, I've been living in the wrong city all my life." That husky, mellow American baritone astonished her enough to stare. As he rode past, he coolly held her gaze and drawled, "Ladies."

And onward he rode, without a backward glance.

Though he said "Ladies" as if also to include Georgia, who had just passed, Bernadette knew those words, that tone and mock farewell had all been directed at her. It was as if he were pointing out that she needn't worry. That he wasn't interested in *anything* she had to offer, even though his patched great coat and worn leather boots were worth far less than half a silk stocking.

Bernadette tightened her hold on the reins until it stung. Churlish though it was, it made her want the man. He didn't even try to flirt.

Unless he didn't find her attractive. Oh, gad.

She glanced after him over her shoulder. He casually rode on with his devil friend as if their paths had never crossed.

Bernadette paused, her gaze sweeping back to Georgia, noticing the redhead was well beyond the path.

Kicking her boot into the side of her horse, Bernadette pushed into a gallop. Upon reaching Georgia, she called out, "Miss Tormey."

Georgia eased her horse and flopped her veil back and away from her flushed face. Readjusting her hat, she choked out, "That was disgusting. I felt like I was being groped by my own brother."

Bernadette aligned her horse beside hers and slowly grinned. "Speak for yourself. I rather enjoyed that." There was something deliciously provocative about a man who knew how to control himself around a woman.

They rode on in unified silence, Bernadette's grin fading.

Perhaps it was kismet that their paths had crossed. After all, what were the chances that her understudy knew this landlocked pirate *and* that he was right here in London all the way from New York? Though he wasn't the sort of man she usually associated with, something about him made her want to— "Might I ask a question?"

Georgia glanced toward her. "Of course."

"The man with the patch. Who is he to you? And is he as gruff as he appears?"

Georgia's jade-green eyes widened beneath the rim of her riding hat. "You aren't actually smitten, are you? And with but a glance?"

Bernadette set her chin, ready to defend herself. "And what if I am? I spent twelve years married to a man forty-three years my senior who, whilst everything kind, was anything but attractive. It was like bedding my grandfather in the name of England. He couldn't even—" She blinked rapidly, realizing she was digressing, and poor William didn't deserve it or that. It wasn't his fault he had been old and had money her father had wanted at the price of her youth. "If I haven't earned a right to a man of my choice by now, Miss Tormey, I might as well be dead." And she meant it.

Georgia sighed. "He's had a rough life, and whilst I chastise him all the time, no, he isn't as gruff as he appears. I'm not about to go into detail about who he is to me out of respect for Robinson, but he is more or less family. He lost sight in his one eye after a fight on the street and then lost his da to apoplexy a few years later. And mind you, that was *after* he'd already lost everything. And I do mean *everything*. He lost his fiancée because he had no money, lost his home and the business he was set to inherit. Everything."

Bernadette's chest unexpectedly tightened. That was where that mocking indifference came from. When a man lost everything, it was either mock or die. She understood that motto all too well. She herself was guilty of it.

She glanced back toward the direction of where the Pirate King still rode on the path and paused. He and his friend had already fully turned their horses around and were leisurely making their way back toward them.

Her heart pounded and her cheeks flushed as the Pirate King leaned forward in his saddle to intently observe her.

Was he watching her?

"Bernadette?" a man called out from somewhere before her on the path. "Is that you?"

Startled that a man was using her birth name, Bernadette snapped her head and gaze past Georgia over to a lone gentleman riding toward them at a half-gallop.

His top hat was angled forward in a most unbecoming fashion. He slowed, dashing amber eyes intently holding her gaze in astonishment. "By God. I didn't realize you were in Town."

Dread seized her. It was Lord Dunmore. Her former neighbor. A man who had gallantly come to her rescue many, many times when she'd been maliciously deluged by suitors after inheriting her husband's heart-stopping million-pound estate.

For weeks, Dunmore had called on her every afternoon, save Sunday, to ask if she needed to be escorted anywhere. He was all things dashing and everything her decrepit old husband had never been.

Then one afternoon, whilst he was discussing something with her—she forgot exactly what—out of stupid, stupid infatuation, she grabbed the man by the lapels of his coat and kissed him. She wanted to know what it would be like to kiss a man her own age, after enduring twelve years of old William's sloppy and slurpy kisses. She didn't think, not for a single moment, that Dunmore would let it go beyond that one kiss.

Only…he'd astounded her by not only tonguing the breath out of her, but then shoving her against the wall and jerking up her skirts. In a lust-ridden blur she just couldn't say no to, she let him pound her into the wall.

It was the first climax she'd ever had at the hands of a man and it earned him a Bernadette-approved medal.

From there on out, it turned into a flurry of unstoppable physicality that ended her respectable name. And she didn't care. She was *finally* living life and had already ended traditional mourning for William. What more did society want?

Barely weeks into their torrid affair, everything grew complicated. Dunmore kept saying "I love you" and wanted her to say it, too. She couldn't. Though she'd grown to admire him, her attachment to him was, for the most part, purely physical. She felt very guilty about it, until she caught the bastard riffling through her financial ledgers early one morning, when he thought she was asleep.

In complete disbelief, she had quietly retreated without him knowing it and had him investigated before deciding on what to do. What she discovered had made her heave. After scolding herself for being so stupid, she ended their association with a polite letter—for she hated confrontations as they were pointless—and dashed herself and all of her money over to New Orleans on a hunt for some *American* liberation. She promised herself from there on out that she would no longer form any attachments. She could not trust them.

"Bernadette." He said her name as if he'd break.

She tried to keep her voice steady. "Dunmore."

Still holding her gaze, he said in an equally civil tone, "Why did you leave? That letter never explained anything."

She set her chin. "I ask that you please refrain, given that we are in public."

"The public be damned, Bernadette," he bit out. "This has been weighing on me for well over a year and I haven't been able to bloody move on because of it and you. What the hell did I do? Can you at least answer me that? *What?*"

How dare he pretend like he cared and that *she* was the villain in this? "Aside from you paging through my financial ledgers?"

He stared. "What do you mean? I never—"

"I know what I saw, Dunmore. I'm not interested in listening to lies."

Glancing over at Georgia, who was awkwardly observing them, Dunmore drew his horse closer and said in a ragged tone, "Whatever you saw, my intentions were that of a gentleman."

She stared him down. "A gentleman. Ah. A gentleman who hid debts from me. Rather extensive ones, actually."

His features tightened. "I didn't want you thinking that I was after your money."

"How very considerate of a man who also sired two children with a sixteen-year-old servant girl whom you no doubt still frisk every Saturday evening."

His eyes widened. "Who the devil told you?"

"I had you investigated."

His face flushed. "You had me investigated?"

"It was obvious the truth wasn't going to come out of your mouth."

Losing all polite measure, he boomed, "How dare you bloody investigate me!"

"How dare you lie to me and how dare you impose upon a young girl who wouldn't know right from wrong? I only need one reason to toss a man. You gave me five."

His chest rose and fell more and more steadily. "Even if I had done everything right, you would have still found a way to give me the toss. Because your one true wish in this, Bernadette, was never to love me. Isn't that true? Even though you licked and swallowed my seed in unending pleasure."

Her throat tightened in disbelief. "This conversation is over. I suggest you, your lies and your lack of funds leave." She quickly steered her horse to move past.

His tone hardened to repulsive. "Don't you bloody turn away from me." He rounded her horse and came onto her side with his stallion, the quick thud of hooves kicking up dirt from the path.

Her eyes widened as a riding crop snapped toward her face. She jerked back in her saddle as a lash of leather fire seared her jaw. A gasp escaped her lips as she staggered in an effort to remain upright. Dunmore had never once raised his voice to her let alone—

"Lady Burton!" With the whip of reins, Georgia veered her horse across the path, back toward them.

The thundering of hooves neared as another quick crop swung at her, stinging her shoulder. Bernadette grabbed the reins and pushed her horse forward to dodge another blow as the tip of the crop seared her arm again and again, stinging straight through the material of her gown. "Cease, you—"

She wincingly popped up a hand when another horse veered in.

A blurring male face and a long muscled arm seized Dunmore's uplifted wrist from behind. With the quick hook of another muscled arm that jumped around Dunmore's throat, Dunmore was yanked back until he was teetering half off the saddle.

Her heart pounded in between heaving breaths.

The Pirate King adjusted, and jerked Dunmore's throat from behind into a vicious choke hold that sent Dunmore's top hat tumbling aside and his pocket watch swinging spastically out of his vest. Their horses battled for position against each other as the Pirate King ruthlessly held Dunmore between both saddles.

Digging his chin into the side of Dunmore's mussed head from behind, the Pirate King tightened a bulk-muscled arm around that throat and seethed out between clenched teeth, "Is this how you Brits treat your women? *Is it?*"

Wide-eyed, Dunmore tried jerking free, gloved hands chaotically digging. He tried swinging the crop in his hand, but couldn't extend it. "Unhand me," Dunmore gagged, still in a choke hold. "I'm a peer of the... realm!"

"Whilst I'm *king* of your goddamn realm and throat right now." His voice hardened ruthlessly. "And it's time you fecking bow before royalty." Yanking the crop from Dunmore's hand, he viciously swung Dunmore right off the horse. Dunmore flew, head down, with a squelched thud that penetrated the ground.

By God, the man and all of that muscle was worthy of a swoon and more.

With a snap of the crop he'd confiscated, he hit the flank of Dunmore's horse, sending the horse darting, neighing and galloping down the path with a plume of dust. Leaning over the side of his saddle, he down-whipped the crop at Dunmore's head, eliciting a *thwack.* "Don't ever go near this woman again or you're dead. *Dead.* Because I'll gladly hang knowing the world has one less arsehole in it. You tell the watch that when you send them after me. Now if I were you, Brit, I'd catch up to your horse before I send you bleeding down Salt River."

Lord Dunmore scrambled up, his chest heaving. He glanced toward Bernadette.

The Pirate King yanked out a pistol from the leather belt at his waist and pointed it down at Dunmore's head. "How fast can you run? Show me. Before I go *click.*"

Dunmore turned and sprinted, his morning coat flapping and his leather boots thudding down the path until he and his crop were gone.

Silence drifted across the surrounding park and the path, which fortunately was clear of other riders and witnesses. The Pirate King, his devil friend and Georgia all turned their eyes and their horses toward her.

Bernadette swallowed, her jaw still pulsing from the stinging heat of Dunmore's crop. It was humiliating. Not only to have been cropped in front of them but to have her entire history with Dunmore laid out like a sermon on Sunday.

The Pirate King shoved his pistol back into his leather belt and slowly brought his horse beside hers, his features tightening. He leaned in, the smell of leather, metal and gunpowder lacing the air. "It left a mark."

Lovely. As if her age didn't mark her up enough.

He searched her face, his brows coming together against that leather patch. "Are you all right, miss?"

Miss? Did he really think she was that young? Even with those annoying wispy grays peering out at her temples? Bless him. "Yes, I am. Thank you."

He half nodded and pulled away his horse, still intently holding her gaze with that coal-black eye. "If you have any more problems with that bastard, I'm staying over at Limmer's. Come find me and I'll take care of it. My only regret is that I didn't interfere sooner. And for that, I owe you."

He thought he owed her. After he'd rescued her.

Her throat tightened. Even worse, he was staying at Limmer's. 'Twas a cheap hotel for the sporting crowd, known for being incredibly dirty and hosting all things dangerous. Even whores didn't like going in there, as they usually didn't come back out. She couldn't let a man like this, who had just rescued whatever was left of her face, stay there. "Might I offer you better lodgings, sir? Given what you did for me?"

He lifted a dark brow. "Define *better*."

She would have invited him to stay at her leased house off Piccadilly, seeing Georgia was residing with

Mrs. Astor over on Park Lane, but she didn't want the man thinking her invitation was permanent. "I recommend the St. James Royal Hotel. 'Tis premier and the best London has to offer. I will ensure your room and board is paid for. Gladly."

He stared at her, his jaw tight. After a long moment, he set his broad shoulders. "Let me think on it."

By God, she admired that pride. He wore it so well.

Glancing over at her understudy, he clicked his tongue. "Georgia, Georgia. We never seem to be able to get rid of each other, do we? Much to our own dismay." He scanned the length of Georgia's Vienna blue riding gown, lowering his chin in a way that caused that windblown hair to fall across his forehead. He snorted. "You look like Niblo's Garden on a stick."

Georgia regally set her chin. "And proud of it. Don't you wish you looked this good."

"Ah, you look all right, I suppose."

"All right?" Georgia circled a gloved finger over her face and gown. "It took me ten months to look like this. And look. No freckles. They're there, but they're cleverly hidden. The toiletries these days are *unbelievable*."

He swiped his jaw. "A waste of ten months, I say." Dropping his hand to his thigh, he huffed out a breath. "Since we're catching up on gossip, I'm sure you'd like to know that your John Andrew Malloy not only went out West, but married. Thanks to you, we're now damn well known as the Thirty-Nine Thieves."

Georgia's eyes widened. "John married Agnes Meehan?"

"Isn't that what I said?"

Georgia let out a laugh. "Well, good for him. *And* Agnes."

"Good for him, yes. Not so good for Agnes. He's not exactly what I call the marrying sort." The Pirate King huffed out another breath. "So. Where are you staying? Coleman and I need to get ourselves out of Town. They bloody stone you like crows out here. Expensive as hell."

Georgia snorted. "It doesn't help that you went and bought yourself horses."

The Pirate King and his menacingly quiet friend paused. They eyed each other, to which the Pirate King adjusted his great coat and drawled, "We didn't exactly buy them."

Bernadette blinked.

Georgia gasped. *"You stole them?"*

He pointed at her. "Ey. A hackney costs a shilling just to roll halfway down the goddamn street. I'm not paying that. And we didn't steal the horses. We're borrowing them for a few days and will give them both back once we're done."

Georgia glared. "'Tis no different than stealing, Matthew, to which I say you and Coleman get yourselves jobs as sweepers, because I'm not giving either of you spit."

Matthew. Bernadette almost uttered his name aloud in adoration and reverence. Despite that "borrowed" horse, he seemed so...genuine. And divine. So breathtakingly divine.

Without thinking, she hurriedly dug into her reticule slung on her wrist and pulled out a Bristol calling card, holding it out to him. "I would be honored to provide you with the money and lodgings you need. 'Tis the least I can do after your noble rescue. Call on me. I insist."

Slowly drawing his horse closer to her own until they were side by side, he leaned over. Slipping the card from her gloved fingers, he held her gaze for a long moment. "Thank you, luv."

That gruff, yet equally gentle voice made her want to throw her arms around him and never let go.

He wordlessly fingered the card she'd given him, still heatedly holding her gaze. He molded and re-molded the card against the curve of that large hand, as if trying to *feel* her.

Bernadette drew in a breath, wishing that card *was* her.

"Milton," his friend called out. "Instead of playing Casanova with the card, give the woman's generous offer a day and the hour you intend to call."

The Pirate King tucked the card into his boot and recaptured her gaze. "This Thursday. I'm thinking mid-night."

Bernadette quirked a brow. "Is that what you're thinking?"

"Midnight is my version of noon," he added, still holding her gaze.

He was clearly interested only in linen ripping. And who was she to deny over six feet of brawn? "Mid-night it is."

His mouth quirked. "I'll see you then." Rounding

his stolen stallion, he glanced back at her one last time, then he and his friend galloped off down the path.

Georgia tsked. "You have no self-control. None whatsoever."

Bernadette smirked. "Coming from you, Miss Tormey, I will take that to be a compliment."

CHAPTER FOUR

M. Falret, a doctor of medicine, has prepared from the official records of the police, a curious memoir on the suicides in Paris, from 1794 to 1822. Of those, some were attributed to:

Crossed in love: Number of men, 97. Women, 157.

Calumny and loss of reputation: Number of men, 97. Women, 28.

Gaming: Number of men, 141. Women, 14.

Reverse of fortune: Number of men, 283. Women, 39.

Let the numbers speak for themselves.
> —*The Truth Teller, a New York Newspaper for Gentlemen*

Limmer's, 12:54 a.m.

THE GLOW FROM THE SINGLE cracked lantern set on the floor beside him illuminated the unevenly nailed wooden planks that lined the slanted ceiling. Stripping his leather patch from his eye and tossing it, Matthew fell onto the sunken straw tick on the floor. Rolling onto his back and stretching out, he held up the expensive ivory card that had been given to him that afternoon. Disregarding the address, he stared at her name: *Lady Burton.*

Holy day. Holy, holy day. The way those dark eyes had held his, the way those lips had curved around her words every time she spoke, and the way that sultry voice had dripped with elegance and refinement about punched the last of his rational senses out. Something about her awoke an awareness he'd thought long dead and whispered of endless possibilities he wanted to roll around in.

Though he couldn't help but wonder about the association she had with Lord Arsehole. That heated argument on the riding path, which had resulted in her getting cropped, hinted at far more than he cared to admit.

Skimming his thumb across that printed name, he drew the card closer. Was it conceivable for a woman like her to want a man like him? And could a woman like her, who appeared to have everything, give a man like him, who had nothing…everything he wanted?

The door to his small room opened. There was a pause.

He didn't have to look up from the card to know who it was. "What do you want? I'm trying to sleep here."

"Sure you are." Coleman snickered. "Shall I leave you two alone?" he said, looking pointedly at the card.

Matthew sat up on the straw mattress, molding the card against his palm. "A touch jealous, are we?"

"Hardly. Women are a waste of breath, man. They're only good for one thing. And I wish I could say it was fucking."

Ah, yes. The man, who'd been married at sixteen to a woman crazier than him, thought he knew it all.

Matthew pointed the card at him. "Ey. Just because you're bitter doesn't mean I have to be. The difference between you and me is that I've been patiently waiting for the right one to come along. And *this*—" He held up the card, wagging it. "This here is about as right as they come. Not only did she agree to meet me at midnight—*in her home*—which means she damn well wants what I want, did you see the way she looked at me when she gave me this card? We're talking more than a night here."

Rolling his eyes, Coleman leaned against the frame of the door. "She gave you the card because she felt obligated after what you did. She's an aristo, Milton. Not exactly your kind of people."

Matthew flicked a finger against the card. "Why do you always ruin everything for me?"

"Because I think you may have taken too many knocks to the head. You seem to think women are moldable to your vision of…whatever the hell you're looking for, but I'm telling you right now, Milton, you can't mold a woman. Women mold you. And when you least expect it, they crush you until your very clay squeezes through their conniving little fingers."

"I pity your cynicism. You know that?" Matthew paused and glanced toward Coleman, noting that the man was not only fully dressed in his great coat, but that his black silvering hair was pulled back into a neat queue. Which the man rarely did. "Where the hell are you going?"

Coleman adjusted the riding coat on his muscled frame and eyed him. "Aside from taking back the horses we 'borrowed,' I'm off to double our money. We need to get you back to New York. And as for me…" He cleared his throat theatrically in the way he always did before announcing something Matthew didn't like. "I'm heading to Venice."

Matthew stared. "What do you mean you're heading to Venice? What about New York?"

"What about New York?"

His eyes widened. "The swipe is over and you and I share responsibilities."

"Milton." A wry smile touched those lips. "I'm honored knowing you still want me around, really, but the Forty Thieves was your vision for a better life, not mine. There's nothing left for me in New York. Not to say I won't miss you. You're the closest thing I have to a brother. But you have your life and I have mine." Lowering his gaze, he sighed. "How much money do you have? I need at least five pounds to make the cards worthwhile."

Matthew glared, feeling as if he'd been walloped in the chest by a man who had clearly moved on from their friendship. "You're not gambling what little we have. If you plan on ditching me and the boys, that's your damn right, but you're not sinking me while you're at it. Instead of *gambling,* I suggest you go put yourself in a few matches. London is big on boxing. As for me, I'm soliciting labor over at the docks come morning."

Coleman leveled him with a mocking stare. "The docks? Since when do you prance about soliciting honest work?"

Matthew pointed, trying not to feel *too* insulted. "I'm not playing with the law here, Coleman. Unlike in New York, I've got no marshals here to protect my arse, and these Brits are crazy. They'll hang you for anything. *Especially* if you're unlucky and Irish. And as you damn well know, I'm both. Now, off with you." Matthew settled back onto the mattress, snatching up his card. "I'd like to be alone with my card, if you please. I have a feeling it'll give me a lot more respect than you just did."

"Christ. Don't make me tear that bloody thing in half and shove it up your ass."

Matthew swiped up the pistol from the floor beside him with his other hand and pointed it at Coleman with a mocking tilt of his wrist. "Get the hell out of my room. I'm not paying four shillings a night to have you in here."

"We need twenty pounds each, Milton, if we're ever going to get out of Town. *Twenty.* My boxing will only bring in a few pounds per match, unless I start dealing with aristos. And as good as I am, I can only take so many hits a week. As for you working over at the docks? You'll only bring in about two pounds a week. At best. Count that on your fingers, man. *You* may have time on your hands, but I'm not staying in this piss of a city beyond two weeks." He paused. "How much do you think you could get out of this aristo, given what you did for her? If you slather on that charm I know you're good for?"

Matthew sighed and set the pistol back onto the floor. "I don't know. This whole idea of me calling on her for money merely for doing something ingrained in me feels dirty."

"No one does dirty better than you, Milton."

Matthew rolled his eyes. "I'm not *that* dirty and you know it." He tapped the card against his chin before glancing down at it. "I still can't get over the way she looked at me. I'm telling you. There was something there. I could see it and feel it. It was as if she and I were meant for bigger things."

"Bigger things?" Coleman snapped, angling toward him. "What the devil is wrong with you? We're not talking about some tea dealer's daughter here. We're talking nobility. Do you know what that is, Milton? It's better known as the trinity. Meaning, there's them, there's the King and then there's God. Notice that I didn't mention you at all. Why? Because you don't exist. And you never will. They don't touch people like us. Not unless it's to their benefit."

"Stop saying 'people like us.' You yourself are of nobility, for God's sake. You're—" Matthew scrubbed his head in exasperation, knowing it. To think that the same man he'd been training with and aspiring to be more like since he was twenty had been an aristo in hiding all along. It was something the stupid bastard didn't have the decency to tell him until they up and boarded the ship over to Liverpool. A part of him felt betrayed, though he understood Coleman hadn't been given much of a choice but to abandon who and what he was.

Matthew dropped his hand from his head. "You came here to straighten your mess of a life out and move on. That's what you said. Only, you're not doing shite. You're up and drinking and playing cards like some fecking sharp with money you don't have, making a bigger mess of not only your life, but mine. Why the hell aren't you facing the reality you came to face? I know why I came here. Because it was better than being dead and it was *your* goddamn idea. And whilst the swipe is over, I'm not leaving until I hold you to your reality. Call on your parents, and that uncle and nephew of yours who dug you up through the papers back in New York. Because seething on and on about a past you can't change isn't helpful to anyone. Especially yourself."

Coleman's features tightened as his blue eyes cooled to rigid ice. "I'll see them when I'm ready to see them. And I'm not fucking ready. Isn't that obvious?" Coleman stepped out and slammed the door, rattling the lantern.

Matthew sighed and hoped the man didn't do anything stupid. Holding up the card again, Matthew stared at the name *Lady Burton* and hoped he himself didn't do anything stupid.

CHAPTER FIVE

All information printed pertaining to the struggles
of others are not necessarily true.
—*The Truth Teller, a New York Newspaper for*
Gentlemen

St. James's Square, Thursday afternoon

THE FOOTMAN GRACIOUSLY gestured toward the open
doors of her father's library. "'Tis a joy to have you
back in London, my lady."

"Thank you, Stevens." At least someone was happy
regarding her return to London. Bernadette clasped her
bare hands together and entered the cavernous library
lined with all those endless books she used to gather
from the shelves as a girl and stack up all around her.
Not to read, mind you, but to build a full deck of a ship
she would then climb on top of and teeter to sail across
the expanse of the…library. The room still looked the
same. It even smelled the same: mildew laced with
cedar and dust.

Her chest tightened. It had been years.

Scanning the brightly lit room, she found her father and drifted toward where he sat, her verdant skirts rustling against the movements of her feet.

Lord Westrop's head was propped and resting against the side of his leather wing-tipped chair, that snowy white hair combed back with tonic. His eyes were closed and his usually rigid features were endearingly soft as the center of his Turkish robe rose and fell with each breath he took.

Bernadette paused before him, quietly observing him. It was the most peaceful she had ever seen him. "Papa?"

He opened his eyes and looked up at her. His astounded features gave way to him sitting up. "Bernadette."

"How are you, Papa?" She lowered herself to his booted feet and gathered his hands that had begun to show their age. She could see the veins.

He grabbed hold of her hands and smiled, shaking them in his. "You came back for me. You came back. I knew you would."

He seemed so happy to see her. Imagine that. He still knew how to exhibit happiness. She'd forgotten how good of a man he was capable of being when the burden of losing everyone—a wife, two brothers and three sisters—didn't eat at him.

She smiled as best she could. "I'm not staying long. New York is my home now. You know that."

His hands stilled against hers as he searched her face with dark eyes. "Why do you always wish to make me suffer? You know I have no one but you."

A deep sadness came over her. The same one that always gripped her whilst in his presence. "I am merely living my life now, Papa. The one I never got to live. 'Tis something I have old William to thank for. He adored me more than I deserved."

"Damn right." His aged features tightened. "Bloody deranged is what he turned out to be, leaving you with all that money and freedom. Look at you. Worth a million, yet living as some no-name Mrs. Shelton in New York City, cavorting with American ruffians like the Astors. I hear that you now entertain men on the hour."

"If it were on the hour, Papa, I wouldn't have time to call on you at all, would I?"

"And what of gossip?"

She lowered her chin. "There is all sorts of gossip, Papa. And it doesn't mean it's true. Which rumor are you referring to?"

"About you standing on the streets in nothing but petticoats out in New Orleans. What was that about?"

She cringed, knowing she was forever cursed to hear of that one awful misstep during her first days of freedom. "I was robbed whilst attending a street masking ball. That was why I moved from New Orleans to New York and took on an alias. The papers, not to mention all of stupid American society, made the incident out to be so much more nefarious than it was."

His eyes widened. "What the devil were you doing attending a street masking ball?"

Why did she feel like she was ten years old again? "I have never been to one and I wanted to go."

"Wanted to go. Indeed. Well. Serves you right. If

you had stayed at home and devoted yourself to being a respectable widow, it would have never happened. I think it time you accept that your days of traveling and frolicking are done, girl. Done."

She heaved out a breath. "I never got to travel or do much of anything. You know that. Neither you nor William ever allowed for it. As you well know, I was married barely two weeks after my debut, which wasn't really—"

"All I want to know is where are the grandchildren I wanted? *Why* won't you remarry in an effort to give me at least one?"

Her throat tightened as she fought to stay composed. After twelve years of trying to become a mother, allowing old William to bed her again and again in the hopes of having a child to love and cherish, she knew it was never meant to be. And in truth, she was done playing the role of a possession. "My days of matrimony are over. I have done my duty to you and to William, and to expect more or to say more is cruel."

Her father's features notably softened. "I did not mean to be cruel." He hesitated and then quickly said, "Honor your father by leaving this New York City behind. Stay here with me. I would like that. You can take your old chambers. I haven't changed anything. I still have all of your dolls and books and those porcelain figurines you always played with. You and I can read and play chess and should we need respite from London, we can always travel to Bath. Bath is a good, respectable place. We can take in the air by walking the Town, and during the summer, eat those flavored ices you used to love so much when you were a tot. Remember? 'Twas a good life. More important, a respectable one. So it's settled, yes? You will stay right here with your papa."

She slowly shook her head, dread seeping into every last inch of her. He didn't seem to understand that she wasn't a child anymore. "No. Though I do love you, I am my own woman now and I am asking that you respect me and my life."

His dark eyes flashed. "Are you intent on stabbing me in the heart, knowing that I have no one but you?"

Bernadette rose to her feet, sensing her time with him was done. No matter how much she gave him, he was always desperately grasping for more until nothing remained. "I am not about to submit to this guilt you keep piling upon my soul. Not when I have submitted to you all these years at the cost of my life. Do you think I ever wanted to marry William? No. But you wanted me to, so I did. And therein my obligation ends." She swallowed, trying to remain calm. "It was good seeing you, Papa. I trust you are receiving the yearly annuity I arranged through William's estate."

He grunted. "'Tis measly."

She half nodded. "I see. Thirty thousand a year is measly. I didn't realize your tastes were so extravagant. If you need more, I can make it fifty thousand."

He grunted again. "If I needed more, I would have asked. Now, are you staying with me or not?"

Why did she always stupidly cling to the hope that he could be the father she wanted him to be? "I am five and thirty, Papa. My life is practically half over.

I have given it to you, I have given it to William and I have given it to society. I do not intend to give up any more. I intend to frolic with whomever I please, whenever I please, and travel until my slippers fall off, regardless of what you and everyone else may think. Men do it all the time and no one even blinks. So let them all blink."

He swiped a veined hand over his face, snatched up his cane from beside the chair and heaved himself up. "I ask that you not call on me again unless you either respectably remarry or decide to live with me. I have nothing more to say." With that, he stalked out, leaving her to linger alone in the library.

An unexpected tear traced its way down her cheek. Annoyed with herself for even caring what he thought, she swiped it away and set her chin. She had done everything to make him happy at the cost of her own happiness and was finished with that and him.

She had spent twelve years of her life serving and bedding a scrawny, withered man who had grunted into her and knew nothing of her pleasure, let alone her happiness. Though she supposed she'd been fortunate, considering. For at least old William had treated her with an adoring, kind regard and devotion rarely found in aristocratic marriages. He had even left her his entire estate, despite her inability to sire a child for him. It was a gesture of the love he'd had for her. She regretted knowing that the old man had died without having ever once earned the one thing he'd wanted most—her heart. Sadly, her heart had yet to genuinely beat with love for a man. And at five and thirty, she wondered if it ever could.

But who was she to complain? Love was overrated anyway. As was holding on to one's reputation. Neither allowed a woman a breath of freedom. And rakish though it was, she was very much looking forward to midnight and whatever salacious adventure it would bring in the guise of the Pirate King.

CHAPTER SIX

An edition of the works of Lord Byron has recently been published in England, expurgated, and omitting Don Juan, deeming all of the passages offensive to decency and good morals. Who are the British to decide what decency and good morals are?

—*The Truth Teller, a New York Newspaper for Gentlemen*

Piccadilly Square, midnight

EVERYTHING IN HER home smelled like fresh-cut flowers, tea leaves and fobbing cinnamon. It was a damn good thing he'd bathed, scrubbed and shaved for the woman before coming over or he would have bloody wilted everything.

Silence drummed as Matthew awkwardly lingered in a lavish, pale green imperial drawing room decorated with overdone wall hangings, marble statuettes and a variety of gilded clocks scattered upon the mantelpiece of a grand hearth.

Matthew scanned the impressive length of the room and angled his way past countless upholstered chairs and pedestal tables. He paused before a white moonstone velvet settee. The woman had more furniture than he had toothpicks. He couldn't even remember what it was like to own furniture just to own it.

He adjusted the patch over his eye, ensuring it was straight. Glancing down at his great coat, which was spattered and streaked with crusting mud from riding about in last week's mud and rain, he cringed. He wasn't going to be making much of an impression. Certainly not the sort she'd made on him.

God. Why was he letting himself face her again at the cost of his own pride as a man? Oh, yes, he knew why. Because of Coleman. That son of a bitch had gambled away and lost everything, and now it was up to Matthew to clean up the mess.

The clicking of heels echoed down the candlelit corridor, drifting toward him through the open double doors.

Setting his calloused hands behind his back, he widened his stance and watched that entryway. His pulse thundered.

Within moments, a curvaceous, dark-haired woman appeared. The same one he'd wanted to seize and mold against himself when he first laid eyes on her in the park. Who knew British women had the ability to rile an Irishman into a full salute with but a glance.

It was felonious.

He tried not to linger on that exquisite appearance. Those black curls, which bore delicate wisps of silver that hinted she was a tad above his own age, were gathered and pinned around an elegant pale face. The only flaw on her face was a welt of a line on her jaw from the crop he'd been unable to save her from.

Since he'd last seen her, her riding bonnet had been stripped and replaced with a gathering of pretty, pale blue satin ribbons that had been woven into her hair, matching the shade of her azure evening gown. That delectable gown clung to her body and full breasts in a way that made him want to bite his hand to keep from biting her.

What he wouldn't do to unravel this.

Realizing she was watching him, Matthew smiled. He gallantly inclined his head toward her, offering his best rendition of a gent.

She met his gaze and also smiled, those full lips curving.

There was a sensual playfulness in that vibrant smile that made him want to trace his tongue all over it and never stop. Knowing his thoughts were treading on uneven hot bricks, he dug his bare fingers hard into the skin of his wrist below the cuff of his coat and locked it hard against his back. He needed to remind himself of the reality he was stupidly disregarding. Women of her caliber didn't associate with bogtrotters like him.

She hesitated, her dark eyes flicking to his leather belt and pistols in quiet uncertainty.

Matthew self-consciously adjusted his muddied great coat over the handles of his rosewood pistols, burying them from sight. "You needn't worry about the lead, luv. 'Tis more for my own protection. Not a lot of people like me." Which was an understatement. To date, fifty-six people wanted him dead for turning them over to marshals for various crimes. Fortunately, they were all back in New York and most were still sitting in Sing Sing Prison. Most.

She sashayed into the room and rounded him, those hips a-swaying as that satin gown flowed ravishingly against the elegant movements of her shapely body. Dark eyes met his as the zing of citrus floated toward him.

He wanted to lick the air *and* every last inch of her.

Her lips widened into a dazzling smile. "I am ever so pleased you came."

That voice was just as he had remembered it. Melodious. "I'm ever so pleased I did, too."

She swept an ungloved hand toward the white velvet settee. "Would you like to sit?"

He shifted his weight from boot to boot. "Ah, no. I'd rather not get mud on anything that pretty or white." He couldn't help but smirk about it. "I owe too many people money as it is."

Glancing toward his great coat, which she assessed indeed had crusting mud on it, she lowered her hand. "I care nothing for the furniture." Her expression brightened as she searched his face. "I know all that you see is a chair too pristine to sit on, but I wish to assure you, that the chair does not represent me. Now, please. Sit."

He eyed her, his smirk fading, noting the genuine dip in that honeyed voice and how she disregarded the mud on him without a blink. This was not your average aristo. There was an endearing earnestness lingering in those dark eyes and that pretty face. Sadly, her delicate jaw was still welted with an angry red line from that arsehole who'd cropped her.

He was beginning to sense that many men—men like Lord Arsehole—took advantage of what appeared to be an incredibly generous soul. And now, the dear was so bloody grateful to him for what he'd done, she was eagerly offering up everything—money, lodgings, a midnight rendezvous and a velvet throne—as if he were worthy of that and more.

Him. Worthy. His throat tightened. Feck. He'd taken money in the name of everything throughout the years, at the cost of everything, including whatever was left of his morals, but the idea of taking money from *her* felt like he'd really be crawling as a man. Coleman was going to maim him, but he just couldn't crawl in front of a woman who made his very chest ache.

He cleared his throat. "I, uh, actually came to personally thank you for your earlier offer in the park. 'Twas very generous. Regrettably, Coleman and I must decline for reasons of integrity." Not a lie. "I should go."

Her startled gaze met his. "You intend to leave?"

"Aye. 'Tis late and I've inconvenienced you enough." He also didn't feel like standing in front of her in a tattered, filthy great coat a minute more. "It was a pleasure. And I do mean that. Good night." He inclined his head and quickly rounded her before he could up and do something stupid. Like ask her if he could stay the night and every night thereafter.

She hesitated and then hurried after him. "Might I offer you tea? At the very least?"

He hated tea. "No, thank you. I don't do tea."

"Are you hungry? The chef always has something in the kitchen. I can have the servants bring everything out. You can have whatever you want. Caviar, wine, wilted cress with quail. What would you like?"

It was like dealing with all the mothers back in the ward who wanted to feed him for bringing their wandering children home. Only, this here woman could actually afford what she offered. He swung back to her, but kept walking backward to ensure he didn't linger. "No, thank you. I ate."

She paused. "I was really hoping you would stay. Will you?"

He jerked to a halt, his pulse drumming. "Why?"

She smoothed her hair, sending those soft, black curls swaying and, after a long moment, said, "I wanted to get to know you."

This could be good or this could be bad. "What do you mean? As a person? Or as a man? Because there is a difference. One involves just talk and the other one involves a hell of a lot more than talk. If you know what I mean."

She blinked rapidly. "Uh…well…both."

He drew in an astounded breath. Damn. Well.

To hell with Coleman's notion of the trinity. He was doing this. Angling toward her, Matthew offered in a husky tone he knew the women in his parts liked, "Have at it. What would you like to know about this here man?"

She stared up at him. "Everything."

Silence pulsed between them.

Everything. Christ, if he was stupid enough to blurt out everything about himself here and now, he doubted she'd let him stay long enough to finish a single sentence.

He cleared his throat. "I suggest we start with the basics. The name is Matthew Joseph Milton. And your full heavenly name is?"

"Lady Burton. It was on the card."

"Right." The one he had fingered to the point of tattering. The problem was, he wanted her *birth* name. Not the prissy title on the card that everyone else got.

Shite. What was he doing? Why was he staying and perpetuating this? A woman of Brit aristocracy would *never* seriously involve herself with a one-eyed third-generation Irishman with nothing to his name but letters. Furthermore, the boys back home, who were all full-blooded Irish patriots, would no doubt knock his teeth out for this. The woman could even have a fop of a Brit husband. Which he hadn't fecking thought of until now. A husband who'd be number fifty-seven of men wanting him dead.

He huffed out a breath. "Before I find myself in a situation I'd rather not be in, are you married or currently involved with other men?" After living almost nine years in what he referred to as "Satan's Circus," he was long past being coy. It was all about the point.

She let out a laugh. "Oh, no, no. I am no longer married. I have been widowed close to four years now. Nor am I involved with any man." She eyed him and added, "Yet."

His brows rose. Luck was at long last on his side.

"Ah. Yet. And, uh…how far are you willing to take this? Are we talking matrimony here? Because I'll admit, despite not looking the sort, that's what I'm going for. You may not know this, but a rough life does one of two things to a man. Disillusions him completely or makes him create a *very* long list of all the things he wants and needs. And I'm the latter."

She lingered for an awkward moment. "Matrimony is for the rest of society, Mr. Milton. A concept I have abandoned out of respect for myself. In truth, I prefer to engage in…whatever adventure presents itself." She smiled brightly up at him as if pointing out *he* were said adventure.

He paused. "Why do I get the feeling you're a bit of a rebel in your circle?"

"I wasn't always a rebel. I used to do everything everyone told me to do. And then I got bored." Those pretty dark eyes held his gaze in a daringly intimate manner. "I should probably warn you of something."

"Amuse me. What?"

"Attachments have not worked well for me in the past. As such, I don't like to give a man more than a night. That is, if he's fortunate enough to get a night."

He dragged a heavy hand through his hair. Apparently, he was dealing with a full-fledged libertine. Not good. He'd sworn to himself long ago, that he'd only take on a woman capable of giving him *everything*. Because after having lost everything, settling for anything less was downright insulting. He had to make this one cooperate or that damn list of the things he'd always wanted—a wife, children, a home—sure as hell wasn't going to fall from the sky anytime soon.

She lifted an inquisitive brow. "You have grown unnervingly quiet. Did I unnerve you?"

"I don't kneel that easily, luv. Believe me. And I'm afraid I'm not willing to accept less than everything. It isn't in my nature to do so." He traced his gaze to those full lips and leaned in, fighting against dragging his palms down the curve of her throat. He was beginning to think this woman was about to make him question his nature. "Can I kiss you?"

"If you keep at this, Mr. Milton, you and I will end up fully unclothed within the hour."

He drew in a steadying breath. "I was hoping."

She wet her lips. "Were you?"

The woman had to go wet her lips. She probably did it on purpose. "What? Am I not breathing on you hard enough? I thought I was being ridiculously obvious here."

"A little too obvious. What happened to us getting to know each other? All I know of you thus far is your name."

"I thought you said attachments have not worked well for you." He mockingly stared her down. "Besides. If I were to tell you anything more about myself, you'd ask me to leave and the night would be over. Is that what you want?"

She smirked. "I knew you were trouble the moment I glimpsed you in that park."

"And yet you not only invited trouble into your home

at an ungodly hour, but are asking him to stay. I wonder why."

She lifted a hand to his chin. "Because when I want
something, I have learned not to deny myself of it. And
yes, I will admit, bold that I am, I want something. Can
you guess what it is?" Holding his gaze, she delicately
grazed the tips of her fingers along the curve of his jaw
in a way that made his breath hitch.

He'd been touched by women before. Obviously.
But something about her and that touch was haunt-
ingly different. *This* was different. He could feel des-
tiny biting into his soul, taunting him to swallow this
and her whole.

He grabbed that hand and savagely pressed its heat
against his chin. Lowering his gaze to hers, he tried to
keep his breath steady and possessively fingered the
softness of that skin, allowing her heat to penetrate
his own.

She didn't pull away.

Which meant she wanted him.

His throat tightened and he couldn't bloody help but
think about ripping all of that expensive fabric from
her body with his teeth. Regardless of what this would
ultimately result in, he was damn well willing to settle
for whatever the hell the woman wanted.

Releasing her, he plunged his bare hands into those
gathered curls. He dug his fingers in and out, causing
pins and ribbons to cascade out as he unraveled some
of the silken strands. "Are we doing this?"

Her chest rose and fell more rapidly, those breasts
taunting him to touch and expose them.

Tugging back on that thick, soft hair, he tilted her face to ensure she was looking up at him. "I asked you a question, luv. Are we doing this?"

Her lips parted, those dark eyes intently searching his face. "Mr. Milton—"

"Matthew. Call me Matthew."

"Matthew."

"Yes?" He waited for her to say something, but no words fell from those lips.

She merely watched him.

Sensing the woman was mesmerized by what he considered to be a simple touch, he slid the tips of his fingers down that soft, pretty face, ensuring he didn't touch or graze the welt on her jaw. His calloused fingers hadn't had the honor of touching something so beautiful or satiny in so long. "I want you to tell me something."

"Yes?" she whispered.

He cupped the sides of her face. "Since we met, have you thought about me at all?"

She hesitated. "Yes. I have."

"Often?"

"More than I care to admit."

She'd been thinking about him. Often. Just like he'd been thinking about her. Often. A little too often and to the point of pleasuring himself in the darkness of his room to ensure he didn't explode whilst waiting to see her again. "And did you pleasure yourself at all whilst thinking of me?" he pressed.

Her eyes widened. "Is there a point to this?"

He tightened his hold on her face. "Did you?"

She held his gaze, those flushed features giving her the appearance of a woman who had just emerged from the throes of six hours of passion. "Twice."

He could see in her eyes that she *had* done it twice. Knowing it was obscenely exhilarating.

"I did it more than twice." He released her and purposefully lingered closer, letting his legs brush against those skirts. "Seeing you and I clearly feel the same about each other, I want you to put your arms around me. Are you up for it?"

Still holding his gaze, she slowly wrapped her arms around his shoulders, dragging him closer against herself until the scent of powder and citrus permeated his very breath.

He asked and she did. Damn. He'd been waiting for a woman like this all his life. He could only hope that her one-night-only rule wouldn't apply to him after this was over, because he wouldn't be able to live with that.

He slid his hands up the sides of those incredible curves, her warmth hardening the last of him. His cock pressed rigidly against the flap of his trousers. "Tell me what happens next."

"I think we both know what happens next."

His pulse thundered and he could no longer breathe. All he could think about was licking those full lips, ripping that dress in half and making her his, all his. "I should probably warn you, I've never been one to take anything slow."

Still lingering, she softly and tauntingly pointed out, "Did I ask you to take this slow?"

He bit back a shudder and, God help him, he knew he was done for.

CHAPTER SEVEN

All that you can do, do not. Unless it will bring
forth good. Unless it will bring forth change.
— *The Truth Teller, a New York Newspaper for
Gentlemen*

EVERY INCH OF BERNADETTE's skin pulsed as those large
hands trailed from her hair down the curve of her
throat, until their blessed heat stilled at her bodice.
His fingers slipped past the edge of her décolletage.

He held her gaze, his shaven jaw tightening until
the muscle below his eye patch flickered. He smelled
of leather, farthing soap and danger.

She knew what he wanted and she wanted it, too.
And though she had never bedded a man this quickly
in all her five and thirty years, be it wicked or not, she
was doing this. For he was all things breathtakingly
alluring and she had never *ever* physically wanted a
man more.

Bernadette eyed the parlor entryway. "We should
close the doors."

He didn't move. "Why waste breaths we're going to need?"

Her cheeks blazed. "I have…servants."

The tips of his roughened fingers tightened against the lace-rimmed edge of her bodice, frilling her skin and breath. "They'll just have to heed the noise and stay out."

Heaven help her.

He met her gaze with that one visible eye that beckoned her to kneel. "Do you really want this?"

Did she? "Yes."

"As in me inside you?"

Oh, God. "Yes."

"Give me one reason as to why we should do this."

If he was by any means being honest when he'd said he wanted a commitment, and if that was what he sought in that moment, he was about to find himself disappointed. Her stomach fluttered as lust hazed the very last of whatever decency she'd ever been born with. "Because I really want to."

"I rather like that answer."

She released the breath she didn't realize she held. He leaned in and erotically traced the tip of his hot, wet tongue across her bottom lip and then her upper one, and between the two again.

Her breath hitched with each wet lick.

His fingers tightened on the fabric of her gown, grazing her skin beneath. "I'm not wasting time with all of these damn hooks and buttons. Can I?"

She swallowed. "Yes."

"Hold still." Gritting his teeth, he gripped both sides

of her gown above each breast and with the quick, violent jerk of muscled arms, shred it open with a shocking rip that sent hooks and buttons spraying and tinkering across the floor.

She gasped, swaying against the aggressive movement, and felt as if her very knees were going to snap. The heat of her skin pulsed against the cooler air sweeping her. Her lilac corset and chemise and the tops of her pushed-up breasts were now completely exposed. Her breath escaped in pants. She tried to hold still, desperately wanting and needing to know what was going to happen next.

She'd never known anything like this. *Ever.*

Flicking his gaze to her breasts, he shifted his large frame toward her and tilted his head just enough to cause strands of sunlit hair to hang against the leather patch of his left eye. "Take off the rest."

Could she do this without fainting? She slid the ripped material of her gown down the length of her arms. It effortlessly fell away from her, cascading down onto her petticoats. She pushed it farther down, past her waist, until it slipped past the fullness of her petticoats and flopped to the floor.

He towered before her, watching. Waiting.

She undid the lacings on her petticoats, her heart pounding at the realization that she was actually doing this. She was about to bed a man she had just met in the park.

Her petticoats dropped and she stood in only her chemise, corset, stockings and slippers. Holding his gaze, she kicked off her slippers, sending them into the folds of her gown on the floor.

She paused, knowing she couldn't undo the corset on her own.

"All of it." His voice dipped low.

She tried to steady her breathing. Tried. "I cannot undo the lacings on my own."

He reached into the pocket of his great coat. Pulling out a folded razor blade, he flicked it open, the metal glinting against candlelight. "Allow me to play tailor."

Her eyes widened as he rounded her. She jerked toward him. "I would rather you not use that."

"Why not?"

"It makes me nervous."

"I like making you nervous." He grabbed her waist hard and spun her back around, jerking her to a halt in front of him, forcing her to face the open doors of the parlor. Leaning in from behind, he shoved her long hair to one side of her shoulder with the sweep of his other hand and slid the hot tip of his velvet tongue down her throat and shoulder.

She closed her eyes against the sensation, letting her head roll naturally to its side as his tongue made its way to the curve of her bare shoulder. Oh, God. He could have slit her throat and she couldn't have stopped him.

He paused. "Don't move." Grabbing the top of her corset just beneath her shoulder blade with one large hand, he wedged the tip of the razor between the upper lacings and…*sliced*.

She winced, feeling the razor work its way through

each lacing just above her skin, down, down, down until he tugged and the corset tumbled onto the floor.

He slowly rounded her, his boots echoing in the parlor, and snapped the blade of the razor back into its handle. Leaning toward a side table beside him, he set the razor on it, then methodically removed each of his two pistols from his leather belt. He set them beside the razor against the polished wood with a gentle clatter.

It was like disarming France.

And, somehow, she didn't care.

Turning, he stepped back toward her and raked his gaze across the sheer length of her linen chemise that showed *everything*. His broad chest rose. He let out a slow, soft hiss. "How old are you?"

Her face burned. Is this where it ended? "Five and… thirty."

He let out a low whistle, adjusting his great coat. "The good Lord loves you. *And* me, apparently. I don't think I've ever seen a woman look this good. And that's coming from a man six years younger than you. Six."

An astonished laugh escaped her as she awkwardly covered herself. The way he said it was—

Stepping back toward her, he pushed her hands away from herself, took hold of her chemise and dragged it up the length of her body and over her head in a teasing sweep. He flung it aside, leaving her completely naked, except for the white silk stockings held in place by matching lace garters.

He paused and lowered his gaze to her breasts, the palms of his warm hands slowly rounding her breasts and nipples. "So why don't you want to remarry? Because, I'll admit, I'll have trouble letting you go after this."

Heat raced beneath her skin as she bit back an exasperated breath, fighting the awkwardness of having him carry on a full conversation with her whilst she was naked. "I am done being owned."

He searched her face. "You obviously haven't been associating with the right sort of men."

She swallowed, the movement of those fingers grazing and caressing each nipple. This man exuded an experience of life laced with an exotic ease toward her body as if wanting to understand her from the inside out. It was liberating.

He lingered for a long, pulsing moment, then leaned down and in. He gently kissed her mouth. The palms of his large hands now hovered intently beside her face, not touching, but their heat emanating toward her skin. It was as if he were afraid she would break.

Blindly reaching up, she cupped the side of his shaven face and crushed her lips against his, forcing his mouth open with the press of her tongue.

He groaned against her mouth.

Her mind blanked as that velvet hot tongue playfully circled against her own. Her hands roamed up, grazing his smooth, leather patch as she reached up and into his hair, her fingers hooking against the leather tie.

They kissed and kissed and kissed. It was a mesmerizing, enchanting blur until he broke away.

Her eyes flew open and their gazes locked.

She was still naked. And he was still fully clothed. Tightening his jaw until a muscle flicked, he tugged off his great coat, revealing a yellowing frayed linen shirt, wool trousers and leather boots. He let his coat slip to the floor.

Still holding her gaze, he grasped his shirt and dragged it up over his head, pulling it off until it also slipped to the floor with the flex of sun-bronzed, well-muscled arms. He leaned into her, that broad chest hovering before her, wordlessly announcing that she give them both bliss.

Ever so slowly, she slid her hands up that smooth, hard chest in lust-hazy awe, rounding the palms of her hands over his broad shoulders and back down again. She'd never touched or seen anything quite like it. His scent of leather and soap, his warmth, and tense muscles surrounded her.

Several scars met her fingertips. She slid a lone finger on the largest, which extended from his left biceps to his shoulder. She leaned in and kissed it gently. "What happened?"

"Life happened," he murmured.

She glanced up, noting he was watching her.

His broad chest rose and fell in uneven takes, as if he were having trouble breathing against her touch.

She wasn't the only one being obliterated in this moment.

Reaching between them, while still holding her stare, he undid the flap of his trousers, pushing it aside, and exposed his thick length. Grasping her waist, he dug his fingers into her hip with the spread of his hand and then used his other hand to slowly rub the length of his erection against her upper stomach. The friction warmed her skin, sending a shiver of awareness throughout her entire body. Why was it she couldn't guess what he was about to do next?

His features tightened. "Turn. Face the hearth."

She slowly, slowly turned and faced the hearth, where the coal embers burned low.

He grabbed her wrists gently from behind and brought her arms up, pushing her forward, using the broad hard length of his body. Bringing her to a halt before the hearth, he guided her hands out to the marble ledge.

Her fingers gripped the smooth, hard ledge that had been warmed by the coals. This was it. This is where she was introduced to something she'd always wanted but never known with any man—*unadulterated passion.*

He draped the length of his large body against her backside, his erection pressing into her bum. "Are you even real?" he whispered from behind, his lips moving against her neck.

"I am," she whispered back. "Are you?"

"I am." He leaned away, tracing his hands from her shoulders to her back. She closed her eyes against that touch as he moved his hands down, down her legs and knelt behind her. Warm lips and the moist tip of his tongue slid across the curve of her lower back. All he did was touch and slide that tongue. It went on and on.

Gripping the marble hearth hard, she swayed. "Please." She couldn't say much more.

He rose, that tongue sliding up her back. "Say it."

"Take me," she choked out.

His tongue traveled along her shoulder blade. "You can do better than that, luv."

She bit back a shudder. "I…I need it."

He licked the other shoulder blade. "Need what? Come on."

She swayed. "You. I need you."

He dipped in and nipped the curve of her neck. "You don't sound desperate enough."

"Do it already!" she choked out in riled exasperation.

"That's more like it." His hands jumped to her waist. Grabbing her hips hard, he positioned himself and slowly slid his thick length between her wet folds. Without warning, he rigidly rammed deep into her—up to the hilt—causing her to not only gasp but jerk against the hearth she clutched.

It was amazing.

He held her savagely against himself, his fingers digging into the skin of her hips before rounding toward the front of her. He fingered and flicked her nub, staying buried deep within her. He didn't stop until her body gave way to stomach-rippling, throat-tightening, breath-catching pleasure that refused to let her go.

This man clearly knew what he was doing.

His fingers rounded back up to her hips. Gripping her waist, he slid halfway out and then slammed into her. She staggered as he thrust again and again, each jerk of those hips determined to break her. Dominating pressure and pleasure crossed and rippled through every inch of her until she was so overwhelmed she was unable to breathe.

He ground into her harder, each forceful thrust sending her moist fingers sliding against the ledge she was having trouble holding on to. The embers in the hearth swayed as did her entire world.

"Give me your name," he rasped from behind in between thrusts. "Your birth name."

She closed her eyes, as pleasure seized her core and tossed her upward. "Bernadette," she choked out in a half moan.

"Bernadette," he repeated as if stroking her name along with the rest of her.

Oh, God. She was about to—

Everything shattered and her body with it. She moaned, letting it take her into oblivion as he rode her faster.

She finally knew what it felt like to embrace real passion. And it was heaven all ablaze.

His slick, hot thrusts continued until he groaned and jerked out completely. Using several quick tugs of his hand, the warmth of his seed spurted against the curve of her back. A longer anguished groan escaped him as he smeared his seed all over her back with his fingers.

Their ragged panting filled the air.

She staggered, still hanging on to the marble ledge in an effort to keep herself up. Dearest God. Bedding him was like gulping freedom laced with euphoria.

Over her bare shoulder, she saw him step back. In between heavy breaths that expanded and further showcased that bronzed muscled chest, he buttoned the flap of his trousers. He paused, holding her gaze.

She swallowed, feeling unbearably vulnerable and naked under that gaze, and turned to gather her clothes.

"Bernadette." He jumped toward her and grabbed her by the waist, startling her. With his other calloused hand, he swept her up and into the crook of his arms, his jaw tightening from the effort. Pressing her against the soothing warmth of his exposed chest, he turned them toward the open doors of the parlor and glanced down at her. "I'll tuck you in. Where is your bedchamber, luv?"

She blinked up at him, in astonishment, clinging to those bare, broad shoulders. Why did she no longer feel naked or vulnerable in his arms? "Upstairs."

Wordlessly, he carried her out of the parlor and took the main stairwell up, taking two stairs at a time until they reached the landing.

"To the right and the last door," she offered.

Within a breath, they were there. Taking several long strides across the length of her pale blue bedchamber, he set her atop the four-poster bed with a sweep. Yanking the linens up from all around her, he folded them up and over her naked body, tucking it around her in unspoken tenderness.

She propped herself up on an elbow, astounded. Did he tuck all his women into bed like this? "Do you want to stay the night? I'm offering."

He glanced up from his task of molding the linens around her. He stared in what appeared to be genuine disappointment. "As much as I'd love to, I can't. I've got someone waiting for me."

She nodded. Though she hadn't planned on wanting

to see him again, annoyingly, she wanted more of him, of this, of his razors and his linen tucking. She'd never known anything like it. "And will I see you again?" She tried being very casual about it.

His gaze held hers. "Do you want to see me again?"

"Yes."

"And what happened to your one-night rule? Hmm?"

What, indeed? She knew the answer to this one. There had never been a man who had offered her a night like the one she'd just had. Not. Ever. She drew in a breath, aware that he was intently searching her face, awaiting an answer. "You appear to be a rare exception. And as such, I suppose I can spare another night."

His mouth quirked. "It'll be a pleasure ensuring that the next time I see you, you'll spare me several thousand more."

Why did she feel as if she had just damned herself? She wasn't even going to comment. For she had a feeling he wanted her to. "Did you need money before you go? How much?"

That quirk in his mouth faded. He lowered his chin. "We're not whoring ourselves here. So keep that dirty talk to yourself. If I want money, I'll ask for it. And I'm not asking."

She stared. This was a first.

He sighed. Leaning over the bed and her, he skimmed a bare hand over the side of her face and searched her eyes. That leather patch had shifted across his cheekbone, hinting at the curve of the eye hidden beneath. "Bernadette." He grazed a thumb against her lower lip. "The next time we see each other, we should talk."

She swallowed. "About what?"

"About what happens next. We got a little ahead of ourselves. Actually, a lot ahead of ourselves, but I have a feeling you and I will be catching up quick." His jaw tightened as he searched her face. "Don't be inviting other men into your bed anymore. You got that?"

The way he said it, so assuredly, without any doubt, as if they had just been married by the hand of the bishop himself, made her inwardly panic. She pointed up at him, trying to keep herself from altogether poking him. "I belong to no one. Let there be no doubt in that. I decide who I get involved with and what happens next. Not you."

He shifted down toward her, leaning against the side of the bed until the muscles in his arms and chest visibly tensed. "I'll give you a week to miss me. We'll take it from there." Straightening, he adjusted the faded wool trousers slung low on his hips and swung away, striding out of the room without another backward glance as if he knew without any doubt she *would* miss him.

His booted steps faded down the corridor.

She released a shaky breath, still in disbelief over what had just happened. All of her lofty dreams involving unadulterated, heart-pounding passion had always been more incredible inside her head than in reality, but *this* was the first time the two had *ever* merged into one.

Which meant…something very bad was about to happen. It always did whenever she took to dreaming.

And the last thing she wanted was to lose control over this entire situation. Especially given the man thought that their one night was about to amount to forever-more.

Sitting up, she quickly wrapped herself in linen and scrambled out of bed. She hurried to the open door and leaned out. Although Matthew had long disappeared, her burliest footman was making his way toward her, eyes downcast, as if announcing that he saw nothing, even though he probably saw everything.

"John," she called out, drawing up the linen farther around her shoulders until all skin was buried from sight. She was long past pretending that her life was anything but what it was: widowhood and scandal.

The large man froze and glanced up. "Yes, my lady?"

"You know the man you just saw? The one with the patch?"

He lowered his gaze. "Yes?"

She quieted her voice. "I will pay you an additional fifty pounds to follow him about Town until he calls on me again. He is downstairs right now, getting dressed. I ask that you follow him out and watch over him. Ensure no one touches him and ensure you tell me everything there is to know about him. Will you do it?"

He glanced up, his brows rising as if he had been bestowed with some sort of a title. "Gladly. I once served in the military. Infantry."

She smiled. "Yes, I know. Which is why I'm entrusting this to you. Thank you. Now, I suggest you bring pistols, for I will warn you, I have no idea how involved this may get. Should you fear for your life at any point, involve the authorities. I do not want you or anyone else getting hurt. For I know nothing about this man."

"I'll heed that, my lady. And you needn't worry. I'll ensure my own safety." With a quick bow, John jogged down the corridor, disappearing.

Bernadette leaned against the frame of the door. In terms of learning more about the dangerous side of Matthew, that was one route established. Next, she needed to speak to Georgia.

CHAPTER EIGHT

Let your memory be of death, punishment and
glory. Not merely the glory.
—*The Truth Teller, a New York Newspaper for*
Gentlemen

OPENING THE NARROW DOOR to the small hackney that
waited for him just down the cobblestone street from
Bernadette's townhome, Matthew angled in. Slamming
the door behind himself, he slid toward the inner wall
of the carriage on the seat beside Coleman, adjusting
his great coat around his frame and the pistols tucked
into his leather belt.

He, Matthew Joseph Milton, was a prick. A worthless prick. Why? Because he was bringing the incredible, edible Bernadette into his mess of a life without
letting her know what the hell she had just gotten herself into. He was damn certain there was a command-
ment somewhere against this in the bible. Like, *"Thou
shalt not covet a woman without informing said woman
that thou art a gang leader."*

"So how much did she end up giving us?" Coleman pressed.

Ah. Yes. That. Matthew reached up and casually knocked on the roof of the hackney to signal the driver to leave. "I didn't take any money."

Coleman sat up. "What? What do you mean? Why not? What happened?"

"Nothing happened."

"What do you mean *nothing* happened? You were in there for two goddamn hours. What were you doing while *nothing* was happening?"

Two hours? It felt like a breath.

As the hackney rolled forward, Matthew could do nothing in that moment but stare at his hands. And although he could barely see them in the waving shadows of the night, he could still feel them. He could feel her softness, her skin, her touch, that fragrance of powder and citrus, and it was as enchanting as it was eerie.

He'd never wanted a woman like this before. *Never.* Not in a way that made him unable to breathe or think. He had left that long, long ago with Miss bloody Drake and the lad who would try to kiss her and stupidly quote poetry, only to realize that while he would have sacrificed everything for her, she couldn't and wouldn't and didn't sacrifice a thing for him. She had let him fade away into the Five Points and went on to marry his best friend from his old life barely a few months later. It was something he'd never forgiven either of them for. But this...this was... It felt—

Coleman shifted toward him. "So what *did* you do whilst you were in there? Because I'm just bloody wondering what took you two whistling hours, only to walk out with nothing."

Matthew tried not to get overagitated with the man. "She and I are officially involved. All right? So feck the money. We'll get it elsewhere. We'll take on five jobs shoveling dung if we have to, because I'm not taking money from a woman I'm looking to make my own."

Coleman paused and then boomed, "You— *What!* What the hell do you mean you're *involved?* You mean, you're fucking her? *Already?*"

"Why do you always make everything sound so disgustingly vile? It wasn't like that at all and I'm not saying any more. But I will say this—I'm not taking money from her. I'm not."

"Oh, I see. It's all about you and into Salt River I go. Maybe I ought to wrap that overambitious cock of yours with a satin bow and sell it to the Queen for fifty to ensure we both get the money we need."

Matthew feigned a not-so-enthused laugh. "Since we're on the topic of cocks and satin bows, why not just call on that father of yours and ask *him* for the money? He's got plenty of it, being an aristo, doesn't he?"

Coleman's voice hardened to the edge of lethal. "I'm not touching coffers lined with the plague. Call me a tad superstitious. If I call on my father, I can assure you, *neither* of us are going to want to be in Town."

God knows what that meant. Matthew shifted against the seat. "Your financial situation is not my problem anymore. I've got a woman to impress."

Coleman kicked his boot into Matthew's. "What the hell is this? A rescue in the park, two hours in her parlor and you're undone? Are you that devoid of common sense? Since when?"

Matthew dug his fist into his palm. "Since now. You have a problem with that?"

Coleman flopped himself back against the seat as the carriage rounded yet another corner. "Was it that good? Hell, maybe I ought to prance myself over and see what my cock is worth."

Matthew narrowed his gaze. Though he couldn't see anything but the hard outlining shadows of Coleman's face in the swaying darkness, he leaned toward him and hissed out, "No one mocks me. You got that? I mock me. And don't you fecking talk of going near her, or you'll wish you were dead. You'll wish."

Coleman coughed out a rough laugh. "For you to be talking to me like this means she blew a hole in your head the size of Manhattan. Who ever thought you'd go down so easy?" Holding out both hands, he clapped jeeringly. "Well, bravo on that. It appears you finally found yourself a girl to fill that stupid list of being a family man. So now what? Do you plan on carrying her off into the Five Points and settling her in with all the rats? Or did you forget to tell her about the rats? And when I mean rats, I don't mean the real ones. I mean the boys."

Matthew pointed rigidly at him. "If I didn't know any better, Coleman, I'd say you were jealous. And to hell with you and that. This woman happens to be the epitome of everything I ever wanted, and if that bothers you, I suggest you go slit your throat. Because I have a right to a life outside the boys."

Coleman shifted. "I'm confused. Are you actually staying here in London? Is that what you're telling me?"

Matthew let out a sigh. He knew he'd have to face this question eventually. "I don't know what I'm doing quite yet. But I do know one thing—I'm not walking away from her and this after what happened tonight."

"Well...you can't hang the boys like this. Especially with me not going back. The swipe is over and they're all waiting for you to do the right thing. And what about Ronan? He's holding your goddamn tenement for you. You know how that boy depends on you for everything. You told him you'd be back."

"I know. Believe me, I know." Matthew threw his head back and hit it repeatedly against the seat, hating his life. He couldn't even get involved with a woman without choking on the guilt of his responsibility to the ward.

They sat in silence the rest of the way.

The hackney eventually rolled to a stop before Limmer's. The side door opened. Yellow light from the dirty gas streetlamp edged in, illuminating sections of the interior.

Leaning forward, Coleman said, "I still need money."

"Damn you for breathing." Though Matthew could grouch for years about it, he knew he owed the man this and more. "Keep boxing and I'll give you whatever I make. All right? I'll simply get back to New York later than expected. Which I don't mind. It'll allow me to figure all of this out."

Coleman hesitated. "Thanks. I appreciate it."

"It's about time you do."

"Limmer's!" the driver shouted from outside in reminder. *"Gents?* You coming out?"

They paused and jumped out of the hackney and into the misty dampness of the night. Matthew tossed a coin from his pocket up at the driver. He rounded toward the entrance of Limmer's. Thick fog hovered all around, dimming the yellow glow of the gas lamps that lingered at the end of the narrow, filthy cobblestone road.

Sensing someone was watching them, Matthew turned slightly. Through his one eye, he glimpsed a sorely misplaced black-lacquered carriage lingering just down the street with a driver and burly footman in the front box watching them.

He turned away, pretending he never saw them. "Coleman," he said through lips he didn't move. "We're being watched."

Coleman hissed out a breath but didn't turn. He lowered his voice. "Why would we be watched?"

Matthew pushed him toward Limmer's. "I don't know. Just keep moving."

"Are they from New York?"

"They can't be. Our sort can't afford to cross an ocean, let alone hire a carriage like that." He paused. "Does your father know you're in Town?"

"As you damn well know, I haven't approached the bastard yet."

"Then who knows?"

"No one other than Georgia."

Seeing it obviously couldn't be Georgia sending men after them, Matthew knew they'd have to unravel this soon.

CHAPTER NINE

INFORMATION WANTED
—*The Truth Teller, a New York Newspaper for*
Gentlemen

The following afternoon
Park Lane

WITH A LOPSIDED GRIN, Georgia whirled her way into the room on quick slippered feet, her chartreuse morning gown swaying against her playful, sweeping movements. "In all but five days, I make Robinson kneel and crawl. And I hate to say it, Lady Burton, but I can't wait."

Between the two of them, it would seem there was nothing left to talk about but men. Bernadette smiled. "I hope everything goes as planned."

"Oh, it will." Still grinning, Georgia hurried toward her. "I haven't heard from you since our little trot through the park. How have you been?"

"Hanging off a cloud, I suppose." Bernadette didn't even give Georgia an opportunity to sit when she went on. "I know how busy you are establishing yourself here in London, and I am desperately trying not to impede upon Mr. Astor's plans, so I will make this brief and scurry off. I need you to tell me more about this Mr. Milton. Can you? Please?"

Georgia jerked to a halt, her gathered strawberry-red curls quivering. A pert laugh escaped her lips as equally amused green eyes met hers. "That one is what I call trouble, trouble, trouble."

This was encouraging. "I'm already in trouble," Bernadette couldn't help but admit. She glanced toward the doorway of the parlor, half-expecting Mrs. Astor to walk in, and prayed the woman wouldn't. Bernadette lowered her voice. "He called on me last night."

Georgia seated herself majestically and arranged her morning gown about her feet before quirking a rusty brow. *"And?"*

If it had been anyone else, Bernadette would have quietly risen from her upholstered chair and walked out the door. But this was Georgia. The girl who snorted. The girl who excitedly clapped at having her freckles disappear beneath cosmetics. The girl who had no qualms about saying words like *piss* and *feck*. The girl who happened to be Bernadette's closest thing to a friend. Actually, the only female friend she had. "I let him bed me."

Georgia's eyes widened. She leaned forward in the chair, clutching the armrests as if she were about to fall out of it. "You let Matthew Joseph Milton bed you? Oh, now, Lady Burton, that's just—" She pretended to spit twice over the side of her chair before letting out a heaving sigh. "Why would you do such a thing?"

Bernadette lowered her chin, annoyed with the idea that she had to defend herself. "Because I find him to be profoundly genuine, irresistible, incredibly attractive, and despite my inability to trust myself in this, I am desperately hoping I don't have to live the rest of my life thinking all men are bastards. That is why."

Georgia leaned back against the chair. "I suppose that's good enough for me. What would you like to know?"

"Everything."

Georgia giggled. "I don't know *everything,* but I do know enough to make the poor man blush."

"Even better. Out with it. Start with his date of birth."

Glancing up toward the ceiling, Georgia tapped a manicured finger against her knee and puffed out a breath. "His date of birth is the twentieth of December. Which will make him...*thirty* by the end of this year. He's incredibly intelligent, though his actions sometimes beg to differ with that. He loves children—though I know I wouldn't trust mine to him, lest they learn things they shouldn't. He leads a vigilante group known as the Forty Thieves and is rather involved in the politics of the city, though sadly, no one ever takes him seriously. The mayor has brushed him off for years, despite Matthew having written over several dozen letters to the man."

Georgia leaned forward in the chair again. "Did you know that, since I've known him, and I've known him since I was fifteen, he hasn't bought himself any new clothes? Nor has he taken the time to steal any. Not a single button's worth. He thinks it's vain and not worth the money, and therefore opts to patch and repatch everything he owns instead. Whatever money he does get, be it earned or not, he stupidly gives away to others, which is why he never has anything. He cuts his own hair whenever it gets too long, because although it only costs two pennies at the barber off Mulberry, he's that cheap. His best friend is Edward Coleman, which should tell you his taste in friends is questionable, because Coleman is a boxer, a gambler and a heathen, though I will say all the women in the Five Points absolutely adore him and are forever trying to get their hands on him."

Georgia paused. "But then again, they're all whores so maybe that doesn't say much. Oh, and if you really want to annoy Matthew, fix his patch for him when it's crooked. He hates that." Georgia pertly returned her gaze to Bernadette's, her finger no longer tapping against her knee. "Is there anything else you wanted to know?"

Despite all of those little snide commentaries, and the man leading some vigilante group, it was obvious this Matthew was unlike any man she'd ever met. He loved children? And wrote letters to the mayor? "Might I ask why he walks around with pistols and razors? Is he a criminal? I know he looks like one, but he doesn't act like one and this talk of him loving children and writing letters to the mayor clearly hints of a soft side.

He mentioned people not liking him. Who doesn't like him and why?"

Georgia rolled her eyes. "When a man gets himself involved in street politics, as we call it over in the sixth ward, *everyone* will eventually want him dead. He walks around with a razor and pistols because, where we came from, it's either shoot, slice or die. And yes, I hate to say it, but he's a criminal. Not your average criminal, mind you. He does good and right by others, but he thieves in order to maintain his group of gallivanting banshees, and whether he realizes it or not, it's leeching his morals dry. He's trying to wrestle hope and self-respect out in the Five Point filth, not caring that it gets all over him. And in the end, he just can't get it off. I'll also say that, sadly, it's all about money for him."

Bernadette bit her bottom lip before dragging it loose to say, "For a man, whom you say only cares about money, he has turned away any opportunity I might have offered him. Are you telling me it's a ploy?"

Georgia paused, squinting at her. "So he hasn't asked you for money? Or taken anything from you?"

"No. In fact, last night, when I asked him if he needed any, he outright scolded me for it."

Georgia's features softened. "You're clearly getting to see a different side of him." A small smile frilled her lips. "It sounds as if you touched him in the right way. It's a pride thing now. He never takes money from his own. 'Tis obvious he already thinks you're his."

Feeling her stomach flutter, Bernadette pressed, "What do you mean by that? I know he and I shared a bed, but—"

"All I can say—" Georgia leaned forward again "—given what I know of him, is that Matthew is very particular about his women and only jumps when he thinks she could be the one. If he thinks you're the one, Lady Burton, well…you are well and done for. He'll put a pistol to your head before he'll let you walk away. So congratulations. It sounds as though you've got yourself a husband."

Bernadette felt herself panicking. "But I don't want a husband. I made that very clear to him last night. Very clear. I was in no way misleading."

Georgia smirked. "It doesn't matter what you say or think. Matthew is the sort of man who leads. Not follows. Which means, he decides what happens. Not you. Would you like some tea?"

Bernadette's eyes widened. "No. No tea." What under heaven and above hell had she gotten herself involved with?

CHAPTER TEN

Not the smallest clue at present remains that is likely to unravel this mysterious transaction, which appears to have been instigated by a robbery.

—*The Truth Teller, a New York Newspaper for Gentlemen*

Days later, evening
Piccadilly Square

BERNADETTE PLAYED OUT her angst and thoughts against the ivory keys of the piano, fluidly leaning in and out, in and out, as her hands moved rhythmically across the length of the keys. Unlike everything else around her, she could always depend on the ivory beneath her fingertips to respond in the way she wanted them to. It was always beautifully perfect once she mastered a piece. If only she could say the same about everything else in life.

"Impressive," a man hollered out. "I didn't realize you played."

She jerked away from the piano, midnote, and froze.

Matthew loomed in the doorway of the candlelit parlor.

How did he get in? Her pulse thundered in disbelief, realizing that one of his large hands fisted a wool sack, whilst the other clutched the collar of her burly footman, John, whom she had secretly tasked to follow him.

Oh, dear. She scrambled up from the piano seat, turning toward them, and paused. Matthew's chiseled face, leather patch and the length of his muscled frame was well spattered with mud, whilst that rain-soaked chestnut-colored hair clung to his forehead like tar.

He shoved her footman, who was equally muddied, forward and into the room. "This is yours, I believe," he rumbled out.

He didn't look like a man who had won a battle.

He looked like a man ready to start one.

Bernadette cringed. "I can explain."

"No need." He headed toward her, boots thudding against the floorboards with a rigid determination that she could not only see but feel. He paused before her and leaned down and in so close, the faded leather patch of his eye blurred against his face. "You have the nerve of Satan sending someone to spy on me."

It would seem men who were out doing wrong didn't like being spied on. She stepped back and blinked rapidly, halted by that muddy sack, which had been visibly torn, beneath his arm. Expensive red velvet peered out from beneath the wool like a blood wound.

She eyed him. "Have you robbed someone?"

"I don't have to answer that."

Which meant he had. Oh, God.

He reached out a hand and directed her toward the open doors. "Walk. We're taking this elsewhere."

The footman quickly rounded them. "Don't touch her!"

Matthew shifted toward her, looking even *more* agitated. "Tell him to leave, Bernadette. Tell him to leave, before I fist him up to Ireland."

Sensing that he really would fist poor John up into Ireland, she insisted, "Leave, John. You needn't worry. Mr. Milton is an acquaintance of mine."

Matthew shifted closer, lowering his chin. "We're long past that and you know it."

The footman hesitated.

Bernadette gestured frantically toward the entrance of the parlor before anything more was said or done. "Go wash up, John. Please. I will be more than fine."

Though the footman still hesitated, he eventually nodded and quietly left the room, adjusting his scuffed livery.

Matthew took her arm, flinging half-hanging straw from his coat onto her gown, and hurried them into the corridor. "Let's talk in the privacy of your room upstairs, luv. I don't want your servants listening in on our conversation."

Her heart pounded as his grip tightened around her arm. He didn't say another word.

The sweeping stairs and the long corridor leading to all the suites whizzed by, finally ending when they paused at the closed door leading to her bedchamber. He had remembered its location.

He released her and leaned toward her, the scent of fresh mud drifting toward her. "Do you honestly think I deserved being followed by one of your servants like that? It made me feel utterly worthless and I can assure you, I already feel worthless enough without having it pointed out."

She shifted toward him, her throat tightening in shame. "Forgive me. I just…I needed to know more about you."

His chest rose and fell against his great coat and his unlaced linen shirt. "You could have just asked."

Her stomach knotted. "I'm not used to getting straightforward answers out of men."

"I'm not like other men. If you ask me a question, there isn't a goddamn thing I won't answer. And that's a fact. Because you see, my mouth has always been connected to a thing called integrity."

"What a lovely, lovely sentiment. One I intend to test." She glanced toward the sack he held and pointed. "Did you steal that?"

He swung away and punched the air twice, still clutching the sack. He jerked back to the door and turned the knob, kicking the door open with a muddy boot. "Get in. We have to talk."

"What about my answer?"

"You'll get it. *In there.*" Gently grabbing her arm, he dragged her into the room, shutting the door behind them. Heaving out a breath, he crossed over to her dressing table and set the small wool sack on it, knocking over bottles of rose water, talc and rouge. "Sorry." He rearranged the bottles with hands that were much larger than all the items he was handling. "What is all this? Cosmetics? Shite. You actually use all of this?"

It was obvious that he was stonewalling.

Whisking toward him, she paused before the mirrored dressing table he lingered by and took up the sack. Placing it back into his hands, she swiped at her own hands, removing the grit clinging to them. "I suggest you take this back, Matthew. I may have many indecent flaws myself, but I am not about to condone this."

He stared. "I hate to disappoint you, but I can't take it back."

"Why not?"

He still stared. "I only came to deliver your footman. But given that you asked, I'll be gracious enough to say that I didn't even want you knowing about this."

Why did she have a feeling she didn't want to know, either? "For heaven's sake, what did you do?"

He huffed out a breath. Widening his stance, he dug his hand into the wool sack and yanked out a stained, red velvet bundle from its belly. He tossed aside the torn wool that had been cradling it and held the bundle up. "I saw the bastard who cropped you, just off Regent Street on my way back from working at the docks today. So I followed pretty boy home, waited until he took off for some arsy-varsy event and cleaned out his vault. The only trouble I had was having to tackle your footman to ensure I didn't get caught."

She gasped. "You *robbed* Lord Dunmore?!"

"Yes. Didn't I just say that?"

Her eyes widened. "But why? Why would you—"

"Because my personal take on justice has a tendency to warp my rational perception from time to time. I robbed him because he deserved it after what he did to you. I don't expect you to understand, given you chose to violate my goddamn pride by having me followed around as if I were a threat to all of England. You're fortunate, Bernadette, that your footman told me who the devil he was, or I could have slit his throat thinking he wanted me dead."

She eyed the bundled material in his hands. A golden threaded shield with the name *DUNMORE* was stitched into its velvet front. Oh, God.

"You have to give it back."

"And hang? For that pig? Christ, no." He stared her down for a long, pulsing moment. "Who is Dunmore to you anyway?"

She inwardly cringed. "No one."

"No one?" He continued to stare. "That pretty mouth of yours is lying. Aside from that shouting match you and he exchanged and the crop you took to the face, would you care to explain why he also has a portrait of you hanging on the wall in his study?"

Her cheeks flamed. Dunmore still had the portrait she'd commissioned for him? Even after all this time? That stupid, stupid fool. "I had the portrait commissioned for him."

"That was incredibly nice of you. *Why?*"

"We were lovers."

"Lovers." His voice darkened. "For how long? Are you telling me you let him do the sort of things to you that I did to you? Is that what you're telling me?"

She edged closer. He was jealous. The Pirate King was jealous. "And what if I told you yes? What of it?"

He hissed out a breath, shifting away. "Forget I asked."

"I will. What is it that you actually stole from Dunmore anyway? I want to see it."

He sighed and slowly and grudgingly unraveled the velvet material, cupping it in the crook of his arm to reveal what was hidden within. "*This* is what my need to avenge you, coupled with a need for money, resulted in. All right? *This*."

Her eyes widened. A dozen gold pendants of different shapes and sizes shimmered in the candlelight against the velvet, an array of red, green, white and yellow stones winking with glistening pride.

She knew what they were. They belonged to Dunmore's late mother. Dunmore had offered them to her one night, and of course, she had refused. And it appeared despite Dunmore's piling debts, which he'd hidden from her throughout their involvement, his inability to part with his mother's jewels, even to this day, meant that there was still a sliver of the glorious man she'd once known. Damn him.

Bernadette glanced up. "You have to give it back. They belonged to his mother. 'Tis all he has left of her."

He continued to observe her, the lines on his face still harsh. "I didn't realize he meant so much to you."

"Matthew." She angled toward him. "This has nothing to do with him. It has to do with what is right. These have to go back to Dunmore. I won't see you hanged for this."

A muscle flicked in his mud-streaked jaw. He set his shoulders and lowered his gaze, rewrapping the pendants. "As if you care if I hang now that you know the sort of man I really am."

Though his stance, words and tone were merciless, as if he didn't give a drat what she thought, his rugged face held a regret even he could not hide. He really was mock or die.

She leaned toward him. "I care more than you realize. I know what it's like to be forced into making decisions that go against everything you are. But that doesn't mean we have to keep going down that path and let it destroy *everything* we are." She leaned a bit closer and grasped the velvet bundle in his arms, trying to yank it out of his grasp. "Now, give it here."

He tightened his hold, keeping it from moving.

She tugged. Only, it still wouldn't move. "Matthew."

He observed her, dirt crinkling the side of his jaw. "You'd make a good nun. You know that?" He pushed her hands away and strode to the side of the bed. Placing the bundle on the linen, he swiped his face with both hands. "Do you still have feelings for him?"

Her heart pounded, realizing he was genuinely upset about her association with Dunmore. "No."

"Is he the reason why you refuse to remarry?"

She sighed, sensing he wasn't about to relent until he had all of his answers. It wasn't as if her life was much of a secret anyway. He could more or less find it in any newspaper. "No. I was imprisoned in a marriage for almost twelve years of my life to a man forty-three years my senior. Though I had requested a courtship, for I wanted time to ease into the marriage, given I was only eighteen, I was denied and handed off two weeks after my debut. William was an old childhood friend of my father's who had offered to pay all of our bills as we had always struggled. All he expected in turn was my hand at eighteen. So, there you have it. Locked away for that long, a lady cannot help but cringe at the thought of being in the same position again."

He said nothing.

Bernadette sighed again and rounded the bed toward the jewels he had set down. "Regardless of my previous association with Dunmore, we have to give these back. 'Tis the right thing to do."

He lowered his chin like any dog would before an attack. "I'm not giving them back to an arsehole who cropped you and marked up your face. I'm not. Furthermore, Coleman needs the money. So we're going to put it to better use."

It would seem Georgia was right about him. Whatever Matthew wanted to do, he firmly believed he had the right to do.

She turned and leaned over the bed to grab up the velvet bundle. "We're taking them back."

"I don't think so." Snatching her by the waist hard, he flipped her around toward himself and then shoved her backward with a flopping bounce onto the bed.

She gasped as he climbed atop her.

He locked her against the mattress with the bulk of his own body. "Did you miss me?"

She froze, staring up at him.

He lowered himself onto her like a nestling lion, pinning her against the mattress with the crushing warmth of his weight, that large frame pushing out her very breath.

She could feel the moist dirt seeping into parts of her gown. "Get off."

His calloused hands grabbed her wrists and drew them up over her head with a slow drag, stretching them out. "Or what? You'll kiss me? Ooh. I'm dithering."

In between hard, crushed breaths, she tossed up at him, "Ask yourself who is the better man in this? The one who rescued me that day in the park? Or the one who cropped me? If you are the better man, you will return these. Does honor mean nothing to you?"

He held her gaze for a long moment. "Honor is the one thing I do own, Bernadette. And don't you ever forget it."

She swallowed, unable to say anything more.

A droplet of soiled water trickled from his chestnut-colored hair, past the leather patch on his cheek, off his unshaven square jaw and onto her face. She winced as it fell on her skin.

He swiped the droplet away from her cheek with his thumb. "I won't be able to lodge at Limmer's after this, should Dunmore come looking for me. Which means I need a place to stay until I figure out what to do next. Can I stay with you?"

Her pulse jolted. "You're proving to be quite the lowlife, do you know that?"

Adjusting his grip on her wrists, he leaned in closer and narrowed his gaze, that patch against his cheekbone shifting. "You, Bernadette of all things aristocratic, who taps a finger and gets whatever the hell she wants, has no concept of what lowlife is. But I do. Have you ever seen the lifeless body of a child dumped into a pile of rubbish as if it were rubbish itself? Have you ever wrestled with savages who take pleasure in ravaging women and children alike in back alleys? *Have you?* I've met lowlife and I don't fall into that goddamn category. Not even with this. So don't *ever* call me that again."

Bernadette felt as if her breath were being cut off. She sensed this man had been through a lot more than even he was letting on. "Forgive me."

His tight, harsh features that hung over her, softened. He half nodded, loosened his grip on her wrists and pushed himself up and away.

Seeing the velvet bundle was still beside her, Bernadette lunged for it.

He jumped, grabbed her arms and flung them away, snatching up the bundle. Holding it high in the air, he angled toward where she lay on the bed. "Don't make me tie you up."

"Oh, I'm not the one who will be in ropes by the end of this night. I'm trying to do the right thing here. Why won't you—" She clenched her teeth and kicked toward him in riled agitation.

He caught her slippered foot with a large hand and shoved it hard off to the side, sending it flopping against the mattress. "No one kicks me and keeps the leg. Remember that the next time you try it." He glared. With the velvet bundle still in hand, he strode toward the closed door.

Pushing herself off the bed, she darted toward the door and, before he could get to it, fell against it. "Those jewels are irreplaceable. They're *heirlooms!*"

He purposefully towered closer, bumping her with his body. "I think we have a problem, luv."

"That we most certainly do." Jumping toward him, she grabbed at one of the pistols sticking out from his leather belt.

He seized her wrist, rigidly keeping her from touching his pistol. "Now that I know where your allegiance lies—this shite ends and it ends now. Before you end up shooting us both."

Tossing the velvet bundle back toward the bed where it landed with a soft thud on the mattress, he yanked out both pistols from the leather belts slung around his waist and set them on the floor. He stepped over them and toward her.

"It appears you don't trust me and I don't trust you. Which means—" Holding her gaze, he unclasped both leather straps from around his waist and held them up. "I'm tying you up. I'll be back to untie you after I deliver the jewels, but if you scream or throw any punches, I'll make sure the belts never come off. You got that?"

She gasped. "You intend to tie me up?"

"You've earned it." He grabbed her hands, pressing her hard into the door with the weight of his muscled body.

Her eyes widened in disbelief. "How dare you— Cease this!" Though she frantically tried and tried to jerk against him, she couldn't budge against that broad frame, which only pinned her harder against the door.

The sound of quick, wrapping sweeps of leather against her wrists that were already tightly pressed and bound together made her realize she would not be able to pry herself out of this mess. Such was the lot of a woman for trusting a thief.

CHAPTER ELEVEN

The devil he whisked his tail to punish every nation. To Scotland he gave the itch and to Ireland
Emancipation.

—*The Truth Teller, a New York Newspaper for
Gentlemen*

MATTHEW HATED TO do it. He really did, but the woman
had given him little choice and he didn't have time to
deal with Bernadette's sentimental fawning over an
arsehole, especially considering that he had well over
six miles to walk back to Limmer's.

When he finished tightening the leather belts around
her feet, ensuring they didn't pinch her skin, he flopped
her back against the mattress he'd carried her over to.
She tried to kick out another angry foot, but was too
tightly bound.

"This is not only for your own safety, but apparently my own."

Her hands sagged against the leather belt as she
plopped them against the mattress. Her black hair had
long since unraveled from its chignon, those cheeks

flushed, with the redness stretching down her throat. Her dark eyes held his for a long moment, waging their never-ending battle for power.

She lifted her head off the bed and squinted. "If you walk out that door without untying me, I will ensure you cease to breathe, you misbegotten prick."

An astounded laugh tumbled from his throat. He didn't realize women of her caliber even knew such words. "Don't make me gag that foul mouth of yours with linen."

"You don't have to gag me, because I am *never* speaking to you again." She pursed her lips as if to demonstrate just how serious she was.

Women. One day fire, next day ice. "You won't be tied for long. I'll be back."

She rolled herself toward the edge of the bed and struggled against the belts again. "I'm not about to let you hang in the name of some bastard friend who—"

"Coleman wasn't in on this."

"That is even worse! Why, that means—"

"What it means is that I was only able to scrape together two pounds on my own through honest work this week, despite putting in ten hours of sweat a day since I last saw you. And the man needs more than that. Another week of honest work wasn't going to miraculously change his financial situation or mine."

She shifted and glared at him. "So instead of coming to me for money, you thought robbing Dunmore was a better idea?"

"I thought you weren't speaking to me anymore."

"Untie me!" she boomed, thrashing against the mattress.

He sighed. Leaning down, he gathered his pistols and the bundle filled with jewels. "I'll be back. Then you can shoot me, and we'll call it even."

She paused, her features twisting. "Matthew. Let me help you. Before you find yourself at the end of a rope."

He tightened his hold on his pistols and the jewels. "You know damn well that if I give these back to Dunmore, I'll be at the end of a rope anyway. Now, stay here. I'll be back."

The following morning

THE SLAMMING OF A DOOR from deep within the house startled Bernadette from sleep. She blinked. Gray morning light peered in through the edges of the embroidered lace curtains that still covered the windows of her bedchamber. She paused and then let out an exasperated groan, remembering the humiliation of having the servants unstrap her hands and feet after the man had left. Damn him. She thought that he was better than this. She didn't know *why,* but she did.

And of course, the bastard never came back.

Men. She hated them. And she was never bedding another one ever again. No matter how well endowed or capable. She was done. Done!

When another door banged open from somewhere down the corridor, this time shaking the furniture in her bedchamber, she sat up, the linen spilling down to her waist. Clutching her silk robe around her chemise, she squinted toward the direction of the doorway. What—

The thudding of approaching boots echoed down the corridor. Bernadette's pulse roared. She pinned her gaze to that closed door. Those boots didn't sound friendly.

She scrambled to the side of the bed and jumped down onto the floor. The door suddenly flew open and slammed against the wall, not only shaking the bed but making her screech.

She froze, her breath hitching.

A tall man, whose long black and silvering hair had been tied back from his chiseled face, loomed in the doorway, dressed in a frayed great coat torn at the curve of his broad shoulder.

Her eyes widened. It was the same man who had been in the park that day alongside Matthew. Coleman. "What do you want?"

He stepped into the room. "You. Who else?"

Panic seized her. She was going to die. In her night-clothes!

Ice-blue eyes penetrated her soul as he stalked toward her, his coat billowing around his body as those whitened-leather riding boots thudded closer. "Milton never returned to his room last night. After spending all bloody morning looking for him, thinking he was dead, I was informed by someone at Limmer's that Scotland Yard up and seized him. So I went over to Scotland Yard demanding to know what he was being charged with, but no one there is telling me shite. Nor will they let me see him."

Bernadette sucked in a breath, slapping a trembling hand to her mouth. Her heart sank down to the tips of her bare feet at knowing he was officially set to hang. *Oh, God.* One of her servants must have gone to Scotland Yard last night, despite her asking for their silence, and now it was going to cost her the life of a man she should have never involved herself with in the first place.

"Get dressed," Coleman said. "You are using whatever title and wealth you have to get him out. I don't even want to know what that stupid bastard did. I used to think *I* was crazy. Until I met him." He whipped away. Stalking over to her large dresser, he threw open its doors, reached in and yanked out a morning gown. Marching it over to her, he held it out. "Put it on."

She tried to focus on what needed to be said and done. "You want to know why Scotland Yard seized him? I will tell you why. He stole heirloom jewels from a former lover of mine. Apparently, you were in dire need of money and he had a point to prove."

His eyes widened. "What?"

"You heard me. One of my servants must have informed the authorities of what he did. That, or Dunmore himself was on to him and he never knew it. Either way, 'tis fairly obvious he is set to hang."

Coleman closed his eyes. "Christ. This is all my fault. I should have never—" Reopening his eyes, he bit out, "We have to get him out." Stepping toward her, he opened the neck of the gown wide and yanked it down hard over her head.

"What are you—" Stunned and unable to see anything but the folds of her lilac gown, she commenced shoving the material away from herself, only to find that he was tugging it farther down and around her body. As if he did this sort of thing all the time!

When her head popped through, she struggled to poke an arm past the sleeve but found her other arm was stuck at her side, the material binding her into place. She glared. "After what he did to me, he does not deserve saving."

He pointed. "If he was good enough to bed, he is good enough to save. You're heading your fancy self over to Scotland Yard right now, dressed as you are, and getting him out."

"Are you daft? I cannot appear pleading for his cause looking like some—some…half-bred, lopsided strumpet. They would only hang me right alongside him!"

He paused as if acknowledging her point.

She straightened and adjusted the dress about herself, attempting to free her other arm. Pressing her lips together, she shoved her arm through the remaining armhole, feeling utterly ridiculous. "Give me time to dress into something more appropriate. I need to not only look presentable but gather my thoughts as to how to do this. We only have one chance to get him out." She glared. "And I highly recommend you remain out of sight. You are as much an accomplice to this as he is, regardless of whether you knew about it or not."

He shifted toward her. "I'm not in the mood for a lecture today. And I don't care what you do, or what you say, just get him the hell out. Aside from his own life here, he's got men depending on him back in New York.

Men whose very lives will cease to exist if *he* ceases to exist. You got that?" He gestured toward the door. "I'll be downstairs, looking for brandy. Get dressed." He swung away and stalked out.

She ground her teeth, refraining from spitting after him. Looking for brandy in *her* house as if it were *his* house, indeed. And she thought Matthew was a man who took what he wanted. No wonder the two were friends!

This was exactly what happened to a woman who'd been locked away from the world too long. She emerged salivating like some fiend for adventure and passion and got herself involved with a one-eyed pirate, and now had to *save* said one-eyed pirate!

Hurrying over to the tasseled calling rope beside the bed, she tugged on it several times, almost ripping it off. It was going to take a lot more than money to get him out. It was going to cost the last of her name. Meaning, the Burton name.

Fortunately, the men over at Scotland Yard had known her late husband very well. William had valiantly supported the implementation of Scotland Yard long before Parliament had the decency to pass the Metropolitan Police Act. And fortunately again, the fading mark from Dunmore's crop was still visible enough for her to use of it whilst pleading Matthew's case before the magistrates. It was now simply a matter of what sort of punishment *she* was going to implement against Matthew once she got the bastard out.

Six hours later
Scotland Yard

A GRAY-HAIRED MAN who had just removed his top hat and set it between them on the table eyed him. Everything about the older gent reminded Matthew of a dead winter day. From his frosty hair to those gleaming, snow-white-colored gloves and rigid white collar and cravat, to his embroidered waistcoat, which matched his ridiculous fop-white trousers. All of that glaring white clothing horridly contrasted with the flat black coat over a stiff back.

Several other men, all of them magistrates of some sort, sat in stern unified silence, lining the far side of a wood bench. Unlike Mr. Frost, they all wore black.

Oh, yes. It was judgment day for a half-blind Irishman against a whole nation of two-eyed Brits. He could have damn well stolen a blade of grass and they would have hanged him.

Matthew leaned far back against the wood chair until he teetered on only two of its legs and set his manacled hands against his thighs. He was going to hang. And his boys and the ward probably wouldn't even know about it until long after his body had been tossed and rotted. He'd hanged not only himself but everyone back in New York, right down to Ronan. He should have never been so stupid as to believe his life could have amounted to anything more than what it always had been—*nothing*.

"You are free to go," Mr. Frost finally announced, examining his snowy gloved fingers. "Once you sign a few papers drawn up by the magistrates, we are done and hope to never see you again."

Matthew brought his chair back toward the table with a resounding thump. His manacles clanged against each other. "What?"

Mr. Frost angled toward him and narrowed his gaze, pointing. "Fortunately for you, Mr. Milton, you had a most prestigious witness step forth—Lady Burton. Next time, try not to blatantly seize justice by the throat."

Matthew blinked rapidly, a pulsing knot overtaking his stomach. By God. The woman who had tried to shoot him in the name of another man, had, in the end, saved him. And he thought he'd seen it all. Mr. Frost gestured to the magistrates and then to Matthew. "Unlock his manacles, have him sign the papers and get him the blazes out. Case dismissed."

One of the men in black stood and rounded over toward Matthew. Humiliation tightened Matthew's chest. He was going to have to face that woman now. Jesus and Joseph. And Mary. No.

In a blur of hands being freed of iron, and a sloppy signature with an ink-dipped quill at the bottom of a parchment he didn't even bother to read, he stood and was escorted out of the room through a side door.

Neither his pistols nor his razor were returned to him.

It was a bad omen.

"Lady Burton awaits outside, Mr. Milton," one of the magistrates tonelessly instructed, directing him to the main entrance.

He was being turned over without any protection whatsoever to a woman who was going to be more interested in castrating him, not kissing him. Drawing in a good breath, he footed it outside into the cold, filmy rain that blanketed the gray afternoon. He halted in the open doorway leading out to the wide cobblestone street.

Three young footmen in red livery lined a black lacquered carriage emblazoned with a crest. Bernadette regally stood before them on the edge of the pavement in a stunning black gown, looking like death and vengeance, whilst lingering just outside the open door of the carriage, which one of the footmen held open. Although her face was hidden beneath a long black lace veil that cascaded down from her bonnet, he had no doubt it was her. He recognized that overly stiff stance and the shape of that luscious body.

Clearing his throat, he adjusted his wool great coat. Descending the set of stairs leading out toward the street, he approached her.

Pausing directly before her, he blurted, "I think I love you. Despite everything." And a part of him meant it. She saved his goddamn life.

Her heel came down onto the pavement with a reprimanding click. "If only I felt the same about you, *Mr. Patch.*"

Mr. Patch. That was new. And he had no doubt it wasn't intended to be a compliment.

She folded her gloved hands before her, her beaded reticule swinging on her wrist. "I trust there is no need for me to lecture you on the gravity of the situation from which I emancipated you." That flurry of stern words ruffled the lace veil that masked her features.

It bothered him to see only the faint outline of her face. It was degrading knowing she didn't want to be seen with him in public. Not that he blamed her.

He shifted his jaw. "Is there a reason for the veil?" He knew the reason, but he wanted to hear her say it.

"No. I simply happen to like wearing veils on rainy days." Her tone indicated quite the opposite. "Now, get in the carriage, lest we both get stoned by respectable society."

"I'm used to getting stoned. So you needn't worry about me." He pulled himself up and into the carriage, skipping the unfolded steps, and eased onto the length of the fine-leather-upholstered seat. He leaned back, noting all of the embroidered blue silk lining the walls and the ceiling of the large space. Hell looked rather impressive from where he was sitting.

With the assistance of a footman, Bernadette was whisked up and into the carriage herself, her hands lifting her skirts enough to allow her movement. The lush scent of citrus seized the air around him, making him instinctively breathe in deep. He couldn't escape her. Not that he wanted to. It was like the woman owned the air he breathed. He fisted his hands hard.

She silently seated herself across from him, still veiled.

The door was closed, trapping him in her world.

He swayed against the movement of the carriage when it pulled forward. Scotland Yard eventually disappeared from his visible peripheral. Thank God.

They rode on in silence.

The veil swayed against her face and shoulders, but otherwise nothing, not even a slim gloved finger of hers, moved. It was as if she were waiting for him to acknowledge the long list of sins he had yet to pay.

He huffed out a breath, setting both hands on his knees, and leaned forward. "I honestly don't know what to say. I didn't expect this. But thank you, Bernadette. It means more to me than you'll ever know. I owe you my very life."

She pushed the lace up and away from her face with gloved hands, her dark eyes and arched brows appearing. "You think a thank-you and a mere apology is going to placate me? Is that what you think?"

"No, I—"

"I just hanged whatever was left of my name to ensure *you* did not hang. And the worst has yet to come, if the testimony I had to give is any indication. 'Tis a testimony that included *why* you stole those jewels and how you sought to slap Dunmore's honor after what he did to me in the park, revealing that you and I are— how shall I say this?—*lovers*. 'Twas the only thing that saved you. Me admitting to a truth and twisting it enough to make everything fit for the magistrates. And given my extensive testimony that is now on public record—a record that includes your full name and *my* full name—by the end of this week, *everyone* who knows how to read a newspaper will know of it. Which means…if I remain in London beyond another week, it would be no different than me taking on the name of Marie Antoinette and staying for the French Revolution! Not even Georgia will be able to associate with me after this. And my own father, who already thinks the worst of me, will probably come to my door merely to cane me. So *thank you* for that. Thank you."

He could feel his heart and his blood pumping fast and strong. If the newspapers printed this, it was only a matter of time before New York knew about it. And if New York knew about it, those that wanted him dead would know about it. And considering that they were all worth nothing, he had no doubt her wealth could result in a kidnapping or two.

Dread seized him. He supposed this is what happened to a man who sought to change his stars. He died with them.

The drizzling rain that had seeped its way through her veil now clung in a soft sheen to her nose and cheeks, making her pale skin glisten. The bruising lash on her jaw had faded considerably, though it was still visible.

He stared at her, every muscle in his body as tense as stretched leather. Why did she think he was worth saving? Was it possible she felt something for him? That certain something that he'd felt for her from the moment he had touched her, obliterating his ability to think about anything else but making her his? "Why did you do it?"

"Aside from getting a bedchamber visit from your bandit friend, who muscled his way past my servants?"

Matthew lowered his chin. "Coleman was in your bedchamber?"

"Yes. That heathen *also* tried shoving me into a gown whilst I was in a state of undress."

His eyes widened. That son of a bitch. "I'll set that arse straight. Don't you worry in that."

Her gaze narrowed. "I would suggest setting your own *arse* straight. For some reason, you seem to think that stealing is acceptable if it is done in the name of revenge or for a friend in need. Stealing is stealing, Matthew. Or did you not know that?"

He shifted his jaw and sat back, feeling as if he'd been slapped. So much for her feeling a certain something. "Given your exceedingly low opinion of me, and your inability to understand that I owe Coleman my very life and have since I was twenty, why not just drop me back off at Scotland Yard? Because I don't want to bloody listen to this. Nor do I have to. I apologized. And it was a heartfelt apology. What more do you want?"

"I *slaughtered* the last of my name because of you, and you think a mere *apology* is going to turn you into Moses and part this bloodred sea for you? Is that what you think, you Irish blackguard!"

He didn't know whether to be irked or irked knowing this British vixen was throwing the Irish at him. He leaned forward again, draping his forearm on his knee. "I never asked you to slaughter yourself for me, but since you did, we now have ourselves a bigger problem. Seeing everyone in London is about to know of our association, it's only a matter of time before those same papers float their way across the ocean. And once they do, one of at least fifty-six people who want me dead might think you'd be worth a good kidnap or two in the hopes of getting a fistful of money out of you."

She rolled her eyes. "Let them try."

"You think I'm joking?" He leaned back against the seat. "There's only one way to go about this. I'm moving in with you until we figure this out. It's not like I have a place to stay and God only knows this is heading toward matrimony anyway."

She gawked and then altogether spat out, "I will hire the entire British fleet in the name of protecting myself, but you are *not* going to be part of it. Nor are we heading anywhere *near* matrimony after last night!"

"Ey. You need to calm down."

She gasped. "I do?"

"Yes. No romantic association is utopian and everyone makes mistakes. And I made a mistake. I'll admit it. There is no need to overreact."

She narrowed her gaze. "Mr. Milton. We have a much bigger problem you do not seem to be acknowledging here. That being—I do not trust you anymore. Nor do I want you around me after what you did to me last night. Do you honestly think I'm about to forgive being strapped like a lamb ready to be roasted on a spit?"

What was a man supposed to say to that?

He swiped his face, too exhausted to even argue after a long night of sitting on a slab of stone on the floor Scotland Yard called a chair. "What do you want me to do?"

"First, I want you to tell me about these men in New

York. The ones Georgia and Coleman keep mentioning. Who are they to you? I want to know."

It wasn't as if he had a reputation to save before her eyes. He sighed. "Coleman and I lead a group of men known as the Forty Thieves. It commenced with a hail to integrity and protecting people in our community that eventually morphed into depending on weapons and thievery due to threats against our lives and how little we have. In the eyes of society, I'm a thief and I fully accept that. For I am. I do steal. But everything I do has not to do with maintaining a lifestyle as much as ensuring that I and others continue to *breathe*. So in answer to your question, Bernadette, these men are, in fact, my family. My mother died when I was twelve, my father died several years ago and I never had any siblings. Which is only one of many reasons as to why I wanted a family of my own. Because as it stands, I have nothing. 'Tis only me, my boys, Ronan and the boots we're all wearing. Which isn't much."

"And what do these men depend on you for?"

"A genuine purpose outside the misery we've all been sentenced to. When each came to me, looking to go up against the violence in the ward, they had nothing. Not even the ability to read. In turn for their loyalty, I gave them an education so that they might understand their rights as United States citizens, while Coleman gave them the ability to fight so we could all maintain a presence. 'Tis far more than anyone has ever given these men. All they ever wanted was a chance to become more. And Coleman and I gave them that chance."

He lowered his gaze and shook his head, knowing she would never understand. It had been difficult trying to even convince his father to understand the necessity of a group in a poverty-stricken area, where the one rule was: *There are no rules.* "The only reason I left New York was because seventeen men in a neighboring ward wanted me dead. Why? Because I work alongside marshals who arrest people all the time and I had to get out. When you've got that many people on you, something as simple as walking down the street becomes a problem."

She slowly shook her head, that gaze of contempt never once leaving his. "I can forgive certain things, including theft and men wanting you dead, but I am not about to forgive what you did to me last night when I repeatedly tried to help you." After a long moment of silence, she added, "I spoke to Coleman. Or should I say...*Lord Atwood.*"

Matthew's gaze snapped to hers. "He told you?"

"Yes. Apparently, he felt a need to confide in a fellow aristocrat. And needless to say, Matthew, you keep very disturbing company."

He held her gaze. "What did he say? What did he do?"

"Enough to make me realize that I am better off without you."

He drew in a burning breath. Coleman had slit the last of whatever opportunity he might have had with this woman. And he had no doubt the man did it in honor of the boys. The son of a bitch. "I don't know what he said to you, but I can say here and now that

Coleman—or rather, Atwood—has a warped perception toward women that does not represent my own.
You're angry with me right now, which I completely
understand, but I have no doubt you and I will figure
this out and move on to something more meaningful
outside of what others think or say."

She stared. "I do not want you in my life, Mr. Milton. And nothing you or anyone else says will ever
change that."

Those words stabbed him a bit harder than he had
expected them to. And that was when he realized he
had a bigger problem. He didn't want to leave her. He
really didn't. Nor was he going to. He was going to
redeem himself. After he beat the shite out of Coleman, that is.

He shook his head and kept shaking it. "Setting aside
everything we've already shared, which you can deny
all you want, but can never be erased, I'm not leaving
you unprotected. It's as simple as that."

"As I said, I do not need your protection. I would
rather hire the British fleet, who will dutifully abide not
only by *my* law, but the law of the land. Something you
clearly have trouble with." Slipping her reticule from
her wrist, she stiffly held it out. "Here. I am giving you
fifty pounds to ensure I never see you again. Which, in
my opinion, is overly generous." She paused and then
added, "And should our paths ever cross once I return
to New York City, which I highly doubt, for my people
are not your people, I suggest you run."

His brows rose. "You don't live here? But I thought—"

"No. I don't live here. How do you think I know

Georgia? Mr. Astor was the one to introduce us back in New York."

His eyes widened as the carriage came to a halt. The footmen thudded down from the box outside to open the door. "I didn't know that you— For God's sake. Don't do this to me, Bernadette. I know I stupidly dirked you, and Coleman isn't the most pleasant of souls, but I'm asking that you give me a second chance. Every man deserves a second chance. Let me show you the sort of man I really am. Outside of...*this*."

"'Tis already obvious the sort of man you really are."

He leaned toward her, biting back the savage need to grab her and make her realize that he was being genuine. "Do you not understand that if you make me walk away from you and this, Bernadette, without giving me a chance to redeem myself, I won't be able to rest, let alone breathe."

"Then you will not rest. Then you will not breathe. And in my opinion, you deserve as much. For I have been crossed too many times by too many bastards to trust you. Once a man proves himself unworthy, he doesn't get another chance. That is how I ensure the crop stays in *my* hand, instead of his." She waved the reticule. "If our short time together meant *anything* to you, Matthew, *anything,* you will respect my decision in this. Now, take it and disappear."

A part of him crumpled. He really couldn't breathe.

She rattled the reticule.

Knowing he had to respect her decision in this, especially as she was asking him to, he reached out and grasped the beaded reticule, slipping it from her gloved fingers. Trying to keep his voice calm, he said, "I want you to hire that goddamn fleet. You got that? Don't toss dice thinking our association is over simply because you say it's over. *Especially* given that you live in New York."

"You needn't worry. I will hire them merely to ensure *you* stay away."

Now, that hurt.

"Keep the reticule," she added. "You can sell it for more money should you need it."

That also hurt. Matthew shifted his jaw, tightening his grip on the reticule until the beads dug into his skin.

The carriage door opened.

The footman unfolded the stairs.

"Limmer's is just outside, Mr. Milton. I thought I would do you the courtesy of dropping you off at your destination."

She was showing him the door. Quite literally.

He drew in a ragged breath, knowing this was goodbye to all that might have been. "My only wish is that you could have gotten to know me. Not as a thief, but as a man," he admitted.

Without meeting her gaze, he rose and jumped out of the carriage, not making use of the stairs, feeling a desperate need to escape her presence before he drowned. It was the first time in his life he ever felt like a lowlife. A real one.

CHAPTER TWELVE

Beware the charmer known to tell everything
but the truth.

—*The Truth Teller, a New York Newspaper for
Gentlemen*

MATTHEW BANGED OPEN the narrow door leading into
Coleman's small leased room. "You are a bloody arsehole, you know that?"

Coleman, who was in a state of undress down
to mere trousers and had just finished securing his
shoulder-length hair at the nape of his neck, swung toward him. Those blue eyes widened as a grin overtook
his unshaven face. "Milton! I'll be. She got you out."

Matthew narrowed his gaze. "I'll probably be
dragged right back in by the time you and I are done.
What the hell did you do? What the hell did you tell
her...*Atwood?*"

Crossing his arms over his bare chest, Coleman's
grin was replaced by an overly stoic expression.
"Whether I had said anything or not, that woman was
damn determined to be rid of you. Not that I blame

her." He tsked. "Tying a woman up with your own leather belts and stealing her lover's jewels? That isn't the way to go about winning over a woman, Milton. Even *I* know that much."

Matthew glared. "I don't need a lecture right now. Not after the one she gave me. Beelzebub himself could hardly desire better company. She actually made me feel…dirty."

Coleman smirked. "I will admit, that woman has fire."

Matthew lowered his chin. "So what did you tell her? Exactly? Out with it."

"Not all that much. A little bit of my life story. Rumors about the lost Atwood heir from New York have to commence surfacing somewhere. I also told her a bit about you, given she asked. Naturally, I exaggerated a few things to ensure she didn't feel the need to change her mind, but that was about it."

Matthew's eyes widened and he could actually feel the veins in his throat swelling in riled disbelief. "Define *exaggerated*. Because, as you well know, my life doesn't really represent itself all that well."

Coleman shrugged. "I can't remember what I said. I was just talking."

Matthew choked. "You call yourself a friend?"

"Yes. Why the devil are you so miffed?"

"Because a *friend*—a real one—would have defended my name!"

"Milton, Milton. You're still that overly naïve twenty-year-old boy I first met, when it comes to women. Unable to swallow reality."

Matthew kept himself from darting forward and punching him. "You want to talk about who can't swallow reality?" he tossed out. "You have a dead sister, whose grave you have yet to visit, and an aristo father with an oversized cock who glories in fecking women *and* men of all ages. Go and swallow *that* reality and then maybe, just maybe, you can call us even."

Coleman's ice-blue eyes met Matthew's head-on. Despite the distance between them, the sharp intent of that stare viciously dug into Matthew, reminding him he had just insulted a professional prizefighter. "Take it back."

Matthew shot up both fists and instinctively positioned his head so that his good eye made up for his lack of peripheral. "Give me back Bernadette first. If you can do that, I won't knuckle the shite out of you."

Coleman rolled his eyes. "You really want to go knuckle to knuckle with me?"

Matthew boldly held that gaze with each fist still stubbornly up. "Come on. Are we doing this or not? It'll be like training. Only better."

Coleman casually and steadily approached with solid movements, those menacingly well-sculpted muscles on his chest and arms visibly shifting and tightening against scars he'd earned since youth. That forty-year-old body bespoke of many, many years of fighting.

Too many.

Matthew shifted his jaw, fists ready.

Coleman paused before him and merely stood there, long arms at his sides and looking completely and utterly bored.

"Scared, are you?" Matthew taunted, sending out half jabs.

"Hardly."

"Then swing it."

"Milton. Whether you can face it or not, your pretty little aristo simply wasn't as smitten with you as you were with her. Or she would have forgiven it. She would have understood and forgiven it. Don't you think?"

Matthew dropped his hands and hissed out a breath. That hurt more than any swing. And it hurt because he knew it was true.

Coleman jumped forward and halted that rigid blow of a fist at his temple. "You lose. Why? Because you got distracted. Which is what women do. You clearly need more training. So let's train. You up for it?"

Matthew winced, realizing he would have, in fact, been hit. "I hate you. You know that?"

Coleman retracted his fist and darted back. He pointed toward his own face, his features tightening. "Always watch the eyes of your opponent, not just the movement of their body. Usually, the opponent will briefly focus on what he intends to strike. Although, sometimes, he'll intentionally try to fool you. Now, focus. I'll stay away from your head and your back, but everything else is fair game. Are you ready?"

"I am not in the mood for this."

Coleman stood back and tapped at his sculpted stomach. "I want you to hit me. Full force. Go on."

Matthew paused. "Why would you *want* me to hit you, knowing that I'm not too happy with you right now?"

"Because I owe you this. I know you want to, and it will relieve that angst. I promise, you won't even be able to knock me over."

Matthew pointed at him with a smirk. "Based on that arrogance alone, don't think I'm going to swing easy."

Coleman tapped at his stomach. "Come on."

Matthew edged toward him and drew back a rigid fist. He hesitated, catching Coleman's intent gaze. "Full force?"

"Full force."

The son of a bitch was crazy. But then again...so was Matthew. Tightening his jaw, Matthew thrust his clenched fist forward and straight into that board of muscles.

Pain unexpectedly shot up Matthew's arm. He winced and stumbled back, shaking his hand out. It was like he'd hit a brick wall with bare knuckles. "Christ, what the hell did you do? That didn't feel right."

Though Coleman swayed against the hit and had pushed out a ragged breath that indicated he'd felt the impact, he continued to stoically stand there. "Something I've been working on. I've decided to take up boxing full-time here in London." He pointed to his stomach muscles, which he visibly tensed, and drawled, "And *this* is why I am about to become known as *Vicomte de Vice*."

Rolling his eyes, Matthew jeered, "Is that going to be your name in the ring?"

"I'm thinking about it."

"Don't." Matthew paused. "Does this mean you're staying in London?"

Coleman was quiet for a long moment. He swiped his face and eyed him.

Sensing the man wanted to tell him something, Matthew lifted a brow. "What?"

"I called on my father, as well as my sister's husband and her son."

Matthew angled toward him. "And?"

Lowering his gaze, Coleman bit out, "My father deserves a knife through the gizzard and a bullet through the head. I'll have you know that I almost…" He closed his eyes, his square jaw tightening. Reopening them, he said, "I wanted to kill him. That prick wouldn't even acknowledge me as being the real Atwood, even though I could see that he knew who I really was."

Coleman sighed. "But I do rather like my sister's husband and that nephew of mine." He half nodded, taking on a distant look. "They seem to have swept me into their circle in all but one breath." He paused and confided, "Instead of going to Venice, as I had earlier planned, I'm thinking I should stay here. I want to see how things work out. What do you think?"

Well, well, well. It would seem Coleman was about to take on London. Matthew couldn't help but smile. "You should stay. Family is family. And don't you ever forget it."

Coleman eyed him. "Speaking of family, you do know Georgia is set to marry my nephew?"

Matthew gaped. "What? But I thought she and that Robinson were…"

"That Robinson is my nephew. Lord Yardley."

"Shite."

"I know."

Matthew heaved out a breath and shook his head in disgust. "Everyone is damn well getting married, for blood's sake. Everyone but me."

"I'm not getting married."

Matthew almost smacked him. "I never included you in that list."

Coleman pounded him several times on the shoulder. "Give yourself time, man. New York has more women than roaches."

Matthew pushed away his hand, that heaviness within his chest returning. "Sadly, Coleman, Bernadette was the one. She was the one, and I fecked it up. I, and all of my damn dirty dealings, fecked it up."

And knowing it depressed him above all else.

CHAPTER THIRTEEN

Yes. Turn away from the truth. Ignore it. Tell them their distress and their destitution must last, says I. Tell them instead of diminishing their misery, their poverty must be aggravated and thus continue. Let them all go down the scale of society until distress drives them to the most violent acts which despair itself can impel human nature to be guilty of.

—*The Truth Teller, a New York Newspaper for Gentlemen*

Three months later
New York City—Manhattan Square

BERNADETTE SMILED AND held up a wine-filled crystal glass to Jacob, Mrs. Astor and, of course, Mr. Astor himself, who smugly sat beside her at the dining table. "A very happy and glorious birthday to you, Mr. Astor. I am ever blessed to be part of it and all the more blessed knowing you all came to dine with me tonight. You are all the only family I ever needed."

Mr. Astor beamed, drumming ungloved hands on the linen table. "Here, here." He shifted in the upholstered cushion of the chair and intoned majestically, "Tomorrow, we celebrate my being young over on Broadway. Now, enough of this toasting. We eat."

He snatched up his silver fork, paused and pointed it at his grandson, who sat across from him. "Now that England is eating American Georgia pie, and loving the taste of it, you and I, Jacob, are darting ourselves over to London come February. And we won't settle for anything less than the daughter of a duke."

Looking up from his supper plate, Jacob's young shaven face stilled. He lifted a blond brow and wagged his own fork back at his grandfather. "I'm beginning to think you want that title more than I do." He glanced over at Bernadette, those green eyes intently holding hers. "You said you had some sort of news. I'd love to hear it as opposed to listening to this old man drone and drone."

She let out a laugh. "Ah. Yes. That." Bernadette set her wineglass aside and announced, "In less than a month, I leave for Port Royal and Kingston." She grinned, glorying that she was *finally* going to Jamaica. She had found herself not one but three guards. Men who were anything but attractive and would ensure *everyone* stayed away, be she in Jamaica or not. "Hopefully, my feet will get stuck in the sand and I never return."

Jacob slowly leaned into the table, adjusting his evening coat about his lean frame. "And how long will you be gone?"

Bernadette shrugged. "I haven't set a time quite yet. Nor do I plan to."

He shifted in his seat, glancing toward her. "Hopefully you won't be gone too long. Because in my opinion—" He froze, his green eyes jerking toward the entranceway behind her, where a noise sounded.

Bernadette paused and turned in her own seat as a large dark-haired man of over six feet, with a thick scar running from his nose to his jaw, stalked into the dining hall. He was followed by five other hefty unshaven men, all dressed in frayed riding clothes. Each pointed a pistol and one of them held a large carving knife. A *very* large carving knife.

Her heart popped.

Everyone at the dining table froze.

"If you move," one of the six announced in a low tone, "we spray blood and make you all lick it up. Including those guards and all of the servants we roped up in the back."

A panicked knot seized her stomach, throat and mind knowing that all three of her guards had been taken down. And without any of them hearing a thing. She tried not to move.

The man with the scar veered in and set a pistol to Mr. Astor's temple. "And what be your name, old man?"

Mr. Astor's hands stilled against the table. "John Astor."

"Astor?" the man echoed, leaning closer. "You mean, that butcher millionaire I read about in the paper?"

Mr. Astor's grandson slowly stood from his seat and

held out an ungloved hand toward the gathered men. "Gentlemen. Tell me how much you want to settle this and it's done."

The giant straightened and glared. "Oh, now, you think this here be about money, do you? I see. So in your refined opinion, I look like some vagrant whose intent can be bought. Well, now that just brasses me off. I think a lesson is in order." With that, the man swung the pistol and aimed at Jacob's shoulder. A loud resounding click, flare, blast and a plume of sooty powder filled the air.

Jacob staggered, clamping a hand to his shoulder. He stumbled back, collapsing into his chair with a reverberating thud.

Bernadette screamed right along with Mrs. Astor as the elder Mr. Astor yelled something out over their screams.

Tears blurred her ability to see as she scrambled up and out of her chair. *"Jacob!"*

The giant handed off his pistol to one of the other men and grabbed another loaded pistol. He swung back and pointed the muzzle straight at her.

She froze.

His gruff, round face held a rancid mocking expression. "Well, well. There she be. I hear Milton has a thing for you. Even after all this time."

She couldn't believe it. He was referring to... Matthew. Oh, God. She swallowed past tears, but swore not to give in to the fear. "What do you want?"

"We'll get to that." He rounded the table and pointed

the muzzle at Mrs. Astor's head on an angle. "Old woman. I know you're worried. Tend to the boy."

Mrs. Astor let out a wrenching sob. Scrambling out of her chair, she gathered the napkins from the table to use them for the wound, and leaned in toward Jacob. She tried to remove his evening coat between sobs but her shaky hands fumbled.

Mr. Astor jumped to his feet, his features twisting.

One of the men approached and shoved him back down into the seat. "Let her tend to it."

Bernadette swallowed hard, unable to stop tears from spilling down her cheeks.

The large man paused before her, the smell of snuff and whiskey permeating the air. His brown eyes hardened to lethal. "Are you Lady Burton?"

He knew her name. He'd come to specifically hunt her down. She only prayed that Matthew hadn't been hurt or was dead. Trying to keep her voice steady, she bit out in riled disbelief, "Does it matter? You just shot a boy."

He fingered the pistol he held. "A boy? That there be a man. And I grazed his arm, is all. He'll be fine."

He leaned over and yelled across the table to Jacob, "Take off the coat and show the woman what a graze looks like, before I shoot you the right way."

Jacob leaned forward in his chair, away from Mrs. Astor, and pushed away her napkins and hands. Holding Bernadette's gaze, he lowered his evening coat from his lean, broad shoulder to reveal the sleeve of his white linen shirt beneath. "I'm fine. It's just a graze. It doesn't even hurt." A small spatter of blood stained his shirt, but it did not appear to be spreading.

Her breath caught, relief frilling her.

"You see," the giant insisted. "That was a wee warning."

Bernadette eyed the man, not knowing what to make of him or this. There was a twisted sense of mercy laced into lack of mercy. What was this? "What do you want?"

He leaned in, stale sweat choking the air between them. "Are you the infamous Lady Burton or not? Because this loyal Irishman whose da is from Cork needs to know."

He appeared to be some crazed Irishman out to shoot himself a few British. "You haven't earned the right to hear my name."

He scrubbed his oily head with the hand that wasn't holding the pistol and swung the pistol to the elder Astor. He cocked it. *"Name."*

A shaky breath escaped her. "I am indeed Lady Burton."

He lowered the pistol. "I thought so." He set his mutton shoulders, his massive frame blocking her view of the dining hall, and smugly searched her face. "I want you to prance on over to the hero of the night. Go on over to Nancy-boy over there."

She hesitated and slowly rounded the table toward Jacob. She paused beside his chair, reached down and grabbed his hand, squeezing it to give herself and him the assurance that they were going to survive. No matter what.

He glanced up at her, squeezing her hand in turn, those green eyes reflecting her own unspoken fear.

The giant waved the pistol toward them. "Now unbutton his trousers and swallow whatever comes out. He's earned it and you're easy like that, right?"

Dread and nausea seized her.

Jacob's hand savagely bit into hers.

"How dare you!" Mr. Astor roared, jumping to his feet.

Every man with a pistol pointed it at Mr. Astor, who sat back down.

Bernadette couldn't breathe. This was personal. Matthew had warned her. He had warned her against this and she had refused to listen. She hadn't accepted protection from him and the guards she *had* hired had been dismantled within mere moments. And now she and the Astors were paying for it.

The giant with the scar shifted closer, tauntingly swinging the pistol from her to Jacob and back again to let her know who was in charge. *"Click, click.* I haven't all night."

Jacob's gaze held hers. He was as terrified as she was.

Bernadette leaned down toward where he sat and cupped that face with trembling hands. Kissing his forehead, she whispered, "I'm not going to dishonor either of us. If he shoots me, and I die, I want you to find a man by the name of Matthew Joseph Milton and have him avenge this and me." She only prayed that Matthew was still alive. And that Jacob would remain so, as well.

Jacob fiercely removed her hands from his face. "I'll die before you ever will." Bumping her away, he rose from his chair to his full lean height of almost six feet and stared the intruder down. "Shoot me. Go on. Only, this time, aim, you son of a bitch, because I'm not impressed."

Laughter rumbled out from the giant. "You're crazy. I like it." He eyed Bernadette and scraped his chin with the side of the pistol. "You don't want me shooting Mr. Crazy. He's entertaining. All I really want is you. There's no need to turn this into a bigger mess. So are you going to leave quietly with me? Or do we need to spray a whole lot of blood for you to cooperate?"

Her heart pounded as she eyed Mr. Astor.

Mr. Astor shook his head and mouthed something.

It was her or their lives. And it was more than obvious this man was deranged enough to use every last loaded pistol in the room if she so much as resisted.

She swallowed and half nodded, trying not to think about what was going to happen to her. All that mattered was that no one died because of her. "All I ask is that you not hurt them."

"This ain't about them. So as long as you cooperate, they'll be fine." He searched her face, the scar marring his own stretching with a smirk. "And you really needn't worry about all the men that'll be riding you in the name of Ireland. Because once we get a good barrel of gin in you, Miss Brit, you won't remember a goddamn thing."

Her eyes widened.

Jacob jumped toward the table, snatched up a carving knife and rounded the table. "She isn't going anywhere."

The man's pistol swung to Jacob's head, that carving knife looking like a toothpick in comparison.

Jacob's gaze narrowed rebelliously against the pistol. "Go on. Do it. *Shoot me!*"

"Jacob!" Bernadette choked out in disbelief. "Drop the knife. Drop it before he turns that graze into the real thing."

Jacob shook his head, his lean body tensing as if ready to jump. "Let him kill me. Because I'm not about to—"

"Drop it!" she yelled in a panic, trying to reason with him. "For heaven's sake, if he had wanted me dead, he would have done it already. I need you to stay alive. Otherwise, what will become of me if you are not there to find me?"

Jacob hesitated. Heatedly holding her gaze, as if to announce he was doing it only because she wanted him to, he tossed the knife, sending it clattering to the floor.

"Rope these three up." The man set a large hand on her lower back and gestured toward the direction of his gathered men. "Follow these here gents. Two are going to stay behind with your friends to ensure the marshals don't get in on this until we're done."

Her heart kicked up a frantic rhythm and tears stung her eyes. Why, oh, why hadn't she listened to Matthew?

MATTHEW COULD PRACTICALLY taste the sooty dampness of the cold, thick fog on his lips. It hovered all around, dimming the yellow glow of the lone gas lamp that lingered at the end of the narrow muddy road. He drew his coat tighter around himself to keep out the chill and quickened his stride.

He kept a firm focus, listening and watching for anything that threatened to wander too close. Though the street remained dark and desolate, it didn't mean he was alone. He never was. Anyone could be watching and waiting.

He paused before the abandoned building where he and the boys kept additional weapons stashed beneath boards and released a breath, wondering why Smock wasn't waiting for him. They had a routine street patrol to do. Glancing around, he could make out nothing more than the looming shadows of wooden time-worn buildings. Dogs barked in the far distance as the wooden sign of the shop creaked on its rusted hinges just above his head.

The echo of running boots made him stiffen. Through the thickness of the fog, Smock sprinted toward him from the other side of the street.

"Where were you?" Matthew called out. "You're never late."

Smock skidded to a halt, blowing out heaving breaths and removed the wool cap from his head with a huff. He rushed into the doorway of the shop. "There's somethin' nasty goin' down."

"What? What is it?"

Unlocking the bolt, Smock shoved the door open. "We shouldn't talk out here."

Looking toward the street behind them, Matthew hurried into the dank-smelling confines of the abandoned shop and closed the door. They stood in complete darkness, the boarded-up windows protecting them from the eyes of the night.

"What is it?" Matthew demanded.

Sparks streaked the darkness as the flint and match jumped to life, illuminating the faded wallpaper around them. "Cassidy done lost his mind." Smock covered the flame with a dark-skinned hand and quickly lit a waiting candle on a crate.

Blowing out the match, he swung toward him. "He's gettin' some woman scuttered over at The Divin' Bell and he's publicly invitin' every man to ride her. And this be Cassidy. *Our own!*"

Matthew sucked in a savage breath. Aside from the poor woman herself, this was going to slaughter the name of the Forty Thieves before the ward *and* the marshals who offered him assistance whenever he needed it most. Marshals who always seized and prosecuted men who tried to kill him.

They'd never support him again.

They'd *let* him get torn to shreds.

Matthew gritted his teeth. "I'm taking him down."

"There's crowds. Riled ones. I wouldn't go in alone."

"Gather as many of our boys as you can. Tell them I'm going in. With or without them."

CHAPTER FOURTEEN

Let your will be constant, obedient and ready.
—*The Truth Teller, a New York Newspaper for
Gentlemen*

WHEN MATTHEW CAME to a sprinting halt less than a
few feet from The Diving Bell, instead of the usual
deserted street of a God-loving Sunday night, an obscenely large crowd of men gathered outside the doors
of that sooty squat building. It looked like ants infesting
a molehill, as men of all ages pushed to get inside the
narrow door, resulting in a mass of bodies and shouts
that echoed up into the misty night air.

Shite. It was one of the biggest crowds he'd seen in
these parts outside of riots and protests during political
campaigns. Jogging into the crush, he weaved through
the commotion. Oily heads, filthy hats and wool-clad
backs bobbed before him, as they all attempted to get
into the building.

Setting his jaw, he shoved through, the stench of perspiration, whiskey and burnt tobacco and its lingering

smoke choking the air. He pushed until he was well inside the tight, dim quarters of the gin joint.

The Diving Bell drummed with countless deep voices.

Since his return from London, Cassidy, one of his best, had taken on goddamn airs, mouthing off more than usual and refusing to take orders. Even though he'd spoken to the man about it several times, and it lulled and faded, it was obvious there was a much bigger problem.

Cracked lanterns hung from the low timber ceiling, bathing the dank establishment in a blanket of yellow, flickering light. He squinted, and peered past heads around him, but couldn't make anything out.

The shrill sound of wood scraping against wood added to the deafening noise of tables and chairs being shoved toward the stone walls to accommodate the growing crowd around him.

He shoved his way toward the back, where the commotion appeared to be. Men stared and moved out of the way, some of them inclining their heads in greeting.

Oh, yes. They all knew he was here to clean it up. As always. Matthew pressed on, elbowing and shoving his way past those who wouldn't move. "*Move!* All of you! I can't believe you rum holes are standing around watching this shite, instead of doing something."

He jerked to a halt well before he could even make it to the edge of the crowd. Beyond the heads before him, and there, across from the rough oak bar was a woman seated on a wooden ale cask, holding a tankard of gin. Cassidy tapped her cheek with a pistol, signaling her to drink.

She guzzled it down, gin trickling from her chin. Long, jet-black hair fell in cascading sweeps and sways around her shoulders, past her corseted waist as she struggled to finish. When she did, she shoved the tankard back toward Cassidy. Cassidy reached in and tossed off the black velvet cloak that draped her slim shoulders, revealing a ravishing moonstone evening gown that swept to the uneven planks of the floor. Not the type of dress you would ever see in the Five Points.

Matthew choked. It was…*Bernadette!*

Cassidy slung a long arm around her, grazing the pistol against her cheek. "I'd say about one more ought to do it. Then we let every last man have a go with all things British." He gestured toward the tankard. "Someone fill that up to its rim!"

Matthew's throat tightened and he honestly didn't know what kept him from lunging across the expanse and ripping Cassidy's throat out with his own goddamn teeth. Given the crowds, however, he *knew* he had to go about this the right way or he'd end up going under before he could even get to her.

"In my opinion, she's still wearing too much!" someone hollered. "I say take everything off. Even those hairpins!"

There was a roar of laughter.

It was officially him against the entire ward who was about to rip off Bernadette's clothes in the name of Ireland. Jesus fecking Christ. He couldn't shoot them all. He had only two shots and a razor.

He had to wait for the boys.

He scanned the crowd around him, but didn't see a single face from the group. Not a single one. Where the hell were they? Some of them should have been here by now.

He paused. What if they were all in on this with Cassidy?

Bernadette staggered, almost falling off the barrel. She caught herself against the bar, her gaze drifting toward the faces beyond. "Someone help me," she wavered and slurred. "I may be British, but that…that doesn't make this…right."

Matthew's eyes burned. He glanced toward the men around him, knowing he couldn't wait or trust that his men weren't in on this. He had to help Bernadette *now*. Even if it meant his throat was going to get ripped open by the crowds. Which it would be.

"Psst. *Milton!*"

Matthew glanced toward a wall of men that now surrounded him in the crowd. His breath hitched seeing Kerner, Andrews, Murphy, Plunkett, Lamb, Bryson, Chase and a few others.

He wasn't alone in this, after all. Thank God.

Barrel-chested Andrews wedged his way closer to him and leaned in, lowering his voice. "If you haven't already noticed, Cassidy has up and drawn lines. None of us even knew about it until half a breath ago, when Smock skidded by, telling us. So what's the plan? If I had my way, I'd just shoot him."

Matthew hissed out a breath, thankful he was going

to get Bernadette out. "He's got a pistol. So I need you to listen up."

Andrews and his fifteen other men all leaned in, wordlessly offering up support and waiting for orders.

Matthew bent toward them, ensuring he was hidden from Cassidy's sight, and lowered his voice. "I want all of you to stay right where you are. I don't want anyone dead and I don't want this turning into a riot. But if the crowd does join in, *that's* when I'll need you all to jump in and keep every last man off me so I can get her out. Because I only have two shots and a razor."

Andrews lowered his voice. "I've got me a razor."

"As do I," Bryson added.

"And I," Chase added.

"Whilst I've bloody got two hands," Kerner ground out, "and I'm not afraid to use them to rip apart Cassidy's throat for this."

"Good. Stand by." Gripping both handles of his pistols, Matthew slid them out of his belt and headed through the crowd, toward the opening of where Cassidy and Bernadette were. Perhaps surprisingly, he'd only ever killed one man since becoming a Five Pointer. It had been a six-and-thirty-year-old man who'd been raping a four-year-old screaming child in a back alley. He'd accidentally snapped the bastard's neck trying to get him off the child. He didn't regret it and the marshals never charged him for murder, given what the man had been doing. The only good to have come of it was that it had made the entire ward realize not only was he capable of killing a man but that he would *never* turn away from doing the right thing.

Matthew stepped out of the crowd and leveled each pistol at Cassidy's head. With the flick of his thumbs, he cocked both weapons.

Bernadette staggered her hazed gaze toward him. Her eyes widened and a sob escaped her. "Matthew!"

A growing silence penetrated the expanse of the tavern.

Cassidy set his shoulders and gestured toward Bernadette with the tip of his pistol. "Is this what you were busy fecking over in London whilst we boys were sweating blood on your behalf to eliminate that swipe? A maggot is what you are, Milton. You've got no loyalty to your own."

Matthew's breaths came in disbelieving takes. Cassidy had gotten hold of London newspapers. Keeping both pistols leveled at that head, Matthew tried to remain calm. "This ends. And it ends now. You've got no right bringing her into this."

Cassidy's features hardened. "You bloody sold yourself out and sliced off what little respect I had for you. Not that there was much left, given that no matter what I did, I was never good enough for you, never honorable enough for you, never chaste enough for you. I was never nothing enough for you, Milton, though I was bleeding out of my nose in honor of you. I was damn well tired of your shite even before I ever knew of this, but *this* is what broke me as a man. Because Ireland is me and I am Ireland, and you knew that. And yet that didn't bloody stop you from stabbing me, did it?"

Matthew's throat tightened. He'd rounded up this wild stallion for a saddle and broke him in an effort to mold him for a larger cause, only to find he'd instilled too much passion in him and in the wrong direction. He'd broken the man beyond his soul. He'd done this. And now Bernadette was paying the price. But this is where it ended. With him.

Darting in fast, Matthew shoved both barrels savagely into each side of that thick throat below Cassidy's chin. "For God's sake, Cassidy, my involvement with her had nothing to do with you or Ireland."

Cassidy raised his own pistol to Matthew's head, pressing it hard against his forehead. He cocked it. "Are we playing Who Pulls First? You know I'm in. By the by, your little black dog, who went about wagging his tongue to gather the boys for you, as he always does, ain't standing with your boys in the crowd, is he?"

Gritting his teeth, Matthew dug his pistols harder into Cassidy's rigid neck until he felt the man's pulse against his fingertips through the metal he was holding. He leaned in against the pistol and seethed out, "Where is he? Where's Smock?"

Cassidy pressed his own pistol harder to Matthew's head, the metal now digging uncomfortably into skin and skull. "He's about to get himself shipped South is where. I ain't giving him up and I ain't letting you lead our Irish boys after this. I ain't."

Matthew always knew Cassidy to be an Irish patriot, but he never thought it would come to this. "Who taught you to read those papers you're now using against me, you Irish feck? *Who!*"

A snort escaped that nose. "I didn't get it from Brit

papers. I'd never touch that shite. I got it from a friend of yours."

Matthew's eyes widened. "I don't know who you're—"

"Lord Dunmore sends his regards. In fact, he's requesting you visit him tomorrow night over on the hill. You know, Kill Hill. Be there at nine."

Matthew almost pulled both triggers. "That you would…that you would let your hatred for a nation come before your morals is beyond disgusting. The only thing stopping me from pulling both of these triggers is knowing that half the ward is watching. Because I still have a name to uphold. A name no one is going to take down by turning me into a murderer."

Cassidy glanced toward the gathered faces that were not only watching but listening with a rare devotion that usually only a priest gave the cross. "They're all with me on this, Milton. And the boys sure as hell can't take on the entire ward. Because the truth be this—we Irish don't hobnob with aristo Brits who, as you know, rape our people and our land. 'Tis a dishonor to everything we represent and why we're about to return the favor. These Brits be the reason why every last one of us are here, an ocean away from everything we love, standing in our own piss and spit with nothing to show but sweat!"

Street sweeper Joseph Moran strode out toward them from the crowd. "That be where you're wrong, Cassidy. Unlike my Ireland, I've earned the freedom to piss and spit wherever the hell I please. And that be why I'm with Milton in this. Sniff the air, boy. You're not in

Ireland anymore and this here girl belongs to Milton. Be she a Brit or not, she's one of us because of it. And damn you into hell for not letting us know!"

Others joined in. "Aye! Go back to Cork with this!"

"Shoot the piss pot, Milton. Your da was a true Irishman!"

"May Raymond rest in peace," murmurs swept across the room.

"If you shoot Milton, Cassidy," someone gruffly added, "you might as well shoot yourself. Because we'll bloody you up for this in the name of Milton's da alone. Don't think we won't!"

As more and more riled shouts reverberated throughout the tavern, Matthew was filled with a sense of pride, knowing that although he'd acquired many enemies throughout the years, he'd also acquired many, many friends. Friends who still remembered his father and everything the man had done for the Irish community whilst he was alive.

Shifting his jaw, Matthew grazed the pistols down the sides of that throat and positioned his head against Cassidy's pistol by leaning into it. "Now what, Cassidy? It seems like you're the one that's outnumbered, not I."

Those brows flickered with uncertainty.

Matthew coolly held his gaze. "You thought you'd take me out by dragging this before the entire ward, did you? Guess you didn't expect to meet with that one Irish trait you never did inherit—*loyalty.* Now, step the hell down and lower your pistol. One last time. Where the hell is Smock?"

Cassidy paused, his features and stance tensing as

he scanned the crowd that was now edging in around them. After a long moment of silence, he grudgingly drew away the pistol from Matthew's head and stepped back. "We tied the dog up and delivered him to Rosanna Peers."

Rosanna Bawd Peers. A bitch known for trading and dealing with Southern plantation owners despite the state of New York being free. "Who's holding him? How many?"

"Patrick and four others."

He'd never once sniffed that five of his own were out. Matthew turned and yelled out to his boys, who were already standing behind him, "Get Smock out of there before he's shipped south."

He handed off one of the pistols to Andrews. "Have Smock call on my tenement in an hour, or I'm bloody ripping apart this ward." Matthew swung back to Cassidy and gritted out, "Expect the marshals to descend, arsehole."

Cassidy smirked. "Oh, I'd worry more about yourself over on Kill Hill tomorrow night. This Brit who calls himself Dunmore is a crazy one, he is. And he's got irons for you."

Matthew yanked the pistol out of Cassidy's hand, handing it off to another one of his men. "Both you and he will be sitting on the same floor in manacles surrounded by marshals who will ensure you never walk again."

Several jumped toward Cassidy and grabbed him. Andrews set the pistol to the man's head as they all wedged their way through the crowd, disappearing.

Matthew pushed out a long breath and uncocked his remaining pistol, shoving it into his leather belt.

Jogging over to where Bernadette quietly sat on that cask, he grabbed her chilled hands and squeezed them hard, trying to quell the trembling in his own hands, knowing he—and he alone—was responsible for this. "Come. I'll take you home."

A half-choked sob escaped her, She grabbed his hands and shook them as if meaning to never let go.

He smiled for her, in a mustered effort to offer up whatever assurance he could and glanced toward her cloak on the floor. Releasing her hands, he swept it up and draped it around her shoulders, adjusting it to ensure she was covered.

She froze and jerked herself and her head away, gagging. A gurgled groan escaped her as she sprayed a mass of vomit that splattered across the uneven floor.

Matthew winced as others scrambled back.

She gagged again and sprayed another mass of vomit. Gasping for breath, she leaned back toward him with a groan and stumbled off the cask.

He caught Bernadette by the waist and swept her up and into his arms with a toss, her gown bundling against him.

Murmurs and conversations rippled through the crowd as she stared up at him through hazy, tear-streaked dark eyes.

"Where do you live?" he whispered.

Her head swayed, as if she were having trouble remembering and keeping her head up together. Her eyes suddenly rolled and she slumped against him.

So much for taking her home.

The rumbling voices in the tavern vanished as Matthew pressed her softness tighter against himself. It was a softness he thought he'd never hold again.

He stalked toward the crowd, staring past them. "Someone hunt Marshal Royce down and let him know about Cassidy. I want that bastard in custody by morning for this."

"I'll tell Royce," a familiar voice called out.

Matthew jerked to a halt and swung toward that voice, drawing Bernadette tighter against himself. "Ronan. What the devil are you doing here?"

"Kerner said I could come." Ronan adjusted his cap and peered in on Bernadette, whose head was tucked against him. "Is she yours?"

Matthew glanced down at her and tucked her better into the crook of his arms. "Hasn't been for some time. And after tonight, I don't think she ever will be."

Ronan smirked, pushing back his cap. "Ah, you'll win her over. Just tell her you love her. Women are easy like that." He thumbed toward the crowd. "I'll dash over to Royce and let him know about Cassidy." He darted, shoving his way past people. Matthew paused, realizing the men around him were also angling and peering in on Bernadette. Clearing his throat, Matthew slanted away. "Excuse me, gents. I need to get through."

Although there was little space to give, every man hop-footed away, some of them reaching out and patting him on the shoulder as he made his way through and out the narrow door.

Matthew strode out into the night and through the

muddy, main street. He didn't dare look down at Bernadette. He didn't want to remind himself of what had once been. He simply walked on, a part of him numb knowing that the wretched misery she had endured tonight was because of her association with him.

He halted before his tenement, knowing there was no other place he could take her. He had to wait until she gained consciousness to get her address, and only God knew when that would be, considering the amount of gin she'd been forced to guzzle.

Matthew made his way through the entrance door someone had left open. He paused, glancing toward two men in the shadows who leaned against the wall, smoking home-rolled cheroots.

The voice of what he knew to be his neighbor, Charlie, called out in his usual dry humor, "Finally found yourself a girl, Milton, did you? About bleeding time. Get her upstairs, right quick, I say, before she takes off."

Matthew feigned a not-so-enthused laugh. "Get back to smoking, you rossie. It's all you're ever good for."

"Ain't that the truth. See you in the morning?"

"Aye. Only, do me a favor. If anyone shows up with Smock, yell out so I know."

"Will do."

Matthew quickly made his way up the narrow and steep wooden staircase. The sooner he got Bernadette out of sight, the better.

When he managed to unlatch his door with his key, whilst she lay draped against his arm and his propped thigh, Matthew gathered her again and pushed the heavy oak door open. Angling himself into the darkness, he slammed it shut and blew out a breath, trying to release the tension in his body. He instinctively latched all five bolts on the door. Bolts he'd had installed after a man in another ward had broken in trying to kill him. The five bolts didn't keep people out. They just gave him time to ready himself against an attack.

Dread clenched his gut as he realized Bernadette had yet to see the worst of him: the way he lived. It had been humiliating enough to wear frayed clothing encrusted with mud in her presence back in London. But this? God.

He veered away from the door, adjusting her limp weight in his arms. Through the darkness he knew too well, for he never lit candles at night given a quarter of a candle cost a penny apiece, he made his way to the low closet where his straw mattress was. Lowering her to the bed, he laid her gently out.

Sliding his hands down the length of her bundled gown, he found her feet and removed the slippers and tossed them.

He strode back to the bolted door and braced it, waiting in the darkness. He waited and waited until—

A knock came to the door. "Milton?" Smock called out.

Charlie hadn't yelled. Which meant Smock was alone.

He sagged against the door. Unlatching all the bolts, he yanked open the door.

Smock lingered with a cracked lantern in his black hand, his unshaven jaw set and his dark features twisted in a morbidly joyous sort of way. Reaching out his other hand, Smock grabbed Matthew hard by the shoulder, but said nothing.

Matthew grabbed him and pulled him close and against himself, relieved nothing had happened to him. "I'm so sorry about what Cassidy tried to do."

Smock nodded against him, but still said nothing.

Matthew had no doubt Smock felt even more betrayed in this than he did. Because Cassidy and the other boys who were in on this had gone personal. They had raped the last of Smock by reducing him to mere color. It was heart-wrenchingly monstrous.

Smock stepped away and sniffed, shifting from boot to boot.

Matthew sighed. "We'll have Cassidy in custody by morning. Ronan went straight to Marshal Royce with this." Pulling out the remaining pistol from his belt, Matthew held it out. "Here. It's a better pistol than the one you have. And if you need me for anything, let me know."

Smock grasped the pistol with his other hand. Melancholy tinged those large dark eyes in the sparse light the lantern emitted. "There's more to me than black."

Tears burned Matthew's own eyes. "I know."

Smock hesitated and gestured toward the stairs. "Got to get back to Mary."

Matthew nodded. Having a family was a godsend he so desperately missed. He missed his da. So damn much. "Do you need money? I've got a dollar to spare."

"Nah."

Matthew watched Smock disappear. Stepping back into his tenement, he bolted all the latches on the door and swiped his face with a shaky hand in the darkness. He drifted back into the low closet and lingered beside the straw mattress.

A groan of discomfort, followed by a long breath and then soft, steady breaths reminded him that Bernadette, his Bernadette, was here...in *his* bed. And he was so damn grateful for it. Because he needed her to get him through this night.

Removing his great coat, boots, his patch, then his leather belt and his razor blade, he set them aside on the floor and slowly slid into bed beside her. That soft, heavenly scent of citrus drifted toward him from her skin and clothing, making him inwardly yearn for her.

It was London all over again.

He dragged her closer to him and achingly nestled against her warmth, using his arms to tuck her against the planes of his body. Nuzzling his nose into those silken strands and smooth cheek, he closed his eyes, reveling in holding her. God, there hadn't been a night he hadn't thought of holding her like this.

She had already long proven herself beyond anything he deserved. She, who had saved his life at the cost of her own name, and she, who had tried to save his soul that night when he hadn't been able to understand what his dignity was worth. He was used to leading. Not following.

In that lull of a moment, whilst holding her close, he knew that come morn, everything he'd ever known would change. Because aside from facing the reality of letting her go—*again*—he also had to face a choking new reality. That the respect he'd always sought as a man, and the change he'd always hoped to instill in society, was never going to be found amongst this…chaos. He needed a real job, a real home and a real life outside this mess of the Forty Thieves before the last of who he was and everything he believed in drowned. He had to find a new way to make a difference. He had to be his own man. A real man. Like his father had once been.

CHAPTER FIFTEEN

I am, perhaps, as you will say, a very curious
creature; For I am changing every day, my name,
my shape and nature.

—T.W.K.

*—The Truth Teller, a New York Newspaper for
Gentlemen*

A FLASH AND THE SHARP crack of thunder startled Bernadette from a deep sleep. Nausea roared to life, clench-
ing her stomach, throat and mind. She sat straight up,
fists tight, ready for battle. Her unbound hair fell in a
long curtain around her, swaying against the sides of
her face. She winced and swallowed back the pinching pain in her skull.

Rain drummed against a small window, whose broken pane had been patched with a rag. Gray morning
light revealed a small, dirty room devoid of furnishings save three wooden crates against a wall and the
straw mattress and yellowing, patched linen she lay on.

A visible and deep indentation of what used to be

the weight of a male body, which had clearly lain beside her, whispered of what had happened. Her skirts were bundled up to her knees, tangled around her thighs, revealing her white silk stockings and missing shoes. Panic seized her as she slapped a trembling hand against her mouth to keep herself from screaming.

Though she remembered nothing after her fourth tankard of disgusting gin—which, after a while, she willingly gulped, knowing it was best not to remember *anything*—she didn't have to remember to know what had happened. She blinked back tears that mingled with the headache piercing against her skull. She slowly crawled across the mattress, praying that the man would let her go.

Lightning streaked the sky beyond the small window again, illuminating the uneven walls that revealed sections of wood lattices that held up the walls beneath. The heavy creak of floorboards protesting against the weight of someone moving within the adjoining room made her almost wretch.

"Oh dear God," she whispered, not knowing what to do.

There was a pause.

She had said it too loud.

Heavy steps made their way over and into the narrow doorway. "Bernadette?" a deep voice rumbled out.

Her heart jumped.

A large, broad-shouldered man loomed in the doorway, shockingly dressed only in wool trousers, with a tattered towel slung on his shoulder as if he'd been washing up. That commanding stance of his well-muscled body and that scattered sunlit hair made her realize it was—

Matthew. Only, he wasn't wearing his patch.

Dark eyes held hers for a long moment in a breathtakingly intimate manner she wasn't prepared for. Though the eye he usually hid beneath his leather patch appeared normal, there was a soft clouding in it that hinted at its blindness. He looked different without the patch. He looked like a gentleman. A real one.

Searing heat crept up the length of her thighs and chest as she struggled to remain indifferent. He was absolutely breathtaking. He'd always been, but…

He came into the room. "You don't remember. Do you?"

Ever so slowly, ever so grudgingly, through a haze of a night slathered with gin, she saw glimpses of a massive crowd, of Matthew with two pistols against her assailant's throat, of her staggering to uphold herself against a barrel, of her realizing Dunmore had ultimately betrayed her and Matthew in the vilest of ways, of her vomiting and then nothing thereafter.

A pulsing disbelief that was laced with glorious relief overtook her realizing that Matthew had protected her when she had needed it most. "I remember what you did for me." She swallowed. "Thank you, Matthew. Thank you for—"

"Your association with me is what led to this. So, for God's sake, don't thank me." He lowered himself onto the mattress beside her, whipping off the towel from his bare shoulder. He tossed it and settled in close, bringing in the fresh scent of penny soap and shaving cream.

The muscles within his chest shifted as he leaned toward her. "I'm so sorry. I truly am so sorry you had to go through all of this."

A disbelieving sob she didn't realize she'd been holding escaped her. "I thought I was going to die."

Grabbing her, he savagely wrapped his arms around her, tugging her close. The heat of his solid body washed over her like a blessing from above.

Bernadette tightened her hold on that warmth, desperately needing it.

They lingered in rocking silence, it being broken only by his breaths and hers and an occasional sniff she couldn't contain.

It had been so long since she'd felt any sense of comfort similar to the one she was cradling now. She still couldn't believe that Matthew, the man she thought she would never *ever* see again, was holding her and comforting her. He was here. With her.

She released him and, after a long moment, confided, "Even long before last night, I regretted the way we parted. I want you to know that."

"Nah. I deserved the boot." He shifted away. "And just so you know, I learned from it. I haven't stolen a goddamn thing since. I took on two other jobs outside the ward and even got all of the boys doing the same." Matthew didn't meet her gaze. "I never got a chance to…genuinely apologize for everything that happened. I know I probably caused quite a rift between you and your da when those papers printed that whole mess about us. I'll admit, when you mentioned that your da would most likely cane you because of me, it weighed on my soul. Because I never wanted any of this for you."

She shook her head. "He didn't cane me. He never even sought me out. I'm used to disappointing him, and in truth, he and I parted ways long before that."

"'Tis a shame to know." He was quiet. "I was fortunate enough to have been very close to my own da." He nodded.

Knowing that his father was no longer alive, Bernadette reached out and rubbed his shoulder. "Georgia told me about him passing. I'm ever so sorry."

"So am I." He sniffed hard, scratched at his chin and shifted on the mattress, away from her touch. "So." He cleared his throat. "Have you been associating with other men? Since we parted?"

Though he tried to sound indifferent, there was a notable ache in his voice that made her twinge. He wanted to know if she had moved on. As if a woman could ever move on after meeting a man like him. She slowly shook her head. "No. I swore off associating with men after we parted."

He winced and swiped his face. "You hate me that much?"

"No. I was very disappointed in you and very angry, but I never hated you." She sighed. "In truth, you held up a mirror to my life. I never took anyone or anything seriously after my relationship with Dunmore. And that was wrong on my part. Very wrong."

He blew out a long, slow breath. "Well. That's good to know. Because I... It's good to know." He searched her face before asking, "Why is Dunmore so intent on

destroying you? What happened between you and him?
You never told me."

Nausea bit into her. "I did not go about the relationship properly. I wounded his dreams, however twisted
they were, and so in some way, I am to blame for all
of this. And that, I will admit, is difficult to swallow."

Matthew said nothing.

Bernadette searched that handsome face, trying to
get used to looking at him without the patch.

He paused. "Why do you keep staring at me like
that?"

Her heart pounded relentlessly. "You look so different without the patch. I have never seen you without it."

"Is that a jab?"

"A compliment." Despite their torrent parting, she
had thought of him so, so often. Too often. And though
most of it had been bitter, even the bitter had been laced
with delicious moments of sweetness.

He leaned back toward her, gripped her arm and
squeezed it hard. "I need to know. How did you end
up with Cassidy?"

"The one with the scar?"

"Yes. Did you ever hire guards? Like I had asked
you to?"

She nodded. "They stayed with me at all times, both
at the house and whenever I went about Town, but he
and a group of men dismantled them."

Matthew shifted his jaw and eyed her. "Did he touch
you at all? Or…"

She shook her head, her stomach roiling. "No. Not
in that way."

He threw back his head and stared up at the ceiling. "I should have walked away that night when you had asked me to stay. I should have had more goddamn respect for you."

She leaned toward him and gently touched the warmth of his bare chest with a hand, offering up the forgiveness he clearly needed. "I don't regret our night. Nor do I regret meeting you. Even after all that has come to pass. I want you to know that."

He leveled his head. Grabbing her hand, he covered it with his own and dragged it over his heart. He pressed it into place there, letting her feel its fast beat.

He held her gaze, but said nothing.

Her throat tightened. "Matthew—"

He released her hand and rubbed his jaw with the back of his hand. "We need to get you home. I'll go get dressed." He pointed toward the floor. "I set your slippers out for you. The floors are dirty. I sweep when I can, but they never get clean."

Pushing himself up off the mattress, he jumped to his bare feet with a thud and strode out, disappearing into the adjoining room. There was a clattering of items and the sound of clothing being shaken out hard.

This was his way of saying goodbye.

He wasn't even asking for a second chance. Even though, after this, she may have considered giving him one.

With a sadness she had never known, she quietly scanned his makeshift bedchamber. The broken window, the exposed wood lattices within the uneven, stained walls and three large wooden crates, one holding a collection of old weapons and the other two holding frayed, mismatched clothing. It made her heart squeeze in disbelief. She couldn't bear knowing that he lived like this. No man deserved to live like this.

Especially a man like him.

Her attention drifted to the lumpy straw mattress she was on, where the indentation of Matthew's body remained. He'd slept beside her. He'd stayed with her the entire night after that horror of an incident. If only she could remember how it felt.

She reached out and smoothed her hand against the indentation, trailing it across the patched linen. Her hand stilled against something hard hidden beneath the linen. She dragged the linen away to see what was buried beneath and paused. Her beaded reticule. The one she had given him when she had told him to get out of her life.

Knowing he'd not only kept it, but slept with it, tears stung her eyes. Bless him for being the sort of man she had yet to earn knowing. She carefully draped the linen back over the reticule to hide it, sensing that his pride as a man wouldn't have wanted her to know about it.

She slid off the lumpy mattress and pushed herself up onto stocking feet, wincing in an effort to rise. She straightened, her evening gown cascading down onto her legs. Seeing her satin slippers had indeed been placed neatly by him at the end of the bed in what appeared to be an endearing and loving manner, she smiled and slid her feet into them.

She wandered through the narrow doorway to peer in on him, and hesitated at finding only one other room adjoining the bedchamber. The furnishings consisted of four mismatched chairs. And nothing else.

One chair was set below a cracked mirror where a washing basin, a razor, soap, shaving cream and his leather patch were laid out methodically on its seat. He stood before that chair and mirror set against the wall, quietly getting dressed, wrapping a yellowing linen cravat around his shirt and throat. A faded blue waistcoat was already buttoned and in place. Two of those buttons were missing.

Another chair, the one opposite him, was stacked high with newspapers that threatened to tilt. The third chair held a humble stack of unevenly cut parchment neatly set onto the center seat, several quills and a half bottle of black ink laid beside it, serving as a desk. And the fourth and last chair held various glass bottles of varying sizes, containing what appeared to be whiskey and other unlabeled concoctions. A tin cup sat amongst them.

A small hearth with an iron cauldron and a wooden spoon sticking out of it completed the room that was as equally small as the one she'd left.

Unlike before, she finally understood his desperation that night. She finally understood why he savagely held on to his pride. He owned nothing else.

"'Tis pathetic the way I live, I know," he tossed out, still watching her through the cracked mirror as he finished adjusting his knotted cravat. "Your taste in men isn't what it should be."

"Oh, hush. Have more respect for yourself."

He grunted and gestured toward the chair with the

bottles. "Drink what's in the cup. It'll help with your nausea."

She nodded and went over to the chair. Picking up the tin cup, she peered into it. The thick, brown liquid sloshed within. She sniffed and winced as a rancid smell penetrated her nostrils, aggravating her nausea.

"Don't breathe in," he offered, "just swallow."

Dreading the contact it was about to make with her mouth, she quickly did just that. She almost gagged as it coated her mouth and throat, tasting of rotten peppered ginger. She set the tin aside, happy to be rid of it and winced against the bitterness.

"Da used to make it whenever either of us were stupid enough to drink too much. He called it *Morning Pepper Brew*. You'll feel better in as little as a few breaths."

The man had not only rescued her, but was now rescuing her from the effects of gin. Was there anything he couldn't do? She swallowed, slowly feeling that the concoction was, indeed, already notably soothing her stomach.

It was amazing. As was he. Why, oh why, had it taken seeing him in this horrid hovel to make her realize that he was unlike any man she'd ever met?

She drifted toward him, knowing she could never leave this man behind and most certainly not here, especially after what he had done for her last night. Upon reaching him, she gently took his linen-sleeved arm. "Matthew."

He stiffened and glanced down at her.

Turning him fully toward herself, away from that

cracked mirror, she reached up and gently placed both hands on that smoothly shaven face. "I want you to leave this place. I don't want you living like this. Come live with me."

He stepped away from her touch and solemnly held her gaze. "No. I'm done taking anything that isn't earned by me for me. I intend to crawl out of this myself and I don't need your pity."

"Matthew. You cannot live like this. Nor will I allow for it."

He turned back to the mirror, grabbed up his patch from the chair and tied it around his head, adjusting the worn leather around his eye. "I have lived like this for nine years. Another nine isn't going to be the death of me."

Maybe this wasn't about pride. Maybe this was about…her. "I know we didn't part on the best of terms and I know we are by no means associating romantically anymore, but—"

"If you think I've moved on, Bernadette, you're wrong. But the sad reality is that even if you gave me another chance to redeem myself, which I know you won't, you and I still can't exist. Because *I* don't exist."

Tears stung her eyes. "I'm not abandoning you to a life like this. I'm not."

"You need to stop. I'm taking you home." He grabbed up his great coat and, shrugging it on, walked to the door, unlatched all the bolts and swung it open. "Out, Bernadette. I've got a long day ahead that includes planning for Dunmore over at Kill Hill tonight."

She panicked. "You aren't actually going to meet the man alone in a place named Kill Hill? Are you mad?"

He snorted. "Whilst I appreciate your concern, I'm not going alone. I'm taking marshals and having his arse arrested. Now, come on. You and I have to go."

She shook her head and kept shaking it. She was not giving up on him or this. Not when he'd clearly given up on himself by depending on nothing but that stupid pride that always got him into trouble. Like it had that night.

Turning away, she went over to the chair before the cracked mirror and snatched the chalk and small brush off it. Aside from the grit of last night still coating every last inch of her skin, she needed to get rid of the gin-and-vomit-laced taste in her mouth. Dashing the brush across the small cube of chalk, she leaned toward the mirror and brushed her teeth, determined to get her tongue and mouth clean from the thought of last night.

He stared. "The next thing I know you'll be requesting a full bath and champagne."

She ignored him. When she finished chalking her teeth, she daintily set everything back onto the chair where she'd taken it from and wandered over to the chair piled with newspapers. She commenced rummaging through them, setting each aside one by one by one and eventually held up the one that caught her interest.

The Truth Teller
A New York Newspaper
for Gentlemen
May 17, 1819

"Rather old." She glanced toward him. "Is there a reason you—"

"Leave that." He stalked back over. "They're organized by date." He tugged the newspaper from her hand and took to carefully organizing the ones she had taken out, placing them gently back into the stack they had been in.

She watched that intent expression. They meant something to him. "Why do you keep them?"

"'Tis all that remains of my da's newspaper. 'Twas rather popular in the Irish community and was one of the few papers that printed what went on not only in New York but in Ireland. My father was treated very well in these parts because of it. That may be why so many men came to my side last night. They were honoring my da, not me." He set his shoulders. "Now go to the door."

Her brows rose. "What happened to your father's paper? Does it not exist anymore?"

"No. Da entrusted a friend, who squandered all the funds of his paper on gambling and whores. Hence why we ended up here."

She glanced toward the pile of yellowing papers, angling back toward it in renewed fascination. "'Tis a shame it was dismantled."

"Yes, it was a shame. Can we go now?"

She paused, noting a small, crudely torn piece of newspaper that had slipped to the floor from the pile he'd reorganized. She retrieved it and turned away to read it, lest he take it.

DIED, in New York City, on the 7th of June 1826, age 53, Raymond Charles Milton, a descendent of Cork, Ireland, and a most distinguished gentle- man of the ward, whose life was nobly dedicated to bettering the lives of others. He leaves behind a son, Matthew Joseph Milton, and a wife, Georgia Emily Milton. His burial will be held this Sunday at Saint Peter's Church.

Her eyes widened. She glanced up. "Georgia was married to your father?"

He winced and cleared his throat. "Yes."

"She never told me that. I cannot believe I never once put the two Miltons together. I often thought it odd when she kept brushing aside how she actually knew you. How old was she when they—"

"Eighteen. By a few days."

Oh, God. She herself was eighteen when she'd been forced to marry William. "I didn't realize Georgia and I had so much in common. She was so young, and he so old. The divide must have been…brutal."

"Hardly." Matthew slipped the obituary from her fingers. "I'll have you know that girl had a thing for my da that men could only dream of. And rightfully so. He was well worth being loved." He placed it gently back atop the newspapers and turned away. "Now, come along."

Bernadette touched her hand to the obituary and the newspapers piled beneath it. It was like touching Matthew's soul. It made her ache. And it also made her soar knowing she was at long last getting to see who he *really* was. He wasn't a thief or a criminal. He was a good man. A man worthy of a second chance.

Knowing who he *really* was, she knew she had to fight for this incredible man before he broke himself in the name of pride. Pride wasn't everything. She should know.

She glanced back at him, noting that he was quietly watching her. She would buy him a new life. It was as simple as that. "I am offering you fifty thousand dollars to do whatever you please with. And I will not accept a rejection of this offer."

He stared. Grabbing her arms, he jerked her fully toward himself and tightened his hold, a pent-up aggression pulsing from that grip. Leaning in, until his face and that patch almost blurred in her vision, he rasped, "Not everything can be bought. Do you not understand that, Bernadette? I know you've been born unto a privilege few touch, but this is where your understanding of the world is that of a bloody child. *Pride* can't be bought. *Honor* can't be bought. *Sweat* can't be bought. I have to make a man of myself without pity or charity. Do you understand? I have to do this on my own, or I won't be able to live with myself as a man. And if that is something you can't understand, then you will never *ever* understand what I represent. Nor will you ever have my respect. Not when you think everything, including me, my pride and my soul, can be bought and controlled at the toss of a dollar. Because it can't. It *can't.*"

She blinked rapidly, those words choking her.

She swallowed and lowered her gaze. "Forgive me."

She'd never felt so ashamed of who and what she was. Here was a man who had nothing, but who savagely held on to his pride because he valued what little he owned, and what did she own? Nothing but superficial trinkets that never delivered her hope or happiness or love. "You are right. Forgive me."

His chest rose and fell, his savage hold loosening. He released her and stepped back.

She knew she had to reinstate a different offer. One worthy of him. One that would allow him to rise above his circumstances. "Allow me to amend my offer, for I only wished to honor you, not dishonor you. I would be willing to…become an investor."

"For what?"

"To reopen your father's paper. It would mean that I would own it until your debt is paid in full, using the funds you make through the paper itself. Once that debt is paid, *The Truth Teller* will become yours and you owe me nothing. Not even gratitude. You would become your own man."

He paused, his brows rising. "Reopen *The Truth Teller?*" He sounded intrigued.

"Yes."

He dragged both hands slowly through his hair, causing his patch to shift. "You would…do that?"

She smiled. "Yes."

"I can't guarantee that I'd be able to make enough to even repay a fraction of the costs. It could take years."

"I place no time on the return of the loan."

He shook his head, dropping his hands. "No. I…I

can't. I haven't earned this opportunity you're giving me."

"Matthew."

"No."

It was obvious he needed time. And she would give it to him. Because this incredible man, who had given so much to everyone around him, despite so many missteps, had forgotten to give back to the one person who needed it most: himself. Which was why she had to adhere to patience and teach him the lesson of receiving. After last night, she owed him that and more.

But first things first. She couldn't even breathe or think in the way she wanted to with the grit of last night still coating every last inch of her skin. She wanted it off.

Bernadette quickly rounded Matthew. Heading to the open door that led to the corridor beyond, she closed it and latched each bolt. One by one by one by one.

He stalked toward her. "You'd best unlatch that door, woman. Because you sure as hell aren't staying."

"Cease being rude. I'm merely ensuring privacy for myself." She turned and commenced undoing all of the hooks on her gown, exposing her corset to the waist. "I need to hand bathe before I leave. Is there enough water in your basin for me to do so?"

He froze. "You can bathe when you get home."

She pulled down the sleeves of her evening gown from her arms and pushed it past her waist and petticoats. "I don't want Cassidy's stench lingering on me for a breath more. His grubby, sweaty hands were grabbing me all night. Please. I feel…disgusting right now. I want it off."

Matthew sighed. "I'll ready a basin." He swung away.

"Thank you." Unlacing her petticoats, she pushed them down around her legs and stepped out of them, now in only stockings, a chemise and corset.

Without offering her even a side glance, Matthew stalked over to a tin bucket filled with water set in the corner of the room, plucked it up and set it beside the chair that held his small washbasin. Grabbing up the basin she knew he'd earlier used for himself to shave and hand bathe, he carried it to the other room, opened the broken window and tossed out the water.

Slamming the window shut, he strode back in and set the basin on the chair again. He poured in some water from the tin bucket and set it down. "I'll be in the other room."

Bernadette rounded him and poked his arm. "Before you go, can you undo the lacings on my corset, please?" She bit back a smile. "Without the use of a razor, mind you. For I will need to wear it again once I'm done washing up."

He hissed out a breath. Rounding her, he tugged and unlaced, tugged and unlaced with the precision of a man who was intent on getting her out the door. He stripped the corset from around her and dangled it out to her from over her shoulder.

"Could you hold on to it for me, please?" she asked. "I don't see any hooks on the walls."

Jerking it back toward himself, he quickly made his

way into the adjoining room with it and disappeared. "You've got five minutes, luv," he called out. "Five."

She smiled. He had called her luv. She wondered if he'd ever use it again. Stripping her chemise, she took to using the soap and water to hand bathe herself.

When she was done washing her torso and everything else down to her knees, and at long last felt clean, she used her chemise to pat herself dry. Pulling it back on, she sighed, feeling gloriously better.

In her chemise, satin slippers and white silk stockings, she walked into the adjoining room where Matthew was. "Thank you. I really needed that. Could you please assist me back into my corset? I'll do everything else myself."

Matthew, who'd been blankly staring out of that cracked window, with her corset still in his hand, turned. His gaze snapped to the sheer fabric of her chemise. He crushed the corset between both hands. "I can see everything, for God's sake."

"You *have* seen me naked before," she tossed out, trying to be as casual as she could, whilst striding over to him. "And I can't very well lace myself. I need your assistance in that."

He jerked his chin to his shoulder, averting his gaze and thrust out the corset, dangling it. "I'm sorry, but you're going to have to figure out how to do it on your own. Because the name is Matthew, luv. Not *Saint* Matthew."

She bit back an exasperated smile, stepped toward him and took the corset. "I appreciate your attempt to save us both from the wrath of sin, but in truth…'twas my hope that you and I would be able to start anew. Outside of this mess we stupidly created for ourselves."

Though he still held his chin to his shoulder and his gaze toward the direction of the far wall, he did seem to notably pause. "What are you saying?"

She fingered the corset and sighed. "I have decided to give you that second chance you had asked me for back in London. 'Tis yours. If you want it, that is."

He edged his head back toward her and searched her face. "Why? I don't deserve it. I haven't earned it."

He was more of a saint than he realized. "Because I deserve to get to know you outside of this poverty and you deserve to get to know me outside of my million. We both have a lot to learn about ourselves and each other and I want you to take my offer of the loan as a makeshift truce. And as an opportunity to make of yourself what you've always wished but have never been able to. Despite what you think, you did earn it. I owe you more than a second chance, Matthew. I owe you my life."

"I didn't think that you'd ever even consider…" His gaze ever so slowly slid its way down toward her breasts. His jaw tightened.

His gaze jumped back to her face, his shaven face actually flushing. "Sorry." He swiped at his mouth and set his shoulders. "If I were to, uh…take this loan, what would it entail?"

She tried not to smile, knowing she had flustered him with her seminudity. Him. A gang leader from the Five Points who had seen it all. "I would have solicitors draw up a contract that would delineate any and all terms you deem acceptable."

He moved closer, still intently focusing on her face as if he didn't trust himself to look at anything else. "And this so-called second chance? What would that entail?"

She felt her cheeks heating. "What will be, will be. The relationship would be determined by what we do and how we do it."

He stared. "I rather like that."

"Good. So do I."

He momentarily closed his eyes. Scrubbing his hair with a hand, he blew out a long breath and reopened his eyes. "If I were to accept both—which I damn well want to—I'll need time. I'm hoping you'll be able to give it to me. Will you?"

"Time? For what?"

"To become the man I want to be. To become the man you deserve to know."

A small smile touched her lips. "I respect that."

He held her gaze. "You would wait for me?"

Her heart jolted. This was where she had to accept that, sometimes, not everything could be controlled, and that when it came to what went on between a man and a woman, there were no rules. Only a blind hope that it would all work out. "Yes. I would wait for you."

A muscle quivered in his jaw. "I'll get your clothes. Before I altogether digress." He quickly rounded her and disappeared into the other room, only to return with her gown bundled in his hands. Coming up to the bed, he tossed everything he was holding atop the mattress and, without looking at her, said in a low tone, "Come here."

She swallowed, sensing something had changed between when he left and when he came back into the room. Bernadette pursed her lips and drifted toward him. She paused beside him, still fingering her corset.

He turned toward her. "What if it took me a year or two or three to redefine myself? Would you still wait?"

Trying to ease the maddening erratic beat of her heart, she nodded. "I would still wait for you. Does this mean you…intend on taking the loan?"

"Only under the provision that I repay it with interest."

"Of course."

He hesitated and reached out. Dragging the corset from her fingers, he tossed it onto the bed beside them and stepped closer. He lingered, lowering his gaze to hers. "Can I kiss you? Before I dress you and take you home and figure this loan out?"

She tried to calm her pounding heart. "Yes."

He grabbed her and yanked her toward himself, startling her. He held her gaze for a long moment. "The moment we kiss, we start anew. Agreed?"

She swallowed and half nodded.

"Good." Molding her against his muscled frame, he crushed his lips against hers, forcing her mouth open with a press of his tongue. He sucked her entire tongue into his mouth, hard, causing her to indulgently melt against him in disbelief that she was being kissed by him again.

Dearest heaven, she wanted more. She wanted more

than this. She wanted all of him. And she wanted him naked. *Now.* Repositioning her mouth against his as she worked her tongue harder, she frantically pushed off his coat from those large shoulders.

Grabbing her hands, he broke off their kiss by jerking away and stumbled back. Between heaving breaths, he affixed his great coat back onto his shoulders and cleared his throat. "Now, now. We should get you dressed and get you back home. It's the right thing to do and this—"

She dragged off her chemise, leaving herself naked except for her stockings and slippers, and lowered herself onto his straw mattress. "If you are going to make me wait a year or two or three, Matthew, you had best give me something to remember you by whilst I wait."

He hissed out a breath. "As if I'm about to say no to that." Turning fully toward her, he whipped off his great coat, heatedly holding her gaze, and unbuttoned the flap on his trousers, a visible and solid erection buried beneath.

A shiver, unlike anything she'd felt before, rippled through not just her body but her very soul. She was more or less committing to this man without knowing what it would bring. But then again…once upon a time, when she was a young girl, she had dreamed of sweeping, heart-pounding adventures, true love meant to make one sigh and unadulterated passion that no music from her piano could ever evoke. If she was ever going to try to make a grab for all of that, she knew it was now or never. And she hoped that it was now. For she was rather tired of never.

CHAPTER SIXTEEN

Never tie yourself to someone else's apron strings.
You never know where those strings have been.
—*The Truth Teller, a New York Newspaper for
Gentlemen*

HOLDING BERNADETTE'S GAZE, Matthew undid the flap
on his trousers, trying to keep his mind and his breath
steady, though he felt as if he couldn't even breathe,
let alone think, knowing that she wanted him. She still
wanted him.

Propped on those hands, she lay there unmoving,
damn her, on *his* bed, those beautiful, incredible pale
limbs and full breasts whose nipples had long hardened, all on display for *him*.

He lowered himself onto the straw mattress, crawling toward her until he hovered like an animal over
the length of her naked body. He dragged his hands
up that body he remembered all too well, outlining its
curves as he slowly went up and across her full, soft
breasts and back down to her smooth stomach. God.
This couldn't be real.

Her full lips parted as she stilled beneath his touch.

He couldn't believe she was giving him *everything*. It was more than a second chance. It was a second life. He leaned into her mouth and achingly devoured it, sliding his tongue between those lips and teeth and savoring that heat and softness he thought he would never taste again.

Her tongue worked against his and he found himself lost in everything known as Bernadette. Again.

He jerked away, his chest heaving, and hovered above her, wanting her so damn much.

She opened her eyes, those sultry eyes capturing and unraveling the last of him.

Wordlessly, he reached down between them and spread her legs wide, holding her gaze. His breaths came in heavy takes as he finished unbuttoning the flap on his trousers. Pushing away his undergarments, he pulled his rigid length out.

Tightening his jaw, he slid himself between her wet folds, letting every inch of that tightness and every sensation it brought clamp down on his cock. He pushed in and out of her, holding her gaze. He let it go deeper and deeper with each stroke and press until not only her body trembled, but his own did, as well.

She closed her eyes. "Matthew." Her hips pushed up against him, giving in to him. "Oh, God. Matthew."

"Look at me," he ordered gruffly, working in and out of her, harder and harder, until his own breaths came in puffs in an effort to keep calm.

She opened her eyes upon command and gasped beneath him.

He slammed into her, making those full breasts sway against the impact. It tightened every inch of his skin. He couldn't stop. He wanted to pour seed into her. Slamming into her again and again and again, he savagely held that beautiful gaze as she half moaned in an effort to keep her eyes open.

Her fingers dug into his waist, keeping him in place against her.

Unable to remain calm, and feeling as if his body and soul were about to detonate, he pumped, intent on ramming every last inch into her.

She cried out and shuddered beneath him.

That cry and shudder was his undoing.

Waves of ecstasy raked the last of his tense body as his cock pulsed out seed into her wet warmth. He groaned, stilling against her, wanting and needing his seed to penetrate her womb so that she could change his life by allowing him to become the father he'd always wanted to be. "Bernadette."

He collapsed against her softness. Closing his eyes, he pressed himself against her, desperately trying to regain his mind and his breath. He'd never spilled seed into a woman before. And that is how he knew she was indeed the one. For his body and soul wanted and needed her to carry his child.

He slowly pulled out and staggered to sit up, rebuttoning his trousers. He wedged in beside her on the small mattress. Wrapping an arm around her shoulders, he tugged her softness against his side and positioned her to look up at him.

He searched those dark eyes, his chest tightening.

"You are giving me far too much. And I keep taking far too much. I have yet to prove myself to you. I have yet to—"

A pounding came against the door, rattling it against its latches and bolts.

Matthew scrambled up and out of her arms, his pulse roaring. Dearest God. He'd forgotten his duty to Bernadette. A duty to protect her from the world he'd dragged her into. A world she was still trapped in because of his stupidity and his inability to resist everything she was. He had to get her out.

He lowered his voice. "Get dressed. Now."

Her eyes widened. Tossing the corset aside, she scrambled toward the rest of her clothing and commenced frantically yanking on her chemise and everything else she could.

He strode over to his crate of weapons and froze. He'd given Smock his last pistol and Andrews hadn't returned his other one. Shite. He grabbed up the butcher knife that was angled downward in the crate.

Glancing toward Bernadette, who was now scrambling to get all the remaining hooks on her gown into place, he pointed at her and then tapped his lips.

She nodded, acknowledging his request, and quickly returned to rehooking the bodice of her gown.

Heading toward the door, he set his shoulder against it and yelled out, "Who is it?"

"Marshal Royce. Open the goddamn door. Now."

Matthew froze. The man didn't sound pleased. But then again, when did he ever? "What do you want?"

"Would you rather I come back at a more convenient time so you can grab a few more weapons? Is that it?"

Matthew tightened his hold on the blade. "As always, Royce, you seem to think that I'll answer to a tone that is anything but civil. You're not dealing with a felon here. You're dealing with a man who has helped you for years. So give me the respect I deserve or I'm not opening shite."

There was a huff of a breath beyond the door. "I want Lady Burton. Is she with you?"

He tried to remain calm. "Yes."

"Good. Now, I suggest you not only put down whatever weapon I *know* you're holding, but open the door."

Gritting his teeth, Matthew tossed the butcher knife, letting it clatter to the floor, and unlatched all the bolts. He pulled open the door, letting its weight swing it wide, and stepped aside. "Shall I set the table for tea? Or do you prefer quail and caviar?"

"I prefer respect, cooperation and, above all, silence." Royce loomed, garbed in his usual blue military regalia with a sword at his side whose tip extended to the top of his black boots. Royce's dark eyes pierced the short distance between them, his rain-soaked black hair clinging to his forehead.

"Silence," Royce repeated tonelessly. "Don't speak unless I tell you to. Right now, you and the rest of this godforsaken ward are beyond redemption after what happened to Lady Burton last night. We've already made over fifteen arrests and the Astors have placed an astounding reward of a hundred thousand for her return. So I suggest we get her the hell out of Five Points before people make a grab for her for the money alone."

Matthew's gut clenched.

The man strode in, a black-leather-gloved hand on his sword. His muddied boots echoed menacingly as he scanned the room beyond Matthew, where the hearth was. "Where is she?" His gaze swept over to the low closet, brows rising.

Snapping back toward Matthew, Royce swept out his sword, the metal clanging, and whipped the sword's tip toward Matthew's chest, pointing it. "What the hell did you do?"

Matthew stared, feeling his face prickling with heat. There were many, many times throughout the years when people on the streets of New York had passed him, clutching their wives and children, all due to a patch and his inability to afford good clothes. He'd learned to swallow that humiliation for years, but *this* was where it ended.

Matthew stalked toward the man. "Get that sword out of my face, you—"

Royce jumped at him, angling the edge of the blade just below Matthew's throat. He grabbed him by the collar hard.

"Cease!" Bernadette skidded into the doorway of the low closet, her disheveled evening gown and unraveled long black hair swaying around her panicked stance. "Sir! Cease this! I will have you know that Matthew is my lover and has been for some time. Now release him!"

Royce's hands loosened as he drew away the sword

and released him with a push. Turning back to Bernadette, he resheathed his weapon with a sweep. "Milton is your—" He paused, his tone hardening. "Did he threaten you to say this?"

Matthew wanted to fist the bastard into the floor, but doubted it would help the situation.

"I beg your pardon," Bernadette coolly retorted. "Do you doubt our association, sir?"

"'Tis my duty to doubt, Lady Burton. People lie to me all the time. And if I believed everyone, the prisons would all be empty, wouldn't they?"

"I see." Bernadette set her chin and swept past Royce with a strut. Leveling Matthew with a heated stare that made him pause, she approached, reached up and grabbed Matthew's face, pulling him down and toward her.

Startled, Matthew stiffened.

And that was when she kissed him. In front of Royce. And she not only kissed him, but tongued him so deep in the mouth, he felt like he was going to stagger and fall over.

Heart pounding, Matthew grabbed for her and yanked her hard against himself, not only because he was enjoying the hell out of this, but because he wanted to let Royce know that *this* was his. And he was damn proud of it.

Royce cleared his throat. "A full demonstration wasn't really necessary."

Bernadette broke away from their kiss, the heat of her hands still holding the sides of his face with the determination her kiss had established.

Matthew opened his eyes, trying to catch breaths, and held her intent gaze in awe of everything that she was. God, how he loved her.

He was in love with the way she fought for him. He was in love with how she'd been able to see past the patch, the clothes and the broken windows of his life that had kept so many people away. She was everything he had ever wanted in a woman and more.

Thank God Miss Drake had let him go nine years ago and he hadn't found anyone since. Or he wouldn't have had this.

She released him, her features tight, and regally turned back to Royce. "I expect an apology issued to Mr. Milton, sir. Or I will address this with your superiors within the hour. How dare you enter his home and put a sword to his throat whilst slapping his honor and mine, insinuating that because of my status, I could never associate with a man like this? Now, apologize to him. He has more than earned it."

Matthew blinked, an astonished gruff laugh escaping him. Damn.

Adjusting his vest with a satisfaction he hadn't felt in years, Matthew slowly strode over to Royce until he was able to angle himself toward the marshal, face-to-face. He stared the man down. The same man who had always thought himself better than he. "Make it heartfelt, Royce. I may be blind in one eye, but the ears are still pretty damn good."

Royce shifted his jaw, his hand tightening on the hilt of the sword hanging by his side. After a long moment of silence, he genuinely offered, "I should have never drawn my sword or grabbed you without having had an understanding of the situation. And for that, I apologize."

It was good enough. Matthew nodded. "Not bad. Now. I want her the hell out of here, given there's a hundred-thousand-dollar reward hanging over her head. Have the Astors cut the strings on that shite right quick, lest we have mobs hunting her down in an effort to claim it. I also suggest you keep an eye on Cassidy and whoever else was in on this. I'll give you a list of the ones who weren't in on it. All I have to say is that if you aren't going to arrest Cassidy and the rest for what happened to her last night, I will damn well let the state know. Because attempted mass rape is no different than accomplished mass rape. That said, by the end of this week, I'm dismantling the Forty Thieves. I'm on a different path now. One that will get me out of this hole I've been in for years."

Royce shook his head, swiping away rain-soaked hair from his forehead. "Everyone in my division is working on this, Milton, and we're still making arrests. Cassidy, as well as four others, are already in manacles."

Matthew felt a whoosh of relief knowing those bastards were already in custody. "Good. There is one other thing, however. The man who instigated this, Lord Dunmore, is requesting that I meet him at Kill Hill tonight at nine. Apparently, he wants me to arrive alone, but I'm not stupid. I need you and other marshals there."

"We'll be there. Don't you worry in that." Heaving

out a breath, Royce gestured toward the open door. "I have a carriage outside you can both make use of. I still have to conduct a number of investigations here in the ward, so take Lady Burton to the Astors' before taking her home. They are beside themselves and need assurance."

CHAPTER SEVENTEEN

Wealth and privilege does mean insinuate Communion and God.

—*The Truth Teller, a New York Newspaper for Gentlemen*

The Astor Home—Hudson Square

IN LESS THAN SEVEN hours, when the sun long sank into the horizon, he'd be at Kill Hill, but for some reason the thought of that didn't unnerve him quite as much as…*this*.

Matthew awkwardly lingered in his patched great coat behind Bernadette in the pristine vast foyer whose gleaming floors were all made of white, reflective marble. A massive chandelier made of at least a thousand crystals lit the expanse of the entryway. Honey-colored silk-brocaded walls clothed the expanse of not only the foyer but the adjoining large rooms that seemed to stretch endlessly beyond it.

A servant in livery stiffly rounded him and cleared

his throat, holding out white gloved hands. "Your coat, sir?"

Matthew patted his great coat into place and tried to playfully push off the awkwardness he felt. "Perhaps another time. When I'm wearing my fur coat and top hat."

Bernadette reached out and smacked his arm.

"Bernadette," a male, timbered voice choked out.

Matthew snapped his gaze up toward a young, dashing-looking man of about twenty standing at the top of the sweeping staircase, dressed in expensive morning clothes and black leather riding boots. His blond hair had been swept back with tonic, making him look more debonair than Matthew, as a man, wanted to acknowledge or admit.

The young man quickly descended the staircase, a gold-and-emerald ring on his finger glinting as he jumped down the remaining stairs. "Grandmother and Grandfather are still resting. It's been a wretched night for all of us. The moment they rise, I'll be sure to let them know you are here. Thank God for you being back with us. Thank God."

Matthew lowered his chin. *Back with us?*

Bernadette hurried toward the man, her long unbound hair swaying against her movements. "Jacob." She flung herself into those lean, muscled arms and buried herself against him.

"Bernadette," Jacob murmured against the curve of her shoulder. His ungloved hands slowly dragged and traveled up the length of her back and into her hair.

Matthew's breath burned watching those hands caress Bernadette's unbound hair as if the man were about to ride her right there in front of him. Matthew fought to remain rational and indifferent. He was overreacting.

Maybe they were distant cousins.

Very distant cousins.

Or friends.

Very good friends.

Jacob grabbed Bernadette's face with both hands and leaned his forehead against hers, the bridge of their noses touching. "I'm so damn glad you're safe. So glad."

Jacob lowered his voice and added something Matthew couldn't quite hear.

She choked out a laugh.

Matthew's breaths now came in ragged takes, sensing whatever had been said was about as intimate as any touch. And he sure as hell wasn't about to stand for it.

Stalking toward them, Matthew yanked Bernadette out of those arms. Dragging in more breaths that were anything but calm, he towered over the youth and ground out, "You're really not all that intelligent if you think I'm going to watch this."

"Mattthew—" Bernadette softly insisted.

Jacob's green eyes held Matthew's. "And who are you?"

"Do I really need to say it?" Matthew flung back. "Or is my displeasure enough for you to figure it out?"

Those blond brows rose. The youth stepped back and scanned Matthew's appearance from boot to patch.

"Surely, this must be some sort of… I didn't realize her taste in men was so…anarchist."

It was damn bold for someone who was almost a head shorter than he. Grabbing the lapels of that expensive gray morning coat, Matthew jerked the youth toward himself. "Say that again, golden boy. Me and my fists didn't quite hear you."

"Matthew!" Bernadette wedged and shoved her way between them, breaking Matthew's hold on the youth. "For heaven's sake. Cease." Her hands popped up, landing firmly on not only his chest but Jacob's.

Jacob's hand slowly came up and clasped Bernadette's. He tightened his hold and stared Matthew down.

This was war. Matthew popped up a rigid fist, holding it in midair beside his head. "You've got two measly breaths to let her hand go."

"Matthew!" Bernadette glanced up at him, her face not only flushed but astounded. "Enough." Both of her hands jumped up to Matthew's own chest, breaking that hold on her hand. She shook him. "Jacob is a dear friend and all but twenty. Surely you don't intend on making a fool and a brute of yourself."

Matthew lowered his clamped fist and set his shoulders, stepping back. A youth of twenty was hardly a threat. And yet…the way this Jacob still held his gaze in an unspoken challenge of *"May the best man win"* didn't sit all that well with him. It silently clung to the air like the soot of gunpowder. And though Bernadette didn't see it, he sure the hell did.

This boy, this Jacob, was in love with his Bernadette.

He attempted to steady himself. It was very difficult to remain calm and rational knowing that when he, Matthew, who had nothing to offer save the heart beating in his chest, was faced with a dashing young man who appeared to have everything, including two seeing eyes and a face untouched by the woes of life.

This golden boy personified everything Matthew had once been. Though not nearly as wealthy, Matthew had also once been well dressed, well respected and had more than just Miss Drake twirling her parasol. And then Mr. Richard fecking Rawson had the gall to pilfer everything and toss Matthew and his father into the pits of an inferno known as the Five Points, bringing a quick end to not only his poor father's life, but turning Matthew into a one-eyed, poverty-stricken freak, whose sense of morals, which he'd once prided himself on, had sunken straight into the mud.

In that moment, in meeting this boy, Matthew knew that he could never compete for Bernadette's affection with the likes of men in her realm. Which was why his plans were about to go *beyond* the resurrection of his father's paper. Once the loan Bernadette was so generously bestowing upon him was executed, she would not see him again until he had a home, furnishings, horses, a carriage and was dressed and looking better than golden boy himself. And when he was ready, and outright *owned* the paper and his life as a man, *that's* when he would make Bernadette his. By the time he was done, she'd do more than fall upon her knee. She'd marry him.

Quickly turning to Bernadette, Matthew seized her

hands, kissing each and squeezed them assuredly. "Forgive me. I'll never act like that again."

She smiled and nodded. "Thank you."

Releasing her hands, Matthew stepped back toward this Jacob and set his shoulders. "I shouldn't have grabbed you or treated you with such disdain, sir. It won't happen again."

Jacob's face and jaw tightened. But he said nothing.

Because the boy knew there was no doubt whatsoever who the best man really was.

BERNADETTE QUIETLY LINGERED on the doorstep of her home, watching Matthew re-enter Marshal Royce's carriage, which would take him back to his tenement.

Damn the man. He wouldn't even enter her home when she had invited him in. All he did was offer her one searing long kiss goodbye. One clearly meant to last them both. He then endearingly thanked her for the ten-thousand-dollar loan that would be in his hands by the end of the week and asked that once a contract was drawn and signed, they not see each other until the debt had been paid. Fortunately, he insisted they remain in touch through letters during their time apart.

That was when she realized that pride of his was stronger than ever. Though, she really wasn't worried about his pride anymore. She was more worried as to whether he'd live to see the first printing of his paper, knowing he was heading out with the marshals that night to Kill Hill to ensure Dunmore saw justice.

Kill Hill. She swallowed. Clasping both hands together, she silently sent up a prayer that the name did not reflect the night ahead.

CHAPTER EIGHTEEN

In an age of corruption that has seized our nation, rise.

Rise and become the soul you know yourself to be before everything you believe in is vilely effaced.

—*The Truth Teller, a New York Newspaper for Gentlemen*

Kill Hill

NOTHING BUT ROYCE'S LANTERN lit their way through the dilapidated house filled with endless debris of broken glass and frayed ropes. Everything whispered of past transgressions. Dead bodies and beaten souls were always dumped into this house by local scum. Hence the name Kill Hill.

No one appeared to be waiting in the darkness.

Not even rats. Not even roaches.

Matthew could feel his muscled arm growing heavy from the saber Royce had given him. He was used to butcher knives, razors and cleavers. Switching the saber into his other hand, he gripped the hilt hard, moving alongside Royce, deeper into the abandoned house.

They eventually paused before a half-open cellar door, where a light wavered from below. A warning chimed. Aside from the light, it had been quiet for far too long and it was only a matter of time before the silence broke. It was called the rule of inevitability.

Fully creaking open the door, Matthew moved toward the narrow stairs leading down.

Royce grabbed his arm. "Let me go in first."

Matthew shook his head. "I know this house better than you. There's a cellar and a storeroom downstairs. Keep holding out your light." Matthew went down.

The stairs were faintly lit by a lone glass lantern hanging from a hook bolted into the rotting timber of the wall. Matthew placed the hand that wasn't holding the saber against the wall and followed the wall downward.

He paused when he reached the bottom step and looked around the narrow, dank cellar.

Royce held up the lantern.

It felt like a trap. And even with five marshals probing the rest of the house, it didn't feel right. It felt like someone was waiting to set fire to the place. "We should leave."

"We aren't leaving until we rope Dunmore."

"It's too quiet. And the rule of the ward is if it's too quiet, get out whilst you can still hear yourself breathing."

Royce stepped past him, holding out the flickering light of the lantern toward the darkness. He pointed the saber toward a narrow wood door at the far end of it. "If nothing is past that door, we leave."

"Fair enough."

The smell of dank, rotting wood and urine grew strong, drugging his senses with its overpowering odor.

They paused before the narrow timbered door. Matthew grabbed the wrought-iron handle and pushed. It squealed in protest, but the latch clicked open. Pushing the door open wider, Matthew peered into the blinding, thick darkness.

Silence greeted them.

"There," Royce said in a low tone. "What is that? Over there."

Matthew grabbed the lantern from Royce and held it above his head, moving into the room. His boots crunched and crushed hay that had been strewn across a dirt-stamped floor. The waving edges of the lantern light illuminated the small storeroom. Overturned barrels lay against an uneven stone wall as he turned the light over to another direction and froze, his breath hissing out of his chest in disbelief.

Amongst piles of wool sacks was a youth's motionless, half-naked body facing the stone wall. Oh, God. Matthew darted over and skidded to a halt beside the youth. He shakily lowered himself, setting both the saber and lantern beside that still form. Grabbing up the boy's limp, cool limbs, he slowly turned him in his arms.

He gasped as he stared down at Ronan's swollen face, which was practically unrecognizable from the amount of blackened blood, swelling and bruising.

Tears blinded him. "Ronan—" he choked. "Jesus Christ."

Royce fell onto his knees beside them. "Is he alive?"

Matthew's hands tightened on the boy as he leaned down and pressed his ear against that chest. The faint thud of Ronan's heart swept a numbing relief through him. He blinked back the remaining tears that stung his eyes.

It was a message from Dunmore. *This* was his revenge. He had no doubt Cassidy had told that son of a bitch this boy was the closest thing he had to a son.

Matthew glanced toward Royce. "He's alive. Though, who knows for how much longer. We need to get him out of here. Grab the saber and follow me."

Matthew quickly lifted Ronan off the dirt-stamped ground and carefully rolled him into his arms, forcing his own legs to rise, which felt weak from having to see Ronan in such a state. He couldn't have this boy's blood on his hands. He couldn't. He was too young. And his mother, damn her, never gave him the childhood he deserved. Matthew swore to himself that if Ronan lived, Matthew would ensure the woman give him full custody of the boy. Because Ronan deserved a real home, real protection and real guidance. The sort he wasn't getting.

Matthew hurried out of the storeroom, Ronan hanging limply in his arms. He focused on every breath and every step, praying that Ronan was going to pull through.

Royce sheathed his sabers, squeezed between Matthew and the wall and jogged up the narrow stairwell, calling out to the other marshals. He disappeared up the stairs and out of the cellar.

Breathing hard in an effort to remain calm, Matthew kept his eyes on getting to those stairs.

Ronan groaned, rolling his head toward him.

Matthew's pulse raced. He tightened his hold. "Shh. Don't move. We're taking you to the hospital."

"Milton," Ronan rasped. "He's…going back to… London. Tomorrow. He didn't know I…heard."

"We'll hang the son of a bitch before he gets on that boat. Don't you worry in that."

New York Hospital

MATTHEW LET OUT AN EXASPERATED breath and adjusted his great coat, shifting toward the rest of the boys, who were all gathered alongside him like carp in a bucket within the small office as they awaited the verdict of Ronan's condition. Matthew glanced impatiently toward the surgeon, who appeared to be far more occupied with tasks involving his desk. "*And?* How is he?"

Dr. Carter finished scribing his notes pertaining to Ronan's condition. Setting aside the quill, he casually reached out and gripped the porcelain cup beside him. Lifting the rim to his mustached lip, Dr. Carter took a long swallow of murky coffee before setting it back onto the saucer beside him with a *chink*. "He will more than live, gentlemen. Aside from some threading on his face, he is doing remarkably well. In fact, you will be able to take him home in a day or two."

A whooshing breath escaped him.

Dr. Carter rose and rounded the desk. "I should check on him one last time. Before I retire for the night."

Matthew strode toward the man, grabbed his hand and shook it, squeezing it hard. "Thank you, Dr. Carter. It means a lot to me knowing you stayed on to take care of him."

The man nodded and eyed him. "Are you his father?"

Matthew's throat tightened. It was inevitable that Ronan was going to be permanently living with him. "No. But I hope to prevent anything like this from happening to him again."

"Good. Because no boy should have endured that." Dr. Carter nodded, released his hand and left.

Matthew swiped his face and lingered in silence, knowing the Forty Thieves had officially met its death. Dunmore aside, too many people kept getting hurt and too many had already died. And this is where he got everyone the hell out before the Forty Thieves ended *everything* he sought to protect. It was time to make a grab for a new life being given to him by an incredible woman he vowed never to fail again. And he intended to include all of his men who had gallantly stood beside him to the end.

Matthew swung toward Kerrigan, Plunkett, Smock, Dobson, Herring and Lamb. "We're calling a meeting on the morrow and gathering the last of the group. I'm putting in a vote that we end the Forty Thieves before it ends us. We're not contributing to the violence ever again. We're done with this."

All of their eyes widened.

Kerrigan and the rest veered in, their expressions tight. "You can't do this to us, Milton. This here be the one thing giving us purpose. It's the only thing that—"

"I know." Matthew held up a hand. "But we can't keep doing this. Your families need you more than the street does. There are other ways of giving ourselves purpose, whilst making a difference. We can become a voice for those that have none and it won't take a pistol or blood. I've a new offer for you boys. An offer that will enable each of you to become your own men. Men who'd *finally* be good enough in the eyes of the city and the land. And the best part? You'd *always* have money in your pocket. Good, honest money. Not swiped money or measly money that will never be enough to feed you and your families. Are you interested?"

They glanced toward each other and then back at him.

Smock stepped toward him. "I'm in. For Mary an' the girls. What be it?"

One man in, and the rest to go. "I'm opening a business and plan to be out of Five Points by the end of this week. I'm looking to hire fifty people, which means everyone standing here has a job, including Ronan and every last man in the group who stayed true. I'll start each of you at two and a half dollars a week, to be raised to three and a half after a month, and I'll put you all in new clothes and boots merely for saying yes."

Kerrigan squinted, his bearded face doubtful. "What sort of business are we talking here?"

"I'm reopening the doors of *The Truth Teller.*"

Almost every last bushy brow went up.

Dobson bellowed, "Your da's old newspaper? You don't say."

Herring drawled, "Oh, now, that there be pride and history. And you're saying we'd actually be a part of it? Us?"

Matthew nodded and swept a forefinger toward them. "Every last one of you. Because I need good men to help me do it. And aside from printing commentaries about Ireland and New York, we'd also be printing what hasn't been put to print yet—the story of our struggles to survive back in the day when we were Five Pointers. That alone will sell papers."

McCabe let out a low whistle. "New York will never be the same once they hear what we have to say."

Lamb chimed in, "Right in that. I remember me uncle always boasting that your da's paper had what all the others didn't—the goddamn truth. It broke his heart when it went under. And I know without me even asking, he'd work there right along with me. He's been in need of a job for a while. Would you be willing to hire him?"

Matthew leaned toward him. "Your uncle is one of the finest men I know. So, yes. He's hired."

Kerrigan eyed him. "This'll be costing you a pretty pile of nickels and dimes we all know you don't have. Where are you getting the money?"

Matthew rubbed his jaw with the back of his hand. "A wealthy patron, the beautiful lady we saved last night, graciously stepped forth and offered me a loan. It's been approved and I get the money by the end of the week."

Plunkett snorted. "These rich lend out money to anyone these days, don't they?" He paused and added,
"Fortunately for us."

Sensing they were in, Matthew held out both hands.
"At the cost of the Forty Thieves, are you all in for a
chance to get the hell out of Five Points, right along
with me?"

There was a moment of silence followed by a united,
"Aye."

Matthew bit back a grin. Much like his boys, he was
damn well ready to rise. And he swore upon his very
last breath that he was going to become the man that
Bernadette not only deserved, but a man she would
swoon to keep.

CHAPTER NINETEEN

A certain judge, (we forget his name) many, many years ago and in England, acquired the cognomen of Judge Thumb, from having decided in a trial rising out of a matrimonial squabble, that a man might beat his wife, provided he did it with a stick no thicker than his thumb. It must be very consoling to ladies who have men of a domineering spirit, and with thick thumbs, to know that a new luminary of the law, (Mr. Justice Park) in a recent trial said he would not admit that the law authorized a husband to even chastise his wife. Justice most certainly is fickle.

—*The Truth Teller, a New York Newspaper for*
Gentlemen

Two months later
30 miles north of New York City—Sing Sing Prison

IN THE NAME OF ALL THAT he loved about her, damn Bernadette for possessing the heart he knew he didn't have. In a letter she had scribed all but a few days

ago—as it was the only interface he would allow—
she had pleaded that he visit Lord Dunmore, given
she had received a most alarming form of communication from the prison's chaplain. Apparently Dunmore
wanted Bernadette to know of his repentance. Should
he die. She was concerned that the man was contemplating suicide. And because women were not allowed
to visit Sing Sing, it was up to Matthew to ensure the
man did no such thing. Even though Matthew was the
last man who'd ever discourage the bastard from doing
the world a favor.

Of course, this whole fuss came about after Dunmore had been dragged off the boat he'd tried to escape
on and sentenced to eight months of labor and incar-
ceration in Sing Sing. Despite protests from abroad
that included scathing letters from countless British
noblemen and British newspapers the State of New
York dug in its heels.

The state wasn't interested in instating justice. God,
no. That wasn't what it was about. They were merrily
slapping England around, hoping to send them a message: *You don't step into our country and feck with our
citizens.* It was an unprecedented political stance Matthew wholeheartedly applauded.

The sweltering heat of the summer sun outside didn't
penetrate the bone-deep chill of the unending limestone
walls surrounding him.

The smell of stagnant rot, rusting iron, urine and
sewage penetrated Matthew's nostrils as he passed each
narrow iron-and-oak-latticed door lining those barren, sooty gray walls. Human shadows and occasional

gruff faces of men with blank, inhuman expressions appeared beyond every one of those bolted iron-latticed doors.

The only audible sounds were those of his and the warden's boots scuffing the uneven stones of the corridor. For a prison that housed over five hundred men, it was downright eerie. It was as though everyone was dead.

"There is but one rule every prisoner is set to abide by," Warden Wiltse intoned. "Silence. Silence when they march in lock-step, silence when they eat, silence when they labor, silence when they read their bibles and silence even as they're squatting over their chamber pots." The warden paused before one of the doors and turned, his sharp gray eyes meeting Matthew's. "It took time, but Dunmore here has at long last accepted his sins. And it's only been two months. Another six ought to make him a saint."

Holding Matthew's gaze, Warden Wiltse retrieved a ring of iron keys from his coat pocket. He unbolted the iron latch. "You have fifteen minutes, Mr. Milton. Talk all you like, and know that he'll answer your questions as best he can, considering he isn't permitted to speak. This is the last visit he'll be allowed by anyone. He's going into solitary confinement due to his inability to take orders and will stay there until the end of his term." The warden swung open the door and dangled the leather cat-o'-nine-tails he held. "I'll be waiting outside with the cat if you need me."

Matthew nodded and stooped to enter the narrow opening. He veered into the small, windowless cell that bore only a chamber pot and an unevenly stuffed straw bed covered with stained linen laid out on a slab of stone. Bloodstained linen that ran in spatters and streaks. An open leather-bound bible sat upon the bed.

He paused, seeing Lord Dunmore sitting on that straw bed beside the open bible, his disheveled dark head in swollen and bruised hands. Matthew's eyes widened, noting that the blood streaking the linen had come from Dunmore himself. The gray-striped linen uniform he wore was stained with uneven rows of blood that seeped and clung to the expanse of his broad back.

Matthew's throat tightened. He rounded the man. Though pity was the last emotion he wanted to feel for Dunmore, seeing blood on a man had never been something he'd easily swallowed.

Drawing to a halt before Dunmore, Matthew squatted down to the man's level to better see him. "I'm here on behalf of Bernadette. Not myself."

The unshaven man lifted amber eyes solemnly to his, but otherwise did not move. He merely continued to hold his dark disheveled head with his hands as if he needed it for the strength to remain upright. His face looked gaunt, those high cheekbones and lean, square jaw were covered with fresh scrapes and bruises.

Matthew searched that face, utterly astounded. The man not only looked severely beaten but it appeared he hadn't seen a half-decent meal since his sentencing. God help him. Why did he even care?

He shifted toward him. "What the hell did you do? Get yourself into more trouble? Are they not feeding you?"

Dunmore said nothing.

"Did you resist orders? Is that it?"

Dunmore slowly shook his head from side to side, his expression and amber eyes devoid of any emotion. There was no sadness or anger or fear. There was nothing. Nothing at all.

This was not the same man. This man was a bit too broken.

And in that moment, Matthew sensed that the message Dunmore had communicated with Bernadette had, in fact, been genuine.

Matthew leaned in, knowing he had a duty to Bernadette to set her mind at ease. "Bernadette is worried, given the chaplain's letter to her. She wished to assure you that all is forgiven and that you needn't punish yourself by contemplating suicide. Now. Is there any one message you want me to convey that can be done without the use of words? Perhaps proof of your penance?"

Dunmore shifted his jaw. He half nodded, shifted sideways and, still holding Matthew's gaze, lifted his linen shirt. He winced against the peeling, but clearly determined to offer proof, his gaze never left Matthew's.

Matthew's eyes widened at seeing black-crusted blood, puss and freshly broken scabs welting with new blood streaking the flesh of Dunmore's back. Jesus. He'd heard of what went on in Sing Sing from others back in those now far gone days of the Five Points, but he didn't realize the street tales of deliberate torture by the guards were true.

He stared, a part of him needing to know what the hell really went on behind these walls. "How many days of lashings have you endured since being incarcerated?"

Dunmore lowered his shirt and stared at his hands, but offered nothing else.

"I know you're not allowed to speak, but show me fingers. How many days of lashings have you endured thus far? I want to know."

Dunmore hesitated. He slowly held up ten fingers, then closed them and held up ten more fingers, and then closed them and held up seven more.

Matthew drew in a ragged breath. The man had been lashed twenty-seven times since coming into prison. That, out of sixty-two already served days, with six more months to go.

Shite. Yes, the bastard deserved punishment. But this? This wasn't punishment. This was torture. The man's clothes were sticking to his goddamn wounds, which were bleeding into the linen he slept on. What was he going to tell Bernadette when he wrote to her about the visit? That he had said and done nothing whilst the man bled? She'd never forgive him. Hell, he'd never forgive himself. He was more than this.

Matthew rose to his booted feet and called out, "Warden Wiltse? Might you come in?"

The warden's hefty frame appeared in the doorway and stooped to enter. The older man gripped the leather cat-o'-nine-tails and whipped the stone wall with it, a resounding crack echoing within the small, narrow room. "Is there a problem, Dunmore? Are you not answering this gent's questions with the nod and the shake I told you to?"

Dunmore closed his eyes, digging his swollen fingers into his head but said nothing.

"He's answering my questions. That isn't the problem." Matthew strode toward the warden and gestured toward Dunmore. "Why the devil is he being lashed like this? And why aren't his wounds being tended to?"

The warden widened his stance, those gray eyes as flat as his expression. "Orders."

"Orders? From who?" Matthew demanded. "The state?"

"Every prisoner has a set punishment they serve, Mr. Milton. That is why they call it a prison."

Matthew shifted toward him. "So you mean to tell me every prisoner is being whipped daily like this? And then forced to bleed into their clothes like this?"

The warden eyed him. "We don't whip them daily. Only once or twice a week."

"*Only?* And how long are these men being lashed for?"

"I hire men who can't count for a reason."

Matthew's eyes widened. "*What?* And you instate this sort of punishment on every last man here?"

"We have to."

"Including those men who might have only stolen bread to feed their goddamn family?"

"Criminals are criminals, Mr. Milton. This is how we keep everyone and everything in order. This is how we ensure there is no sense of self. They're here because they all had too much sense of self."

Dearest God. This could have been his life, seeing as he had done so much stealing himself. And knowing it punched him straight to the soul. For he considered himself a good man. "I see. So Dunmore and the rest of these men aren't being punished for the crimes they committed but because they have a sense of self that needs to be obliterated. Is that what you're telling me?"

The warden raveled the ends of the tasseled cat around his calloused hand. "I'm only here to oversee these men and these walls. If you have a problem with the way things are being done, Mr. Milton, I suggest you take it to the state."

Matthew leaned toward the older gent and bit out, "I'll do better than that, Warden. I'll print this and let the public take it to the state. Because punishment is one thing. Torture is quite another."

"I'd like to see what becomes of that. If you must know, no prisoner to date has been allowed a single visit from the outside world. Him being nobility gives him privileges all the other prisoners here don't have."

Matthew whipped a finger toward Dunmore. "You call *that* receiving privileges? Dearest God, I would hate to see what all the other men look like."

Warden Wiltse grunted. "You've got five minutes. I suggest you make use of it. Because no one is going to be seeing him again until he's done with solitary confinement in six months. *Orders.*" With that, he stooped through the door and stepped outside again.

Matthew swung back toward Dunmore, his pulse thundering. Christ. Despite this being the same man who had cropped his Bernadette in the face, had almost seen her raped and who had hired no-gooders to brutally beat Ronan before dumping him over on Kill Hill, *this* reciprocated form of brutality only made them *all* animals. Even worse, knowing that hundreds of other men who had done far, far less than Lord Arsehole here were suffering equally alongside him was unspeakable. It was no better than the injustice on the streets of the Five Points. However, Matthew's new path in life would ensure everybody knew of this particular injustice.

Matthew quickly strode back to him. "I want you to listen to me, Dunmore."

Dunmore stared up at him, his features tight.

"You deserve to rot for all the shite you pulled, but in the name of Bernadette, who I know would agree with me, if you truly are repentant, you deserve a second chance. Which is why I'm going to personally ensure we get your back tended to, and that these lashings cease."

Dunmore blinked rapidly and glanced toward the open door. Edging toward Matthew, he rasped low enough so the warden wouldn't hear, "I never sought to have her raped or that boy hurt. That was not what I agreed to when I paid those men. I stated that repeatedly to the court and it is as true as the blood sticking to my shirt. You tell her that." Leaning back against the unevenly stuffed mattress, Dunmore winced. He carefully grasped the leather-bound bible beside him and dragged it onto his lap. A trembling hand drifted to the page of Psalms he was reading.

Matthew drew in a calming breath before letting

it out. It would seem this lost soul was trying to find peace in a world that held none. "I'm not saying this makes us friends, Dunmore, but consider Sing Sing front-page news. My newspaper debuts in fourteen days and this is worth a debut. People have a right to know what the hell is going on behind these state walls. We, the people, pay taxes to protect the rights of our people. We don't pay taxes to whip the skin off them."

Dunmore glanced up and slowly rose, closing the bible. Though pain twisted his face into pausing, Dunmore reached out and tapped the tip of his finger against the bible, then Matthew's forehead and then Matthew's chest before whispering, "My father once said, rare do these three ever come together. And that is why you are free and I am not."

Nineteen days later

ALL OF NEW YORK CITY WAS in an uproar. Not that it ever took much to rile New York, since as a whole, it was overly opinionated, but as all uproars went, there was always at least one definitive source behind it. And Matthew was damn well proud to say that this time *The Truth Teller* was that source.

Due to the ramping escalation of blistering opinions, *The Truth Teller* had sold out every last printed copy in all but five days, which for a weekly newspaper that was in its debut and first printing, was rather impressive.

No one truly cared about the prisoners, per se, or the fact that they were dying, but the good people of New York City did care about how much it was costing the state every year to implement ineffective punishment: a grand total of $53,571 and a whole penny. People wanted to know what the hell was going on and took to protesting all across the city with placards bearing the dollar amount the state was paying.

As a result, Sing Sing Prison's daily routines quickly came under such close scrutiny by enough state officials Matthew was well assured that the remaining months Dunmore had left in prison would be, at least, tolerable. It was still a prison, after all.

Of course, Sing Sing wasn't the only thing to come under close scrutiny. The mayor, who had never once bothered to respond to *any* of Matthew's eighteen dozen letters, which he'd written throughout the years whilst in Five Points, had sent Matthew his very first correspondence. It was unprecedented.

And it read:

Dear Mr. Milton,
I realize the purpose of a newspaper is to convey news, but do try to remember that you have a responsibility to ensure that all of the state representatives are not assassinated in the process. I ask that you call upon me and the entire council *at once* so that we may all privately discuss the particulars in how to best avoid any and all riots that may ensue in what I still consider to be a respectable city, despite its ineffective spending of funds.
Sincerely,
Lord Mayor

Matthew refolded the letter and with the flick of his wrist, tossed it onto his desk with a well-satisfied smirk. His father had once told him that a good paper could be more effective in knocking people over than the plague. Bless the man for being right. And if he continued to sell papers the way he had with the first printing, not only would his ten-thousand-dollar debt to Bernadette be paid in full, but the woman would be his in...oh, eight more months or less. Not bad for a man with only one seeing eye to guide him through life. Not bad at all.

CHAPTER TWENTY

Few have the patience of God, and those that miraculously do harbor that patience, find it does not last very long, given that they themselves are not God.

—*The Truth Teller, a New York Newspaper for Gentlemen*

Six months later
Manhattan Square, early afternoon

"Damn you, Matthew," Bernadette muttered, glancing about her empty parlor. "Damn you, damn you, damn you." She paused and then added another, "Damn you. I cancelled my trip to Port Royal for this?"

They were the only words she had left.

To date, barely six months after being in weekly print, *The Truth Teller* had turned into the bestselling newspaper in all of New York City, selling out from hands and stands and the print shop itself barely hours after each paper was freshly printed and dried every Saturday. It wasn't all that surprising. After all, its controversial debut covering Sing Sing Prison ensured it was now being read by far, far more than just the Irish. *Everyone* wanted to read it, if only to get their hands on the Five Points page alone, which printed real-life stories about the sixth ward, all written by Matthew himself. It read like a dagger-sweeping adventure out of a book. Only…better.

Apparently, the mayor, who at first had been explosively wary, had soon bowed into giving the newspaper accolades along with some sort of prestigious award Bernadette had never even heard of. In fact, the mayor had grown such an adoring fondness for Matthew that, in no time, the two had become the best of friends. According to New York gossip, Matthew and the Lord Mayor met every Friday evening over cigars and brandy.

She hadn't realized Matthew smoked. But then again, there were a lot of things she'd never realized about the man who had also legally acquired guardianship of a boy by the name of Ronan Sullivan, whom he'd pulled out of the Five Points. It was as endearing as it was frustrating not to have been part of it.

Though she had tried to glimpse Matthew and his young ward over at a high-society charity event that had been written up in all the papers, she found herself physically escorted out of the event by Matthew's own entourage. The three men had politely explained to her that Mr. Milton did not wish to be seen by her until *after* he owned the newspaper. Something Matthew had repeatedly asked her to respect throughout their months of written correspondence.

It was annoying that he was keeping her to that promise. Worse yet, women, both young and old and every age in between, all across Broadway and well beyond every well-to-do square, dithered on and on about Mr. Matthew Joseph Milton as if he were some newly discovered Egyptian ruins in need of excavation.

Yes, well, she had found him first.

Only, the man seemed to have forgotten that.

Through it all, throughout all eight torturous and utterly ridiculous months of bowing to all of his wishes, she still hadn't seen him. Not. Once. He had refused every visit she'd made at the print shop. He'd also refused every visit she'd made to his new Italian row house just off Broadway.

Though they'd corresponded through lengthy weekly letters throughout these eight months, his letters were always one-sided and he answered only the questions that he wanted to. In fact, she knew more about his ward than Matthew himself.

Ronan loved playing whist, especially if there was money involved. He immensely enjoyed eating cross buns dipped in wine, preferred playing the violin as opposed to reading and was astoundingly proficient with mathematics. The biggest problem Matthew had with the boy was Ronan's fondness for…as Matthew put it…the lifting of skirts. Something Matthew tried to choke out of Ronan at every turn by keeping the boy as respectably busy as possible.

After the first few months of feeling as if she would die from the anguish of not meeting this Ronan *or* seeing Matthew, she had lost all patience and scribed the following letter:

My dearest Matthew,
It has been far too long. Though I consider myself to be capable of patience, I desperately need assurance in this and us. I would like to call upon you, if even for the briefest of moments. Five glorious minutes in your presence is all I ask. Although, I will even settle for three. I humbly leave that for you to decide.
Yours,
Bernadette Marie

In response, Matthew wrote the following letter:

Patience.
Ever yours,
Matthew

Nothing else had been written on the page. Nothing at all. Which signaled rather blatantly that he had denied her request. So she swallowed her pride as a woman and gave him that patience by continuing to write and hoped he deserved it.

When he'd astounded her by paying off his entire debt of ten thousand all but a week ago to her bookkeeper—which meant he was making that and more—she thought it would finally bring the man to her door. Only, it didn't. She hadn't received a single correspondence from him. Not even a note saying thank you for the loan.

She'd broken four strings on her poor Clementi piano because of it.

Gritting her teeth, Bernadette rolled up the latest printing of *The Truth Teller* and started thwacking her writing desk with it, hoping to God that Matthew could *feel* his newspaper being mangled.

The butler hurried into the parlor and jerked to a halt.

Bernadette paused and awkwardly set aside the newspaper on her writing desk, patting it into place as it unrolled itself.

Emerson held up a small red velvet box with a dainty white satin bow and cleared his throat. "I hope this brings a measure of cheer, my lady. The servant who delivered it requested you open it at once. It wasn't formally announced as to who it was from, but it has a card."

Her heart pounded as she hurried toward him. Could it be from Matthew? It had to be. She would have grabbed that box there and then, but her stupid, stupid hands started to quake and she knew she would only have dropped it and broken whatever was inside. "Can you read the card for me? Please. Whilst I attempt to remain calm."

"It would be my pleasure." Emerson brought the box to his chest and tilted his head to one side, causing his graying hair to shift over his forehead. Skimming his hand around the side of the bow, he found a small, ivory card tucked beneath.

Oh, for heaven's sake. Breaking it might have been better than this waiting. "Shall I take it?"

"I have it." Slipping it out, Emerson held it farther away from his aging eyes and, after a squint, read in a dreary boarding-school tone, "To the ravishing Lady Burton who held the patience of God. Compliments of Mr. Milton."

Her breath caught. At long last. "Does it really say ravishing? Or did you add that knowing I have been waiting to hear from him?"

Emerson sniffed, clearly not amused. "I will set this out on the table with all of your other correspondences. As you always have me do." He turned and made his way back out of the parlor.

Heart pounding, she gathered her skirts and hurried after him, feeling as if the box were Matthew himself. "Emerson, please. I was being silly. Give it here."

Emerson turned back, dutifully holding out the red velvet box. "Of course."

Bernadette hesitated. Even though the man now held the box out, for some reason, she couldn't bring herself to take it, let alone open it. A part of her dreaded that this was goodbye and not the hello she had been achingly waiting for. She pressed her hands against her cheeks, digging her fingers into them, unable to open it.

Waiting with that box still held out, Emerson stared.

Knowing she ought to take it, she let out a calming breath and retrieved the surprisingly light, small box from his hands.

She paused, admiring the beautiful white satin bow tied perfectly and beautifully around the red velvet. It was so pretty. It appeared a lot of thought had gone into it. Which had to be a good sign.

She brought it up to her ear and gently shook it, wondering what was inside. Something shifted within, but it didn't sound like jewelry. She shook it again. It didn't sound like much of anything.

Emerson leaned in. "Shall I open it, my lady?"

She paused.

"I thought perhaps you needed prompting," he added.

Sadly, the poor man had dealt with every single one of her fits these past eight months pertaining to Matthew. "Will you please stay with me, Emerson? Whilst I open it? I may need someone to catch me, should I faint."

"It would be an honor to catch you."

She smiled. "Thank you." She fingered the satin bow, then gently tugged at its end. The smooth ribbon unraveled. It slipped from the box and her fingers, floating soundlessly to the floor. She left it there. All that mattered was what was inside.

She carefully removed the lid and peered in. There, sitting primly atop beautifully folded white lace was a...calling card.

His calling card. And nothing more.

She stared at it, stunned, and honestly didn't know what to make of it. Printed on what she knew was a very expensive ivory Bristol card, which she herself used for her own calling cards, it read:

M. J. Milton
28 Broadway

And on the very bottom corner of that elegant card written in his own scribed hand were the initials of *p.p.*

Her lips parted. By heavens. The man had learned the art of calling-card etiquette. Because *p.p.* was French for *pour presenter,* which signaled to its receiver that if there was anyone the receiver wanted to be introduced to, one merely had to send their visiting card and an hour they wished to visit and it would be done.

He was asking her to call on him. She was going to see him! Though more important, he *wanted* to see her and was *asking* to see her.

She removed his card from atop the soft lace and held it up before her, handing off the box and lid to Emerson. Matthew was at long last his own man and *this* was his way of announcing it.

She smiled. Tilting the card, whose inscription had been elegantly scribed across its smooth surface in black ink, she grazed the tip of her finger across it, knowing he had touched it.

Heart still pounding, she glanced toward Emerson, who bent to retrieve the white ribbon at her feet. "Emerson, will you please have a footman send my card over to Mr. Milton's and announce that I intend to call within the hour?"

Emerson straightened, ribbon in hand and inclined his head. "Of course." He reached for the card.

She set it protectively against her bosom. "Oh, no. This is mine." She knew this card was going to change her life.

Emerson paused. "The footman needs the address, my lady."

Bernadette inwardly cringed. "Of course he does." She held the card back out. "Please ensure the footman returns it."

"I will ensure it." Taking it, Emerson disappeared to hand off the card.

She now had an hour to look…ravishing, as Matthew had called it. Oh, God. She hadn't given herself much time, had she?

Bernadette frantically gathered her skirts from around her slippered feet. Seeing her lady's maid rounding the corner, she pointed and called out, "Samantha! Samantha, by all that is blessed, I need you like a horse needs hay. Bring out every last gown, all of my boots to match, as well as my fur mitts, as it's snowing outside. And, oh! Lay out every last perfume I own."

CHAPTER TWENTY-ONE

Oh, Ireland. Is there not as bright an hour re-
served for thee? Yes. Yes, there is.
—*The Truth Teller, a New York Newspaper for*
Gentlemen

RECOGNIZING THE SQUARE up ahead enclosed by the wide
snow-covered road and tall, stone-washed Italian row
houses, Bernadette inhaled a breath of crisp, cold air
and gripped the edge of the upholstered seat of the open
sleigh to keep herself steady.

In a blinking blur of softly falling snow, the sleigh
pulled to a halt. The footman hopped down and bustled
toward the small door at her side, yanking it open. He
leaned toward her and held out a hand.

She stood. Though barely. She was so nervous. What
if these past eight months had changed him and he was
no longer the Matthew she adored? What if he had forgotten what had once been between them?

Taking the footman's white gloved hand, she stepped
out. "Thank you." Once her booted feet touched the

snow-covered stone walk leading to Matthew's home, she drew in one last steadying breath.

The large gray stone townhome was surrounded by bare oak trees and black wrought-iron gates rimmed with gathering snow. It was elegance at its finest. She felt a swell of pride. Matthew no longer lived with broken windows and walls with exposed lattice.

Gathering her full skirts, she hurried up that path, past the gates and up the wide stone stairs that had been swept clean of snow. She rang the bell, not once but twice, and faced the double doors, untying the satin ribbon on her bonnet so as not to waste time.

Moments later, the doors edged open. A thin, gray-haired man dressed in dark blue winter livery peered out. He inclined his head. "Lady Burton, I presume?"

She bit back a gushing smile. "Yes. I am, indeed."

"A pleasure, my lady." The man dutifully pulled the doors wider and stepped aside.

Bernadette swept into the large foyer. As the door closed behind her, she paused well beyond the entrance, shaking off the snow from her skirts. She slowly removed her bonnet in dazed disbelief, along with her gloves and fur mitt. Countless beeswax candles illuminated a stunning chandelier. Paris pale palomino silk-brocade clothed the expanse of endless walls that nestled a sweeping mahogany staircase.

The butler rounded her and extended his hands.

She handed off her bonnet, gloves and mitt. "Thank you."

The man set everything on a carved mahogany side table and then dutifully brought over the silver calling-card tray, which already held at least a dozen other cards. Apparently, Matthew was popular in New York society, to have collected so many in one day. And though she wasn't supposed to peer at the cards, which were spread out to display the visitors who had called, she rudely scanned them all the same and was rather pleased to see that there wasn't a single female name amongst them.

She paused and confided to the butler, "I already sent over my card. An hour ago."

The servant inclined his head, acknowledging her words, but continued to hold out the tray. "Mr. Milton respectably instructed that you deposit your card again, given this is your first visit into his home. He is hoping to keep the card permanently in the tray for all to see."

Oh, now this she had to donate to. Opening her reticule, she deposited her card. "There. For good luck."

The butler smiled and set aside the tray. "He will be most pleased. This way, my lady." He ushered her toward a large parlor through paneled doors he slid open and pushed into the walls. "Mr. Milton will be down shortly. There are a few pending matters he must tend to first." He departed.

A few pending matters? Ha and ha. With Matthew now owning a successful business that printed well over five thousand papers every Saturday, whilst attending countless charities and events all across New York *and* playing guardian to Ronan, whom she was anxious to meet, she had no doubt the man had *more* than just a few pending matters.

Lingering in the parlor alone, the ticking of a French

clock set above a marble hearth pierced the deafening silence. Wood crackled and popped against flames, emitting a warmth worthy of a winter day. She paused when she reached the middle of a most impressive parlor.

Embroidered green velvet curtains framed sweeping windows that displayed the large treed square beyond, allowing the remainder of the day's gray light to pour through. Countless candles in sconces beautifully brightened the elegant room as gold hooks displayed paintings of what she knew to be Ireland.

There was even a piano set in the far corner of the room. A smile touched her lips. No parlor was complete without one. By heavens. Everything was just perfect. Nothing was overdone. The room was elegant but gloriously simple, holding no clutter aside from necessary basic furnishings. She slowly wandered from one side of the parlor to the other and back again, glancing toward the open doors.

She seated herself, slipping her reticule from her wrist. Setting it aside, she folded her hands. Five minutes passed. Then ten. Then fifteen.

Exasperated, she stood and wandered over to the lacquered mahogany piano. She paused before it. The small bronze plaque above the black-and-white ivory keys read: *Conrad Graf.*

She leaned toward it and blinked in astonishment. It had come all the way from Vienna. A Graf piano was esteemed and coveted by all the greatest pianists. And here it was sitting in Matthew Joseph Milton's parlor. Huh. Imagine that.

"I bought it for you," a deep voice rumbled out from behind.

Her heart jumped. She turned, her gaze darting toward him. "Matthew."

A broad-shouldered man loomed all but ten steps away, dressed in expensive gray morning attire, consisting of a white silk cravat, embroidered waistcoat and matching trousers with leather boots. The commanding stance of his solid and well-muscled body told her he was not only the master of this here house but of himself. That sunlit chestnut-colored hair had darkened considerably to a rich brown and had been trimmed and swept back, tapering down neatly to the sides of his stiff, white collar.

He wore no patch. His dark eyes, including the one clouded by blindness, heatedly captured hers.

She fought from locking her knees together.

He wordlessly lingered. That clean-shaven jaw tightened as his gaze slid down the length of her body from face to breasts to waist to slippers, making no attempt to hide that he had missed her in *that* way.

Searing heat crept up the length of her thighs and chest as she struggled to remain indifferent. Even if she did have any words to share outside of how incredible he looked, she doubted she'd be able to utter them.

That silk embroidered, seam-pinched waistcoat sat against his firm, narrow waist in the most tantalizing of ways. Those well-fitted trousers were as equally tantalizing, being kept taut with foot straps buttoned beneath black leather boots. He looked nothing like the Matthew she remembered.

Still holding her gaze, he now made his way toward her, shrinking the parlor with his presence, that long stride pulsing with an assurance and dominance that was as alluring as it was intimidating. The room hummed until his large frame paused before her, barely a foot away. The sweet, earthy scent of expensive cigars drifted toward her.

Apparently he really did smoke cigars.

He folded his strong arms across his chest, the broad outline of his shoulders straining the tailored fabric of his fine gray morning coat. Still observing her, he eventually provided in a low tone, "How have you been?"

She didn't know why, but she didn't quite expect those words. She blinked and managed a mere, "Good. And you?"

His voice dipped into the realm of smooth and husky. "Incredibly well." He scanned her face and hair, lingering. "Would you like to sit?"

Again, she didn't know why, but she didn't quite expect those words. It was like this man had been domesticated. She shook her head from side to side, never once breaking their gaze. "No. Thank you."

He lifted a dark brow. "Are you hungry? The chef always has something in the kitchen. I can have the servants bring everything out. You can have whatever you want. Caviar, wine, wilted cress with quail."

She blinked again. Why, he was— Her eyes widened. It was London all over again. Only, this time, the roles had been reversed. "Very amusing, Matthew."

He smirked. "I thought it was." His smirk slowly faded. He searched her face. Unfolding his arms down to his sides, he stepped closer. So close, his black leather boots touched the hem of her pale pink gown.

Her breath hitched and though a part of her wanted to grab him and kiss him and never let go, she felt that in doing so, she'd be ruining this incredible, aching anticipation tightening her throat and chest. It was without a doubt the sweetest thing she'd ever experienced. In fact…she'd never felt it before.

He set his jaw. "I missed you. So goddamn much."

Her breaths now came in uneven takes. "And I missed you. So goddamn much."

He leaned in close. Close enough for the heat of his mouth to brush against her forehead. "Court me until you are ready. Will you?"

Her heart pounded. She stared up at that masculine mouth that had uttered those unexpected words. She knew what this meant. It meant matrimonial bells would be ringing all across New York City in honor of them the moment she wished it. Surprisingly, the idea didn't send her into a panic. At all. And she knew why. Because she trusted him. Completely.

Trying to keep her voice steady, she whispered, "Yes. I will court you until I am ready."

He lowered his gaze to her mouth, his broad chest falling and rising more visibly. "Good. We start now. Before I digress." He took several steps back, setting a respectable distance between them.

Her breath whooshed out in astonishment. Whatever rules the man was abiding by, they most certainly weren't adhering to the beat of her poor heart. "Aren't you going to kiss me in greeting? At the very least?"

He stared. "As much as I want to kiss you and never stop, luv, no. I specifically remember you once telling me that your first husband never courted you despite you asking for it. And I know I never gave it to you, either. As such, I've decided to give you the courtship you never had. In truth, I want us to get to know each other outside of all things physical. We already know of our attraction for each other, but what about everything else?"

She swallowed. This was— "I…this is certainly all-embracing." She shook her head slightly, still endlessly astonished. "That you want to get to know me in that way and that you even remember that conversation astounds me."

"Of course I want to get to know you in that way. And of course I remember." He held her gaze. "When it comes to you, there is nothing I want to forget."

She drew in a soft breath. How, oh how, was a woman to define a moment like this one? The distance he'd deliberately set between them made her want to burst. "Matthew?"

"Yes?"

"I would really like a kiss hello. Just one. If you don't mind. I have waited eight whole months for it."

He smiled. "Bernadette."

"Yes?"

"Whilst I'm flattered, from what I know, traditional courtship doesn't include kissing or touching. Am I wrong in this?"

She blinked. "No. You are not wrong."

"I thought so. Which means…no kiss hello. Sadly.

Now, please: Try to respect this courtship you just agreed to. I'll have you know that I've been planning this for months."

"Months?" Her voice cracked.

"Months. So bear with me. I want to get this right." Huffing out a breath, he strode past, making his way to the other side of the parlor.

Stunned by him and this and everything that was happening, she turned, unable to resist watching that long-legged stride. Without a great coat covering the length of his body, there was a lot to admire. A lot. And God save her, if he was expecting them to adhere to the rules of traditional courtship, it also meant she couldn't touch him. It wasn't fair.

He paused before a mahogany sideboard stacked with unopened letters and glanced toward her. "You look incredible, by the by. Even better than I remember."

She consciously smoothed her hands against the fullness of her muslin morning gown, pleased to hear that her fussing over her appearance had amounted to something. "Do I really?"

"Cease being coy, woman. You know you do." Swiping up a stack of letters, he paused. "Though I will say that rose perfume you're wearing is a bit strong and not to my taste. I prefer the citrus fragrance you used to wear. If you don't mind me saying."

Her lips parted. He actually remembered the perfume she used to wear. He remembered everything. "I only wore the rose because I thought that maybe you would like it. I can go back to wearing my citrus perfume. It is my favorite. Would you like that?"

He intently held her gaze. "Yes."

The intensity of that stare practically burned her skin and made her only all the more aware of the distance he had set between them in honor of their courtship. "Then I will."

"I was hoping." He lowered his gaze, going back through all of the letters in his hands and shifted from leather boot to leather boot.

Sensing he was waiting for her to initiate further conversation, she bit her bottom lip. She honestly didn't know what she was supposed to say or do next now that they were...*courting*.

She paused. This moment truly was unprecedented. Old William had never courted her, Dunmore most certainly hadn't courted her, unless walls and beds were considered courtship, and none of the other countless men who had tried to seize her and her million had bothered to go beyond superficial flowers. Not that she would have let them go beyond superficial flowers.

So now what? It was indeed time that she and Matthew got to know each other outside all things physical.

Dragging her bottom lip free from her teeth, Bernadette eventually offered, "I hear you plan on opening another print shop in the city. Is that true?"

"Yes." Matthew set aside the stack of letters back onto the desk, except for one. "'Tis remarkable, actually. We've outgrown ourselves a bit faster than anticipated." Glancing toward her, he turned over the letter and broke the wax seal.

Silence prevailed.

Why was she so annoyingly nervous? It wasn't as if they had never touched or kissed. And yet…this idea of them courting and focusing on everything *but* the physical really changed everything. It was like being eighteen again.

He angled and re-angled the parchment in his hands. It was as if he wanted to taunt her into knowing that he wasn't truly interested in reading it but was waiting for her to give him a reason to break away from it.

Drat him. He wasn't going to make this easy, was he? "So. Given we can't *do* anything, what would you like to talk about?"

He strategically unfolded the parchment. "Us."

"Us?"

"Yes. You know, you and me. Me and you. Us."

She swallowed, and for some reason she was now envisioning him completely naked. She envisioned those hard, bronzed muscles and that lone scar on his chest that her finger had trailed and grazed. She brought her hands together to prevent fidgeting. "What about us?"

He eyed her. "You have no thoughts on the matter, despite agreeing to court me?"

"Not rational thoughts worth listening to," she confided all too honestly. "If you must know, Matthew, my thoughts as of now are wandering into the realm of indecency, given the amount of time that has passed since we last saw each other."

He grinned, the edges of those handsome eyes crinkling. "I've already undressed you at least sixteen times in the past fifteen minutes. So we're even." Still grinning, he casually returned to reading the letter he held.

She let out an exasperated laugh, rolling her eyes. By God, this combination of debonair yet raw man was utterly fascinating. He was still the Matthew she'd once known and adored, and yet...he wasn't.

She made her way toward him, watching him read his correspondence, that grin fading as his expression returned to that of being serious. She paused beside him and the sideboard stacked with letters. "Are you really reading?"

He glanced up from the letter. "No. Not at all."

She smiled. "You seem beautifully content with yourself and life, Matthew. Are you?"

He tossed the letter onto the desk and shifted toward her. "I am, luv. And I have you to thank for it. You and only you."

She felt as if her heart would burst knowing it. "So how goes fatherhood?"

He huffed out a huge breath, deflating both cheeks, and leaned back. "He's a handful, that one. I'll introduce you to Ronan another time. He's over at the office right now, helping out with the trays. We're setting up for the next press. It's something he likes to do and, more important, it keeps him out of trouble."

"I see." She hesitated and couldn't help but ask, "And have you been keeping yourself out of trouble, Mr. Milton, since I last saw you? For I will confess, it seems the women of New York have been dithering on and on about you."

He leaned in. "They can dither on and on all they want. I'm all about Bernadette. Didn't you know?"

Her heart squeezed. Unable to stay away, she stepped toward him. Reaching up, she cupped the warmth of that shaven face she had missed so much.

He froze, as if startled by her touch.

"Matthew. I am so proud of you and all that you have accomplished. I want you to know that."

He lowered his gaze to hers. "Thank you. I'm still adjusting. It's overwhelming to go from having nothing to…everything." Gently taking her hands, he removed them from his face and squeezed them hard before releasing them. He stepped back. "No more touching, luv. I'm trying to survive this. It's not easy."

"No. It isn't."

She set her chin, intent on proving to him *and* herself that she could survive this. Though, who knew for how long. "So. Tell me more about your new life. Whatever you did not scribe about, that is. What did I miss?"

He rubbed at his chin before letting his hand drop back down to his side. "Everything. It's all a blur of events."

"Ah, yes. A blur wrapped in a glorious cloud of expensive cigar smoke. Apparently, you have joined in on puffing cigars like the rest of upper New York male society. I can smell it on your clothing."

He eyed her. "I only smoke on occasion. Because as much as I enjoy it, they're expensive as hell and I feel like I'm burning money. Quite literally."

Despite all of his success, he was still Mr. Practical. Bless him. Bless him for being a man still worth swooning for. "Anything else?"

He was quiet for a long moment and lowered his gaze. "Dunmore departed back to London a few days ago."

She paused and nodded. "I know. The prison chaplain informed me of his release."

"He...called on me. Before leaving New York."

Her brows went up. "Did he? And?"

"It was brief, but civil. He came to thank us for our mercy. Eerily, he spoke in a whisper the whole time. It was as if he thought he was still in Sing Sing." Matthew sighed. "Whether he is reformed or not has yet to be seen, but I will say he is not the same man."

Bernadette swallowed and nodded, remembering Matthew's letters pertaining to the inhumane suffering Dunmore had seen. Guilt still dug into her over it. Despite everything.

Matthew sighed again. "I'm sorry. I shouldn't have mentioned it, but I thought maybe you would want to know."

She tried to smile and push past all that had been. "Thank you. I'm glad you told me. Perhaps he endured enough to understand the suffering he had imposed."

"Indeed." Setting his shoulders, he cleared his throat. "I, uh...don't mean to bring an end to our beautiful tête-à-tête, but I've got a meeting with the mayor in less than forty minutes. He isn't all that pleased with a recent commentary I published about him. I tried to reschedule it, knowing you were coming, but that only brassed him off more. I don't want to go, but I have to."

Wonders never ceased and neither did he. She loved knowing that he was doing far, far more than making money. He was using the paper to expose the government for what it was. "Bravo. I'm glad to hear it. I actually read that commentary you're referring to."

"Oh? And?"

"It was well worth the ink. I know the mayor through the Astors, actually. All in all, he is a good man. He simply has too many voices in his head. Those voices being the council who never want to do much of anything unless it involves an opposition dinner. He does listen to his wife, though, whom I like very much. I donate to her charities all the time. She is what I call moral divinity on carriage wheels, looking to make changes. My advice is that if you ever have problems with the mayor, you bring her into the conversation. He adores her above all else and she always sides with the humanitarian aspect and not any other. Use that adoration to muscle him in. Mr. Astor does it all the time."

Matthew's brows rose. "I'll remember that. You follow politics, do you?"

She shrugged. "Not often. Male politics are always superficial, at best, supporting mostly business and not the real people of this nation. Which is why I genuinely admire the mayor. He steps outside of all things superficial."

He heatedly held her gaze for a long, pulsing moment. He shifted toward her. "I'd like to see you again. When can I? Soon?"

Smug satisfaction hugged her. "I have a few dinner parties and a charity event to attend this week, but I

do suppose I can fit you into my schedule somewhere."
She lifted a flirtatious brow. "What were you looking
to do? Will it involve clothing?"

He stared. And yes, it was one of *those* stares, which
seemed to say "I want you naked."

She tried not to preen too much. "I suppose that answers my question. You may want to ask yourself if
either of us is capable of sainthood. Which is what we
are attempting here. I will wager one hundred dollars
that by the end of this week, one of us will topple the
other. 'Tis simply a matter of who will topple whom."

He lowered his shaven chin against his cravat.
"Which is why I have a few rules I'd like to instate
to ensure neither of us muck this up. Are you ready
for them?"

She groaned. "Matthew. Surely you don't intend
to— Must we really attempt to over-orchestrate this?"

He glared. "Yes. We must. I'll have you know that
a lot has changed since we last saw each other. *A lot.*
Our courtship isn't meant to amuse you or me, nor is
it superficial. Astounding though it may be to you, it
also represents the respectable life I now lead. Aside
from running a political and social paper that makes
well over four thousand dollars a month and hinges itself on *everything* I say or do lest people sink me, I also
have a fifteen-year-old boy living with me. A boy who
has trouble adhering to respectable paths himself due
to his upbringing. So if you want this and me, you're
going to have to follow *my* rules. And I don't appreciate you mocking them."

This was probably going to be the quickest victory

he ever knew. "I understand and will not mock you or your rules again. Go on and name your rules and I will abide."

"Thank you." He huffed out a breath. "*Rule one*— my bedchamber is off-limits. *Rule two*—your bedchamber is off-limits. *Rule three*—our lips never touch. *Rule four*—we only see each other during calling hours or in public or at events where crowds are assured to ensure that rule one, two and three are never trifled with. *Rule five*—all rules cease to exist when you ask me to marry you. Allow me to repeat that. I won't be asking for your hand. You'll be asking for mine."

She couldn't help but smirk. "You seek to force my hand."

"I do." He shifted away. "So how does your schedule look for tomorrow afternoon? Say…two?"

"Two is absolutely glorious."

"Good."

"And will I be meeting Ronan tomorrow?"

"No. Not quite yet. I've got something else in mind for us. Something I haven't done in years."

She lifted a brow. "Years?"

"Eleven, to be exact. Just know that me and my sleigh will be veering your way tomorrow at two. Dress warm."

She was officially intrigued. "I will do that."

"I'm looking forward to it." He sauntered backward. "I never thought I'd hear myself saying this, but the mayor awaits me. I must therefore see you out." He swept a hand toward the parlor entryway beyond. "After you, luv."

And so it was goodbye after what seemed like the briefest but nonetheless most glorious of hellos. Bernadette turned, gathering her skirts from around her booted feet, wandered over to pluck up the reticule she had almost entirely forgotten about and made her way back into the foyer.

She paused by the main entrance door.

Matthew gathered her bonnet, gloves and mitt from the side table against the foyer wall, strode toward her and handed them off to her himself. "Allow me to play butler."

"Thank you." When she had pulled everything on and affixed everything into place, he opened the entrance door leading toward the square and inclined his head. "My lady."

She smiled and inclined her head in turn, before stepping out into the cold throes of winter beyond. She glanced back at him.

He gallantly offered a refined bow, also smiling. Holding her gaze for a long moment, he closed the door.

Bernadette drew in a shaky breath and let it out, the frosty air smoking the heat of her breath. It would seem Mr. Matthew Joseph Milton had declared a delicious amorous war unlike anything she'd ever had the pleasure of knowing.

Blowing forth an adoring kiss to that closed door, she turned and hurried through the snow, toward her waiting sleigh. She rather enjoyed this whole idea of them courting. It was very...*romantic*. Yes. That was the word. It was a word she had never once associated with a man before. Romantic.

CHAPTER TWENTY-TWO

'Tis obvious the mayor has no time to address the vile issues plaguing the dark corners of this city. I dare say, it may be because the man is far too busy sipping on brandy and smoking those nine-cent cigars.

—*The Truth Teller, a New York Newspaper for*
Gentlemen

THE MOMENT MATTHEW SHUT the entrance door after Bernadette, he leaned both palms heavily against it and closed his eyes. Jesus fecking Christ. He was never going to survive this.

He'd bit back telling her that he was madly in love with her at least three different times. All whilst clutching a stupid bill he'd almost wrinkled to death in an effort to remain calm. The last thing he wanted or needed was to send her darting out of his life, thinking he had lost the last of his rational mind by instating a full courtship *and* professing his love. Pushing away from the door, he blew out a breath. It was all up to her now. Which, in truth, scared the shite out of him.

An hour later

THE MAYOR SLAMMED the sliding doors into each other and stalked across the length of his study, those polished leather boots thudding as he headed for the cigar box set on the sideboard against the silk-covered wall. He flipped open the hinged wooden lid and paused. Scrubbing his large head until his graying-brown hair stood on end, he snatched up an Esparteros cigar out of the box, snipping the end off with a cigar blade, and glanced back at Matthew. "Do you want one?"

Matthew shook his head. "No, thank you. Not today."

The mayor stuck the cigar into his mouth, holding it with his teeth, and leaned toward a lit candle set on the sideboard. He set the cigar's rolled end into the flame until it hissed, before drawing away. Letting it burn for a long moment before puffing on it, he blew out a white cloud of smoke through thin lips.

Fully turning that short, stocky frame toward Matthew, the mayor pointed with the tip of his lit cigar. "I thought you and I were friends, Milton. What the hell are you trying to do? Hang me before the eyes of my own constituents? Or better yet, get my house burned?"

Matthew shifted in the wingback chair he didn't bother rising from. The man wasn't royalty, for God's sake. "I told you I'd print my opinion if you didn't get more involved with the issues plaguing the sixth ward. I gave you two months to take up my offer of walking the Five Points with me, and in those two months you did nothing but drink brandy and smoke cigars with the council."

The mayor glared. "Just because you run a newspaper doesn't mean you run me. I own this goddamn city. Not you."

Matthew tsked and rose, knowing he couldn't sit this one out. "You don't own this city, Lord Mayor. The city owns you. 'Tis something you and the council seem to forget whenever you all twirl your little quills and dip them in ink. Not only did I vote you in, but so did sixty-three percent of the population over in the sixth ward you're now avoiding. Why the hell do you and the council seem to think that this city is comprised of only merchants and high society? Merchants and high society don't bloody need another parade. They do that for themselves."

The mayor swiped a hand over his face, a gold ring glinting. "As your friend, and not the Lord Mayor, I'm here to advise that you cease printing articles pertaining to the Five Points. You're riling far too many citizens and they're beginning to throw gravel at me and the council. Despite your popularity with the public, Milton, the council is looking to shut you and that paper down. I've been telling you this for months now."

Matthew narrowed his gaze. "I don't submit to intimidation. I'm fighting for my own here."

"Your own? You call those savages over in the sixth ward your own?" The mayor drew in a large breath of smoke, before taking away the cigar from his lips and letting the smoke hiss out through his nostrils. He grunted. "Every last one of those men are nothing but thugs, soap locks, pickpockets, rapists, murderers, political sluggers and no-gooders. And you damn well know it. Is that what you're fighting for? No-gooders?"

Anger streaked through Matthew. *This* was why he *loathed* New York high society. They associated poverty with scum without having any basic understanding that poverty created scum.

Matthew strode up to the man, leaned in and snatched that cigar from those lips. Holding the man's stunned gaze, he snapped the cigar in half, scattering ash and brittle tobacco leaves and handed it back to the man. "Criminals aren't born. They're made. And by doing nothing but smoking your bloody nine-cent cigar, you're investing in not only their misery but the misery of others."

That bearded face stilled. "And what the hell do you expect me to do, Milton? Go in there and start handing out money to everyone who needs it?"

"No. These people need more than money. They need to know that the city cares enough to create opportunities that will give them jobs and an education beyond writing their own name."

The mayor rolled his eyes. "And how is it the city's responsibility to educate and provide jobs for men, when there are already schools in place and plenty of jobs waiting for those willing to take them? The state of New York has over five thousand almshouses that bring a bloody expense of over two hundred thousand a year. Two hundred thousand! These men have to learn how to stand on their own two feet if it isn't enough. You did it. And so can they."

"I did it with the generous assistance of a wealthy patron. These people don't have wealthy patrons to get them out of the abyss they're in. And if you think I'm only fighting for no-gooders, that's where you're wrong. I'm fighting for voices that have long been silenced. Did you know there is an orphanage just off Five Points with seventeen bolts on each door and all the windows nailed shut, because children go missing from it weekly, only to be found either dead or sold into brothels? Some of these children are as young as six. Six! And guess what? No one gives a damn."

Matthew angled closer. "Have you not read the paper? Forget what you think you know. You don't know. There are countless women and children forced to fester alongside these criminals. And when they're not living in fear for their bodies or their lives, they spend their last breaths picking curled hair out of rubbish bins to sell to wigmakers that upper society slaps on their heads. There isn't a lack of morals amongst these people, Lord Mayor. There is a lack of wage and a lack of support from its own state and country. And *you* have the means to do something about it. All I can do is print the issue at hand and hope you'll get brassed off enough to actually lend a hand."

The mayor blinked hard several times, tension etching his large brow. Glancing down at his broken cigar that was still lit on one end, he muttered, "You should have been a politician, not a rag printer."

"I prefer being my own man, thank you, as opposed to being owned by thousands. My will is to challenge you into becoming a leader capable of assisting those who need it most, not those who already have more and only want more." Remembering Bernadette's advice, he adjusted the sleeves on his coat and casually added, "I've always wondered. Does your wife have any opinion when it comes to politics? Does she dabble in it at all?"

The mayor eyed him. "She has too many opinions and dabbles in it far more than any woman legally should. Why?"

God love Bernadette. For he sure as hell did. "I'm glad someone is holding you over the fire. Perhaps we ought to invite Lady Mayor in on our conversation? I'd love to hear her opinion on this."

The mayor blinked and then slowly shook his head from side to side. "Damn you, Milton, don't you be doing this to me. Don't you be declaring war by throwing my own wife at me. Who the hell have you been talking to anyway?"

Matthew couldn't help but chide, "Someone who knows your wife incredibly well apparently."

"Yes, well, damn you both. It's already a mess without including her in it. Because the council would rather tear down the entire sixth ward and never speak of it again. They aren't going to be happy about me investing what little funds the city has toward what they believe are misbegotten delinquents in need of termination."

Matthew patted him on the back. "And this is where

you prove yourself as a leader to your faithful constituents. Here's what I'll do. I'll deliver close to four thousand letters into your hands, which you can give to the council. Tell them they were all sent to my office just this past month, demanding the city do something."

"Four thousand?" The mayor muttered a curse and brushed past with a breath. "There is strength in numbers."

"Yes. I know."

"Yes, yes, you know everything, Milton." The man sighed and then sighed again. "Go walk yourself right quick to the door and call it a win."

Matthew grinned.

"I'll send you a whole new box of cigars. Just know that I'm here if you need me to print anything on your behalf."

"Good. You'll be hearing from me about all of this by the end of next week."

"I prefer tomorrow."

The mayor grunted. "If only the government could blink that fast. Now, get the hell out of here. I'll have you know my wife is waiting. Don't you have a woman of your own to harass?"

"I'm working on it."

The mayor paused, those bushy brows darting upward. "Oh, are you now? This is news." The man eyed him. "Do I know her?"

Matthew adjusted his coat. "Apparently you met her through the Astors. Lady Burton. She also went for a bit of time under the alias of Mrs. Shelton due to an overdramatized robbery in New Orleans."

The mayor paused. "Ah, yes. 'The Petticoat Incident' as they called it." He lowered his voice. "By God, isn't she worth more than a factory of cigars lined with gold?"

Matthew pointed at the man. "That isn't why I plan on marrying her. So don't you be getting me into trouble by gossiping otherwise."

"No, no. Of course not. Well, congratulations on that."

"Thank you."

"And did you ask for her hand already?"

"No. I'm waiting."

"Waiting? For what?"

"For her to ask. Which, sadly, may take a while. Attachments aren't really her forte."

A boisterous laugh escaped the mayor. "Milton, Milton, Milton. You're a sop in the guise of a panther. You know that? God bless you, for no one else will."

CHAPTER TWENTY-THREE

Let your countenance be cheerful.
At the very least.
—*The Truth Teller, a New York Newspaper for*
Gentlemen

BUNDLING HER THICK FUR coat against her chin, Bernadette wandered out toward the expanse of the snowy road before her house and lingered. Though the air was cold enough to nip her nose and cheeks, the sun brightened the wintery white world around her like magic.

In the distance, the thudding of hooves drew closer. She turned toward it.

A two-horse open sleigh with Matthew seated casually behind its reins, dressed in a black great coat and top hat made her stomach flip.

He tugged on the leather reins, slowing the horses to a subdued walk and brought the black lacquered, two-seat sleigh to a perfect sliding halt before her. Draping the reins on a hook attached to the latticed snow shield, he gathered the oversized wool blanket draping his lap, bundling it aside and rose.

Jumping down from the sleigh into the thick snow before her, he snapped out a black-leather-gloved hand. "Are you ready to ice skate? I've got skates for both of us."

"You are taking us ice skating?" She slowly placed her hand into his. "I will warn you, Matthew, I have never skated before. London isn't particularly known for its winters or its ice."

He leaned toward her. "I look forward to catching you at every turn."

She smiled. "I will ensure I keep you busy."

Helping her up and into the sleigh, he waited until she was seated before pulling himself up and in. He settled his large frame beside her, his arm pressing against her own, due to the small size of the seat. Methodically draping their laps with the blanket, he pulled his top hat down harder onto his head and grabbed up the leather reins from the hook.

He glanced toward her. "You may want to hold on, luv. I drive fast." He snapped the reins, sending them jerking full speed ahead and through the snow.

"Oh dear God!" Her heart nearly flew out of her chest as she grabbed hold of his arm and the snow shield before her to keep herself steady against the unexpected thrust. The cold wind whistled and whipped at her face as they slid faster.

Matthew grinned and yelled above the wind, "This is my idea of winter!"

She tightened her hold on his arm and the snow shield, feeling as if she was about to get whipped off the sleigh. "Or a quick death!" she yelled back.

Still grinning, he snapped the reins again, sending them even faster. The horses galloped at full speed, thudding and spraying snow. "I used to do this with my father back when we had money," he called out. "Every first snow, he'd take us out and sprint us through all of New York. God, did he ever know how to drive!"

Bernadette leaned farther back against the seat, without letting go of him or the shield. It was like sailing a ship across an ocean of endless snow. An unexpected bubble of joy overwhelmed her. She'd never known anything so glorious.

Peering over at Matthew, she noted the flush staining his cheekbones and the excitement that brightened his handsome face. She'd never seen him so full of life. It was...breathtaking. Absolutely breathtaking.

He leaned toward her, veering them down another wide road that took them out toward the fields spread beyond. "Hold on."

She gripped his arm and the shield harder. They rode on and on and on, the sun glinting off the snow with a brightness that was almost blinding.

A small frozen lake appeared in the glittering distance, surrounded by flocks of parked sleighs and horses. Women and children bundled in colorful cloaks, hats and mitts skated across the ice. Various men used canes to balance themselves, whilst others darted effortlessly through those scrambling to stay upright on the ice.

As the sleigh drew closer, Matthew leaned his large frame back, tugging on the leather reins. The horses slowed from a full, snow-flinging gallop to a mere trot, their nostrils and mouths puffing out clouding breaths. Matthew tugged on the reins once again, bringing them to a peaceful sliding halt that settled them all but a few feet from the frozen lake beyond.

The calls and shouts of children made her smile.

Gathering the wool blanket from their laps, Matthew bundled it into the corner of the seat and grabbed up a tied sack from the attached space behind the sleigh. He jumped down and held out a hand. "Come on."

She stood, grabbed his hand and jumped down beside him.

He leaned in and drawled, "Whoever gets to the lake first drives the sleigh back. Are you in? Or are you in? Because you don't want this devil of an Irishman driving."

Bernadette set her chin, casually gathering her skirts from around her booted feet and waded politely through the snow. "Don't be silly. As if I'm going to—" She sprinted toward the lake, thudding through the snow as fast as her huffing breath would allow. "That sleigh is *mine!*"

"Cheat!" he shouted, crunching through the snow after her in a dash.

She gargled out a laugh, pushing as fast she could. "It takes a cheat to know a cheat!"

"I'll make you swallow that." Matthew darted past, his great coat billowing around his frame as he ran faster, moving far beyond her within moments. He disappeared down the hill and skidded to a halt at the edge of the ice beside a half-cut log. He swung back and triumphantly held up the sack with the skates. "Ireland scores one and Britain scores none. As it damn well should be."

Bernadette laughed, finishing her run down the hill, and stumbled to a halt beside him, pushing out breaths. "You try running in a corset."

"Excuses, excuses." He pried open the sack with a smug grin. Pulling out their skates by their leather straps, he tossed the bag onto the log beside them. "Sit. I'll get your skates on."

Rounding the log, she sat, lifting her skirts above her ankles and jerked up both booted feet, dangling them out. "Will they even fit?"

Matthew knelt, setting aside his skates. Grasping one of her booted feet, he set it against the wooden shoe with the slim curving blade pointing upward and tightened the leather straps. He did the same for the other and patted them both into place. "There."

Bernadette clopped the ice skates into one another in astonishment. "They fit perfectly. How did you…?"

Matthew grabbed up his skates and seated himself beside her with a smile and strapped on each skate to his leather boots. Glancing toward her he said, "I had your chambermaid give me your measurements early this morning so I could buy them."

She blinked. "You did?"

"You were still sleeping when I came by." He stood, skates in place, and held out a hand. "Are you ready?"

"To fall? Yes." She grabbed his hand and wobbled toward the edge of the frozen ice leading toward the crowds of skaters.

Matthew released her hand, stepped out onto the ice and turned with the scraping of ice against blades. "Don't try to skate when you first come out. Lift your feet as if you're walking." He held out his hand.

She grabbed his outstretched hand and, holding on to it tight, she set each skate on the ice. She awkwardly tried to push herself forward. Her blades darted forward as she fell back with a screech.

Matthew seized her waist, jerking her upward. Still holding her hand, he set her against his side. "Slide one foot at a time, balancing yourself."

Gripping his hand hard, she did just that.

Though it took time, and they never wandered far, Bernadette eventually mastered staying upright. Then she mastered sliding, and that was about all she mastered in the two hours they spent on the ice. Though it was exhausting, she enjoyed it very much and cherished each moment against Matthew's side, his large hands holding her waist.

The brightness of the sun soon disappeared behind thick, graying clouds that now draped the expanse of the sky, threatening snow.

Releasing her waist, he gestured toward himself. "This is where I impress my girl." He caught the tip of his tongue between his teeth and with the turn of his great coat, skated across the lake. He darted past other men, using his body and the turn of his blades to veer left and then right, carving paths into the smooth ice.

Bernadette lingered, dreamily admiring the way he moved so effortlessly. It reminded her of how her hands moved across the keys of a piano, so fluidly.

Matthew skated back toward her and skidded to an angled halt beside her, lifting a brow that demanded applause.

She grinned and enthusiastically clapped, turning her skates toward him. "That was—" Her skates slid and skidded. Her eyes widened as she toppled forward and against him with a gasp. She seized the wool of his great coat to keep herself from falling, her blades skimming the ice.

His hands jumped around her, those muscled arms yanking her back up and against him. His hold tightened.

She lifted her gaze to his, still clinging to his coat.

He stared down at her.

A gusting wind blew in around them as snow drifted down from above, quietly falling in large flakes that slowly, slowly gathered against the satin rim of Matthew's top hat. His full lips parted as if he meant to say something. The air between them frosted against the heat of that mouth.

Being tightly held in his arms and looking up at him like this whispered of unending happiness. She had never known anything like it.

Is this what real love felt like?

Breaking their gaze, he drew away, dragging his arms out of hers. "We should get back." He lapsed into silence, then added, "I have an appointment at five."

She nodded, pushing away her disappointment in knowing this moment and their day was over. "Of course."

When their skates were removed from their boots

and back in the sack, he grabbed her hand, squeezing it and, together, they made their way back up the hill toward their waiting sleigh, where the horses restlessly shifted.

He assisted her up and into the sleigh and settled into the seat beside her, taking up the leather reins from the hook. "Looks like we're going to get more snow. I suggest we make a dash for it. Are you ready?"

Bernadette leaned over him. He paused. She shyly dragged the bundled wool blanket buried at his hip and pulled it over his lap and then her own. "There."

He smiled. "Are you ready now, luv?"

She tucked her arm beneath the solid warmth of his and also smiled. "Yes."

Turning the horses toward the main path leading back toward the city, he snapped the reins, sending them through the snow that whirled above and below them.

She clung to him the whole while, and he in turn glanced down at her every now and then, his gaze meeting hers only long enough to silently assure her that a genuine adoration lingered there.

When he finally pulled the sleigh to a halt before her townhome, and the snow now fell in heavy drifts that chilled her through the fur coat she wore, he jumped down and assisted her out. Releasing her hand, he leaned toward the sleigh and retrieved the sack, pulling out her skates. He dangled them out by their leather straps. "These are yours. That way, you're ready do this again."

Grasping the leather straps, she cradled the skates

and glanced up at him. "Thank you, Matthew. For the skates and for the most glorious day I have ever known."

He inclined his head, slowly walking backward. "We'll have to do it again." Turning, he hopped into the sleigh and gathered the reins. He glanced toward her. "I'd love to introduce you to Ronan. Would you be able to call on us this Thursday afternoon at four? Afterward, you and I can head over to the opening of *Ireland Redeemed.* 'Tis a new drama over at the Park Theatre. I've got box seats. Are you interested?"

Realizing she was going to *finally* meet Ronan *and* go to the theater, she gushed, "Yes and yes."

"I will see you then." Still holding her gaze, he snapped the reins. As he pulled forward, he called out, "Melt all of this snow for us, will you? Think about me well into the night."

She grinned, pressing her skates tighter against her chest and called back, "Only if you think about me."

"Oh, I will, luv. I will." With that, he and his sleigh disappeared out into the falling snow and the road beyond.

Bernadette took a long steadying breath and, knowing she was alone, threw back her head and arms and whirled twice, her heart spinning right along with her. The metal blades of the skates he'd given her chimed against each other as they swayed from the leather straps she swung around with her. This had to be what real love felt like. It had to be. And if it wasn't, may she never know anything else as glorious as this.

CHAPTER TWENTY-FOUR

Manners. They are something this city does
not own.
—*The Truth Teller, a New York Newspaper for*
Gentlemen

Thursday, late afternoon

MATTHEW SHIFTED IN HIS chair and eyed Bernadette.
So far, she appeared to genuinely like Ronan. Thank
bloody God. Though, he wondered how much longer it
would last. The boy was still a bit rough when it came
to addressing and associating with women.

Ronan rounded the parlor with a leather-bound book
perched on his head. "According to my tutor," Ronan
tossed out, "this'll make me walk with less of a swagger. But the swagger, in my opinion, defines a man.
So I'm torn between the swagger and the book. See?"

Bernadette lifted a brow. "I suggest you learn to
master both, Mr. Sullivan."

"Oh, you're no fun. That's more work."

One of the young servants, Miss Greene, appeared

in the doorway, adjusting her white mop cap against her dark, bundled hair. "Mr. Milton?"

Matthew leaned forward in his chair. "Yes, Miss Greene?"

Ronan flipped off the book from his head, sending strands of brown hair across his forehead, and tossed it, also glancing toward the servant.

Miss Greene offered a quick, polite bob. "My apologies for the interruption, but the cook needs to know if another setting should be placed for supper, giving you have a guest."

Matthew stood. "Tell Mrs. Langley that Lady Burton and I are heading out to the theater shortly, and therefore it will only be Mr. Sullivan tonight."

"Yes, Mr. Milton." She turned to leave.

Ronan rounded the parlor. "Miss Greene."

The servant paused and turned back. "Yes, Mr. Sullivan?"

Ronan strode toward her and upon reaching her, draped his backside on the door frame. "Do you and the footman plan on using the pantry again? Because I'm rather concerned you and he are contaminating the food with bodily fluids that shouldn't be there."

The young woman swiveled toward Ronan, her round cheeks now a deep red.

Matthew sucked in a breath. *"Ronan."* And he thought *he* was blunt. He stalked over, chanting that he wouldn't hit the boy upside the head. "Go upstairs."

Ronan's eyes widened. "But I didn't do anything. I'm merely pointing out my concern, is all. Isn't that my right? Given we're paying her?"

Matthew lowered his chin. "Don't make me get out the pistols."

Ronan sagged against the door frame. "Yes, sir." He eyed Miss Greene who, in turn, eyed Ronan. Pushing away from the doorway, he veered into the corridor and jogged up the stairs and out of sight.

Miss Greene swung back to Matthew, still flushed. "He's looking to get me terminated."

Matthew paused. "Is it true about you and the footman?"

She winced, wringing her hands and lowered her gaze. "Yes, Mr. Milton. It is."

Matthew stared the woman down. "Which footman?"

"Mr. Lawrence."

"And how does Ronan know about you and Mr. Lawrence?"

She glanced up, her dark eyes widening. After a moment of silence, she said in an odd, tense tone, "He saw us when he tried to fetch something out of the pantry on his own."

Matthew's throat tightened. "How much did he see and when did he see it?"

She squeezed her eyes shut. "He saw more than he should have and it was…last evening, sir."

He drew in a breath that was anything but calming. "When I hired you, Miss Greene, did I not line you and every servant up and explain as to what your responsibilities were toward Mr. Sullivan?"

Pinching her lips, she nodded.

"And what was the one responsibility that I placed

upon each of you and emphasized without mercy lest it result in termination?"

Tears welled in her eyes. "That he never see anything a boy oughtn't, given he never had a childhood."

"Exactly." Matthew shifted toward her, narrowing his gaze. "That boy, Miss Greene, has endured far too much throughout his youth for me to stand here and find your behavior acceptable. As such, you *and* Mr. Lawrence are officially terminated. Whilst I will generously compensate your pay, don't ever use my name for a reference, lest it result in words that will shame you. Is that understood?"

"Yes, Mr. Milton." She choked back a sob and darted down the corridor.

Of all days. Of all fecking days. When Bernadette was sitting in the goddamn parlor and he was trying to show off his *respectable* way of life. He hissed out a breath.

Bernadette, who had already long risen from the chair, paused beside him and gently offered, "You did the right thing. You were firm but respectful."

He cleared his throat. "I'm sorry you had to see that."

Ronan jogged back down the stairs and veered back toward them. "Don't be too hard on yourself, Milton. It wasn't your fault. And it's not like I saw something I never saw before."

Matthew stared at Ronan. "Didn't I ask you to go upstairs?"

Ronan stared back. "You said to go upstairs, but you

didn't say to stay there. I assumed it was to talk to Miss Greene and seeing you were done, I…"

Matthew inwardly winced. Why was it he couldn't get this parenting thing right? "No. You're right. I didn't specify. And I should have." He sighed. "Lady Burton and I have to leave soon anyway. You don't mind entertaining yourself tonight, do you?"

"Not at all." Ronan crossed his arms over his narrow chest and shifted from boot to boot. "Before you two head out to the theater, though, I'd like to talk to Lady Burton. Alone. In the parlor. Can I?"

Bernadette's dark eyes darted to Matthew.

Their gazes momentarily locked and his pulse thundered. God only knew what the boy wanted to talk to her about, but he supposed it was good the two had a chance to get to know each other better. For the obvious reasons.

Matthew pointed at Ronan. "Ten minutes. Be a gent."

Ronan placed a hand over his heart. "No worries in that. Everything I know I learned from the best—*you*."

Matthew shifted his jaw, dropping his hand to his side, somehow not feeling all too confident in that particular sentiment.

Bernadette's lips quivered, as if she were having trouble keeping a blank expression in response to Ronan's statement.

With the sweep of her verdant evening gown across the floor, she sashayed back into the parlor, her slippers clicking against the wood floor.

Ronan pointed at Matthew. "If I were you, Milton,

I'd talk to Mr. Lawrence right quick before he darts off. Miss Greene isn't the only servant in the house he's been pounding into. Just thought you might want to know." With that, he stepped into the room after Bernadette, took hold of each sliding door and slid both doors into each another.

Matthew lingered awkwardly for a moment. Muttering a curse, he stalked straight for the servants' quarters.

BERNADETTE EYED THE tall, lanky youth lingering before her.

Ronan held up a finger, then used both hands to sweep his wavy brown hair across his forehead as if readying a thoroughbred stallion for a showing. "Have to look good before the mouth opens. Otherwise, what's the point, right?" He adjusted the sleeves of his dark wool coat. "Given you're a real lady and all, and I've never met a real lady, I've got no idea how I'm supposed to act. But I do hope it's acceptable for me to say what I need to say. I don't want the Queen of England coming after me."

She tried to retain as serious a face as she could in honor of their conversation. "I can assure you, Mr. Sullivan, the Queen has no interest in my life or yours. Speak freely."

"I will." He thumbed toward the closed doors. "Milton is what I call a good man. Actually, he's better than a good man. He's like the father and the brother and the uncle I never had. And I'm concerned about his interest in you. He simply doesn't need a woman in his life right now. Especially a fluff of a woman like you."

Her eyes widened. *Fluff of a woman?* He might as well have called her a bitch. "I will wholeheartedly agree that Matthew is indeed better than a good man, but I do think, Mr. Sullivan, that you are being exceedingly bold with your sentiment, given you know absolutely nothing about me."

He lowered his chin. "I know all I need to know."

Oh, dear God. "Do you? Well. I breathlessly await your opinion of me. Especially as you and I met all but…what is it…an hour ago?"

He rolled his brown eyes and folded his arms over his pin-striped waistcoat. "Let me lay out the bricks before you bring out the cement. I don't want you two getting married. Marriage doesn't solve anything and only creates problems. And Milton doesn't need problems. I'll have you know he hasn't been around women like I have and doesn't know what he's doing. You're going to drown him. And I won't stand for it."

Bernadette stared at him, not in the least bit amused knowing that he was actually being quite serious. "Have you ever been married, Mr. Sullivan?"

Ronan dropped his arms to his sides and leaned toward her. "I think you know the answer to that one."

"Exactly. Which means you have no more of an understanding of what marriage entails than you have an understanding of what I entail. Whilst matrimony isn't a subject I preen and fawn over, given I was, in fact, already married, and in my opinion, matrimony is but a glorified form of female slavery, Matthew is a subject I will preen and fawn over until I cease to breathe and live. So out of respect for me *and* Matthew, I am asking that you allow whatever should happen to happen. If I ever do create a problem in which you become concerned for his well-being, I am hereby giving you the authority to reprimand me in any verbal manner you see fit. Profanity included."

Ronan's brows rose. "Profanity included?"

"Profanity included." She extended a hand. "Now. Shall we call ourselves friends until then? Because I genuinely think Matthew would like that. And I know I would, too."

Ronan huffed out a breath and eyed her hand. Shifting from boot to boot, he finally took her hand, shaking it hard, once. "Friends. Until then."

She smiled, returning that firm grip and shake before releasing it. "I am ever so pleased to know it." Leaning toward him, she added, "And I do beg your pardon, Mr. Sullivan, but I am not fluff."

He blinked. "Sorry."

"No worries."

"Can I go now?" he blurted.

She bit back a smile. "Yes. You may."

He awkwardly turned and hurried toward the closed doors of the parlor. Pushing them apart and into the walls, he disappeared.

Bernadette sighed. *That* felt like an introduction to parenthood. And the best part? She survived. Wandering out of the parlor and into the corridor, she paused in the large foyer and peered up the mahogany staircase, as well as down the narrow corridor leading to the back of the house.

Every door in sight had been shut as if everyone had abandoned ship. "Matthew?" she called out.

The ticking of the hall clock was the only answer she received. She sighed and glanced around.

Noticing the calling-card tray, she wandered over to it. Pinching her lips together, she leaned in and pushed aside each card to see if her card, the one he had promised to keep in the tray, was still, in fact, there.

"It's still in there," a deep voice drawled from behind.

Startled, she turned.

Matthew leaned against the main banister of the staircase barely a few feet away, his muscled arms crossed over his evening coat and embroidered ivory waistcoat. He observed her in what appeared to be clear amusement. "You doubt my devotion, luv?"

She consciously rubbed her palms into the sides of her skirts. "No. I just… I spoke to Ronan."

He unfolded his arms. "And? How did it go?"

"Rather well. He and I are friends now. Or at least I hope we are."

"I'm glad to hear it. Two of my favorite people ought to be friends."

She smiled.

He hesitated and then with two long-legged strides, veered in so close she could make out every last thread and silver button on his waistcoat.

He lingered, lowering his gaze to hers. "I have something for you."

The pounding in her head matched the pounding of her heart, though she tried not to let on. "Oh?"

He slid his ungloved hand into his coat pocket and slipped out a diamond necklace, which shimmered as he draped it over his hand to display it.

Her eyes widened, thoroughly stunned. She touched a forefinger to the smooth, teardrop stones lining its length and breathed out, "Oh, Matthew. 'Tis beautiful."

"I bought it some time ago. I wanted to send it to you, but thought it'd be best to give it to you in person." He hesitated. "Can I put it on?"

She grinned. "Of course."

Taking each end, he lifted it and leaned in, draping the weight of the stones around her neck, his fingers grazing her skin. The heat of his body lingered as he affixed it into place.

Her grin faded, that heat penetrating the last of her rational mind. She peered up at that shaven face hovering above hers. She purposefully tilted her own face upward and toward his, hoping he would just…kiss her.

He lowered his eyes to hers, sliding his fingers from around her throat, allowing the necklace to settle into place. "Don't look at me like that."

Her senses blurred. "Why not?"

His gaze never left hers. "Because now I want to kiss you. Like I wanted to that day on the ice."

A knot rose in her throat and the air between them grew hot and almost unbearable. That day on the ice had clearly meant as much to him as it had to her. "So why didn't you kiss me?"

A snort sounded from somewhere above.

They both jerked away from each other, snapping toward the stairwell. Bernadette's cheeks blazed as she glanced up at Ronan, who lingered at the top of the staircase, smugly watching them.

Matthew pointed rigidly up at Ronan. "Ey. Snorting is not how you go about announcing yourself."

Ronan grinned and clicked his tongue, before swiveling away on the landing and disappearing around the corner.

Matthew swung back to her. "We should depart." He said it as if absolutely nothing had happened between them. At all.

Bernadette sighed, knowing that the moment between them had passed. Again.

CHAPTER TWENTY-FIVE

MISSING: Annabelle Netta Carson
—*The Truth Teller, a New York Newspaper for
Gentlemen*

Park Theatre

IF ANYONE WERE TO ASK Matthew what the hell was happening on that lantern-lit stage below, he would not only have snorted but spit. *Ireland Redeemed* had turned into a dancing, prancing pandemonium of poorly dressed men with too much eye makeup that made them all look like Pharaohs and Egyptians, not Irishmen. And all of it had been set against poorly painted scenery of bogs that looked *nothing* like Ireland.

It was a waste of seven dollars.

As everyone applauded and the heavy curtains lowered onto the wide stage, he glanced over at Bernadette. She had an equally pained expression on her face and stared at those curtains as if she genuinely feared they might be pulled up again.

He bit back a laugh and quickly leaned toward her.

"I suggest we leave. Before I fist every last one of these actors and show them what Ireland is really about."

A laugh escaped her. She squelched it with a gloved hand. "I would love to see you fist every last one of them and then write a full commentary in your paper about the performance's lack of script. What was that?"

"I don't know. I don't. But I'd rather you not encourage this madman." He rose, extending a hand to her. "Come."

She grasped his hand and also rose.

Guiding her out of the box and into the corridor beyond that would eventually lead them downstairs and out of Park Theatre, he released the warmth of her gloved hand, trying to focus on everything but touching her. It was damn hard playing the role of a saint.

He eyed the diamond necklace draping the curve of her throat and wondered if she really liked it or was pretending to like it. He continued walking them toward the main stairwell, trying to come up with something to say. "I have three hours available tomorrow in the afternoon. What would you like to do?"

She glanced up at him, her dark eyes brightening. "Jamaica."

His brows rose. "Jamaica?" He searched her face. "What made you think of Jamaica?"

A breathy sigh escaped her. She stared out before them as if seeing the water and islands. "I have been in love with all things privateering since I was eight. And Port Royal and Kingston are well known for their privateering history. I'm hoping to go. One of these days. I had planned to go prior to that whole mess with

Cassidy, but then you returned to my life and I…canceled the trip."

It was obvious he was going to have to make Jamaica happen. Perhaps not tomorrow afternoon, but at some point. If he could get the woman to cooperate, that is. She hadn't said anything pertaining to their courtship or him or—

A regal-looking and large-breasted blonde dressed in a flamboyant silk moiré evening gown bustled toward them, interrupting their path to the main stairs.

Dread seized him, recognizing Mrs. Klauder. The same Mrs. Klauder who had relentlessly extended various invitations to…um…her bed, despite her being married to a very prominent, city council member.

"Mr. Milton. Do you have a moment?"

Bringing himself and Bernadette to a halt, he tightened his hold on Bernadette's hand. "No. Not really."

Bernadette gasped and glanced up at him. *"Matthew."*

Mrs. Klauder paused and eyed Bernadette with sharp, blue eyes that were anything but friendly. "I don't believe we have ever met." Her voice was much cooler than he was comfortable with.

Matthew gestured to Bernadette. "This is Lady Burton." He paused and felt the need to add, "My fiancée."

Bernadette glanced up at him again. He grabbed for her hand and squeezed it hard. They had been officially outed.

Mrs. Klauder sighed and rounded toward Matthew's side as if no longer wishing to associate with Bernadette. She touched his arm with a gloved hand

and leaned in, intently and heatedly holding his gaze, "Might we speak, Mr. Milton?"

Matthew refrained from sounding *too* agitated. "I'm actually on my way out."

"This will only take a moment." She angled closer, adjusting her cashmere shawl in a way to better display her sizable breasts. "I have been meaning to ask about setting up another charity event for the orphanage next month. It would require time to coordinate. I was hoping for your assistance. Might you be able to call on me sometime this week?"

The woman was interested in entertaining far more than charity. Stepping back, he rounded over on Bernadette's other side to set a good distance between them. "Call on the office. Mr. Kerner will ensure you receive free advertisement, seeing you wish to assist the orphanage."

"I will do that." Mrs. Klauder paused and eyed Bernadette. "Good evening to you both."

Christ. It was like being back in the Five Points and dealing with whores who only wanted his trousers around his ankles for the purpose of taking off with whatever they could. He'd never been stupid then and most certainly was not now.

Mrs. Klauder sashayed past, her silk moiré evening gown provocatively dragging against the carpet, and disappeared around the iron banister and down the stairwell.

He huffed out a breath, thankful the woman was gone.

Bernadette poked him not once but twice. "What was that?"

He shook his head and kept on shaking it. "You don't want to know. She's married to one of the council members. All I have to say is that the city is trying to hang me. The mayor has been warning me for months. They're looking to mar the name I've created through the paper. They're morons, is what. Every single last one of them. She isn't even attractive enough for me to pause."

She blinked, a flush etching her cheeks. "I did not realize there were women who *could* make you pause, Mr. Milton."

He reveled at the idea that she was jealous. He leaned into her. "Are you jealous? Or are you jealous?"

She puckered her lips. "I may have to talk to the council about this."

"You do that."

"Mr. Milton?" a man suddenly inquired from behind. "Do you have a moment?"

Matthew bit back a groan. So much for reveling. He swiveled toward a mustached gent he'd never met, whose overgrown graying hair was snipped in all the wrong places. That evening attire, however, exuded prestige. "Yes, sir? How might I be of assistance?"

The gentleman hesitated, then stepped toward him. "The name is Mr. Grigg. I was hoping to call on you regarding an article pertaining to a disappearance."

Matthew paused. "A disappearance?"

Mr. Grigg glanced about and lowered his voice. It cracked from strained emotion. "A close friend of mine, the owner of this here theater, had their six-year-old daughter disappear from her bed fourteen days ago. Someone broke a window and got in. Though the marshals have been relentlessly investigating the matter, I thought a well-circulated newspaper such as yours might be able to assist in their investigation."

Matthew's throat tightened. "Yes. Of course we'd assist. Please. Call on the office tomorrow morning at nine. We only print once a week, but I'd be willing to push out an extra edition for it."

The man nodded, blinking back tears. "Thank you. I will call in the morning. Good evening to you."

"And you." Matthew stared after the old man, who set his chin and slowly made his way out, his gloved hand tightening on his cane. When a child wasn't even safe in her own bed and in her own home—much like Coleman's own sad story—what hope was there for those children who wandered the street alone? The world deserved to burn for it.

He glanced toward Bernadette and grabbed her hand, tugging her onward. "We should leave." He heaved out a breath, desperately trying to shake off the acrid feeling that this poor six-year-old girl was already dead.

Bernadette allowed herself to be hurried down the staircase, toward the entrance hall and through the crowds leading out to the line of carriages.

When they were inside his carriage and had pulled away from the theater, he swiped his face and confessed, "I hate this piss of a city." He closed his eyes, shaking his head. "It's been too many days. That poor child is dead."

"Do not say that! For heaven's sake, if you hold no hope for that child, what hope does she have?"

"Hope is a pointless emotion to cradle in the real world, Bernadette. It breaks you when you're not ready to break."

The rustling of her gown made him open his eyes. She seated herself beside him and wrapped her arms around him, tucking her head against his arm.

He tugged her close, fitting her beneath his arm, and buried his face into her hair, drawing in that soothing scent of citrus she was back to wearing again. They swayed against each other with each movement of the carriage as the night wavered beyond the glass windows.

She eventually shifted in his arms and peered up at him. "Do not say such things, Matthew. Hope is the one thing everyone can touch and is the one thing that keeps humanity afloat."

He glanced down at her, his heart pounding. Hope. Did it still exist in this misbegotten world? In her eyes it did. And it made him want to believe in it just for the sake of this six-year-old girl.

She smiled brokenly up at him in the shadows of the dim lantern hanging above them. "We will bring her home safely. I know we will. Especially with the vast readership you have."

He set both hands against her beautiful face, wishing life could be as noble and just as she was. "I pray you're right." He lingered and searched her face, desperately wanting to kiss her but knowing if he did, he'd never stop.

He released her, rose and seated himself opposite her. "I'll take you home. I'm going to have a long few days ahead of me. We probably won't be able to see each other this week."

She nodded, her gaze lowering to her gloved hands. "Of course."

Sensing that she was disappointed, he added, "Actually...promise me you'll be at the office tomorrow and every day thereafter until we can get back to finding time for ourselves again. I could use you there. I could use a smile and this thing you call hope."

She glanced up and smiled, her sad eyes brightening. "I will be there every day until we find her. And I know we will."

This was exactly why he not only wanted but desperately needed Bernadette in his life for the rest of his life. Because she gave him hope when there was none.

Four days later

NOT EVEN A DAY AFTER an extensive front-page article had been printed pertaining to the disappearance of six-year-old Annabelle Netta Carson, her naked, mutilated and ravaged body was discovered floating in the Hudson. The heart-wrenching news was delivered by none other than Marshal Royce himself right there in the office of *The Truth Teller.*

Tears blinded Bernadette as she struggled to bite back a sob. It was like losing her own child. She had hoped and hoped and hoped. The girl was only six.

Matthew raked both hands through his hair and fell against a nearby wall with a thud. "Christ."

Marshal Royce inclined his head and departed, clearly aware that no one was capable of hearing or saying more.

Swallowing back tears, Bernadette rounded toward Matthew.

He continued to hold his hands against his head.

She reached up, gently drawing those large, warm hands down toward her. "Matthew."

A lone tear slid down the length of his shaven cheek. Lifting a trembling finger to it, she smoothed it away.

He turned away his face from hers and sniffed, pulling away. He jerked toward the wall. "Jesus fecking Christ. How could anyone—" Gnashing his teeth, he slammed a rigid fist straight into the wall, thudding his knuckles deep into the plaster.

She jumped and grabbed his arm before he could hit that wall again. "Matthew. Please. Don't—"

He yanked it away and paused, glancing toward her. "I don't want you seeing me like this." Seething out a breath, he rounded her and boomed across the room, "*Kerner!* Pull all the goddamn trays before they press. We're going to rewrite the main page. Everyone, from street to heaven, is going to know every last rancid detail of what happened to that poor child. Humanity deserves to choke on what little is being done. We're also going to ensure we find the son of a bitch who did this."

Bernadette didn't know how she found her voice again, but somehow, she did. "I will take the expense of a fifty-thousand-dollar reward on any information pertaining to an arrest. Print that."

He swung toward her, his stern features acknowledging her for the first time. He pointed. "Done."

Lowering his hand, he exhaled. "I want you to go home, Bernadette." He paused, his expression stilling. "Not to your home. Mine. I want you to go and stay there. Ronan will take you. I've got a long day ahead of me, but I need to know that you'll be waiting for me when I'm done. All right?" He set his jaw.

Bernadette nodded, sensing that he was struggling to remain composed.

He commenced swiping up parchment after parchment from each table he passed. He riffled through them and disappeared into one of the back rooms leading to the printing floor, where a long line of men hovered over tables placing individual letters into iron trays.

Ronan wandered over to her and after a long moment quietly offered, "I'll take you. If you don't mind me doing it."

Bernadette grabbed the youth and hugged him. "Thank you."

Ronan nodded but didn't say anything.

She shook him, desperately needing assurance. "I want you to come right back here afterward. I want you to be with him for however long he stays. Promise me you will stay at his side and ensure he remains calm and doesn't hit any more walls."

Ronan stiffened and pulled away. "He'll most likely bloody up his knuckles by the end of the day. It's what he does when injustice rides in a bit hard. He's never been one to take these things well."

She swallowed, searching those young brown eyes. "I cannot have that, Ronan. Do you understand? I cannot. And given that he is like a father to you, you shouldn't allow for it, either."

He winced. "He does what he wants. Always has. You know that much about him, don't you?"

She half nodded and prayed that her Matthew didn't return at the end of the day with bloody knuckles.

CHAPTER TWENTY-SIX

One particular gentleman, whilst out driving his
chaise, was met by another gentleman also driving a chaise. Neither would accommodate the
other, despite the narrow road, and as if by mutual impulse, they drove furiously against each
other. Both were, on the instant, precipitated to
the ground and lacerated beyond comprehension.
If only one had the sense to pull the chaise aside,
both would have been spared.
            —*The Truth Teller, a New York Newspaper for*
                                            Gentlemen

Late evening

BERNADETTE PACED MATTHEW'S parlor and glanced again
toward the doorway, wondering if it was time to go
back to the office. All of the servants had long retired
and it had been well over nine hours since she'd last
seen him or any sign of Ronan.

The chiming of a bell announcing that someone was
at the main entrance made her heart leap. Was it him?

It couldn't be. Why would he be ringing the bell to his own door?

She hurried out of the parlor and glanced down the corridor. Knowing that all of the servants had already retired for the night, she paused.

The bell chimed again.

What if Matthew had sent word from the office pertaining to something important? What if—

She hurried to the door and unlatched the bolt. She edged the door open, a whirl of wind and snow breezing in.

A tall youth with soft green eyes, dressed in evening attire and a top hat caked with snow, lingered on the step. It took a moment for her to realize that it was Jacob Astor.

Her eyes widened. Heavens, she hadn't seen him in…months. From what Mr. Astor had told her, the boy had thrown a fit about going to London. Mr. Astor was still anything but pleased. "Is everything all right, Jacob? What are you doing here?"

He removed his top hat, scattering blond hair across his forehead and shook off the snow from it. "Emerson informed me that you'd most likely be here." He leaned toward her. "Might I come in? The weather is a bit rough."

She hesitated, the cold wind scraping her into feeling a chill that went beyond mere skin. Given the late hour and that it wasn't her house, she honestly didn't feel she had the right to invite him in. She gripped the door, edging it back toward herself. "Forgive me for being rude, Jacob, but it's late and I have no right inviting you into a home that isn't my own. But you most certainly can call on me tomorrow in the afternoon. I will be at home." She smiled. "Good night, and I look forward to seeing you then." She stepped back to close the door.

"Wait!" He shot out a gloved hand, pushing the door back open. "I have something for you. It's why I came." He dug into his embroidered vest pocket and retrieved a letter. "My grandfather received this in the afternoon post. He only opened it because it was addressed to him, but it's for you." He held it out.

She hesitated, drawing the door wider, and took the letter. She lowered her eyes to the piece of parchment in her hands. Recognizing her father's crest embedded in the broken red wax seal, her eyes widened.

It could mean only one thing.

She hurriedly unfolded it and turned away from the door, veering toward one of the oil lamps set on a side table in the foyer to better illuminate the scrawled words she knew, in fact, to be her father's.

Mr. Astor,
If you would be so kind as to deliver this to my daughter, I would be most grateful. The old fool that I am, I never asked for the new address she was forced to take after that most unfortunate incident in New Orleans. Please inform her that I regret the way we parted and I wish to see her again, if she is willing to travel and forgive. I intend to be a better father and wish to be a part

of her life in any manner she sees fit, for however long I have left. Which, I fear, may not be long at all.
Lord Westrop

Bernadette choked, tears blinding her, thankful that the news wasn't pertaining to his death or an illness. For him to have written this letter, it would seem her father's loneliness had devoured the very last of his soul. He was probably sitting alone in the library, as he always did, reading a book or silently praying, as he always did, or staring out the window, as he always did. Damn him. Why did she have to love him?

Jacob stepped inside and closed the door behind himself. "Are you all right?"

"Yes." She sniffed, trying to compose herself and refolded the letter. "Thank you for delivering this."

"Of course." He set his gloved hands behind his back and set his shoulders. "Does this mean you're going back to London?"

She fingered the parchment. "He is old and has no one but me. So yes, I must go to him."

He nodded. "You and he will reach a mutual understanding in this. I know you will."

"Thank you, Jacob. I hope so."

He nodded again and glanced around. "I was rather concerned that you hadn't returned to your house at this hour. As was Emerson. I'll be sure to inform him that you are, in fact, here, as he had hoped." After a long, pulsing moment, he added, "Might I ask what you're doing here, given the late hour? Is everything all right?"

She awkwardly glanced toward him, knowing full well she had to protect Matthew's name in honor of not only him but his paper. "I am here merely awaiting Mr. Milton's return after a most tragic incident. I haven't announced it quite yet to your grandfather but…he and I have commenced courting."

His lips parted. "You and he are courting?"

"Yes. As of this week."

"As in to marry?" he echoed.

She rolled her eyes, knowing full well his astonishment was going to reflect his grandfather's. "Yes. As in to marry. This wild little cuckoo has finally found a nest."

Jacob momentarily closed his eyes and threw back his head. He sighed, his shoulders slumping.

She blinked. "Jacob? Are you all right? What is it?"

Opening his eyes, he leveled his head and tossed his top hat, causing it to roll across the marble foyer floor. He stepped closer and lowered himself to one knee, his gloved hands gently skimming the length of her skirts as he went down. "Bernadette. My dearest, dearest Bernadette."

She sucked in a breath, crushing her father's letter in a fist, and lowered her gaze to his as he continued to kneel before her. Panic seized her ability to breathe or move. "Jacob…what are you doing?"

The door at the far end of the corridor suddenly opened and Matthew strode in, stripping his snow-covered black riding coat from his muscled body.

Her eyes widened. "Matthew!" She almost staggered as she crushed her father's letter to her heaving chest.

Matthew jerked to a halt, his rugged face taut. His gaze snapped to Jacob. "What the hell is going on?"

Her hands trembled right along with the rest of her in disbelief of what was happening. "Matthew. I am as equally astounded as you are. If not more so." She frantically gestured toward Jacob in exasperation and stepped back. She couldn't believe what was happening to her. Jacob Astor!

Ronan, who had also entered by now, raised his dark brows as he lingered behind Matthew, glancing at Jacob, who was still on one knee.

Matthew tossed his riding coat onto the railing of the staircase, his broad chest and embroidered waistcoat rising and falling more heavily with each stalking step he took toward them. "Might I ask why he's even here?" It sounded like a gruff accusation. "How did he know you were here, Bernadette? Because I'm trying to make sense of what I'm looking at."

She cringed and, trying not to whine at the incredibly bad timing of it all, held up her father's crushed letter. "Emerson told him that I would most likely be here. He merely came to deliver this to me and—"

"Fell upon his knee," Matthew provided in a very dark and anything but understanding tone.

She winced. "Yes. More or less." She really needed to get Jacob out of the house before Matthew maimed him. Quickly turning back to poor Jacob, she said, "Whilst I am genuinely touched by all of this, surely you know that this could have never amounted to anything."

Jacob tightened his hold on both her hands and stubbornly jerked her back toward him, remaining on his knee. "I must say it. Allow me to say it. I won't leave until I do."

Her eyes widened. "Jacob, please—"

Matthew stepped toward them and rigidly hit his chest hard with a clenched fist, the sound thudding through the foyer like a war drum. "*This* is my genuine attempt at remaining calm. Now, I suggest, *Jacob,* you get the feck up off that knee and get out of my goddamn house while you still *have* a knee."

Oh, dear. That was the Five Points talking. Bernadette quickly leaned back toward Jacob, shaking his hands with both of her own. "Jacob. Please. For the love of your grandparents, do not perpetuate this."

Jacob tightened his hold on her hands and set his shoulders, capturing her gaze. In a low, self-assured tone, he announced, "I realize, Bernadette, that I'm about to be mocked and rejected and cuffed until I bleed for what I'm about to say, but I have carried this with me for far too long and must be rid of it."

Jacob drew in a breath and exhaled. "I love you. I do. I've loved you since I first saw you on the streets of New Orleans fighting off those men with more fire than I've ever seen in a woman since. My only regret is having never told you. I just…I never thought a woman like you would ever see me in that way. And I was right. After all, I've only ever been a boy in your eyes." Jacob lowered his gaze and kissed each of her hands for a lingering breath with warm lips before altogether releasing them. "And now it's time for me to go." Jacob slowly rose. Straightening, he stepped back and back, his youthful face twisting in silent anguish.

Tears stung her eyes, and a few even escaped and rolled down her cheek, knowing how much heart and soul and strength went into those words. *This* is what she should have done for Matthew. On the ice that day. She had missed her moment out of stupid doubt and it took this moment to make her realize she was never going to get that day on the ice back. Not ever. "Jacob. I admire your strength and your heart. I'm ever so sorry that—"

"There is no need to say it." Jacob held up a hand, not meeting her gaze. "I seized my moment when I thought I never would. And that is all that matters." He half nodded and turned away. Retrieving his top hat from the floor, he angled toward the door and jerked it open. Stepping out, he quietly shut it behind him.

Bernadette closed her eyes, trying to steady herself in between uneven breaths. And so it was Jacob Astor, a boy—or rather, a man, for he had earned it—had taught her more about life and love in that one moment than she had ever been able to teach herself.

It was all about seizing your chance.

Even if it never amounted to anything.

Opening her eyes, she swung back to Matthew, who still lingered in the foyer. She paused, noting his disheveled hair and…that right hand of his, which he rigidly flexed, was swollen and smeared with scabbing blood.

She shook her head, angst overwhelming her. Ronan had rightfully predicted bloody knuckles. Striding toward him, she grabbed Matthew's wrist hard and held it up rigidly toward his face. "Why would you do this to yourself?" she choked out. "What purpose does it serve? Would it have brought her back?"

He yanked his hand from her grip and stepped back. Glancing toward Ronan, who still quietly watched them, he rasped, "Ronan, can you give us a moment please?"

Ronan only stoically stared Bernadette down. "If we hadn't come back when we did, Milton, who knows what would have happened. She probably would have been pounding into him by now."

Bernadette's eyes widened.

Matthew jumped toward Ronan and grabbed him by the collar hard, jerking him toward himself. "You listen to me, boy." Matthew shook him. "You need to cease comparing every goddamn woman to your mother. You're going to end up hurting far more than just the women around you. You're going to end up hurting yourself. What you just saw there was a genuine exchange between a real gentleman and a real lady that would have played out the same if we were here to see it or not. Now, I want you to apologize to Bernadette. Because she is and will forever be a lady. And don't you ever bloody forget it."

Bernadette dragged in a much-needed breath. *This* was why she was in love with her Matthew. Because even in the throes of being tested by having a young boy fall upon his knee for her, he had, in the end, remained true to himself and to her, and was everything other men were not.

Ronan slowly pulled himself out of Matthew's grasp. "I'm sorry, Milton. You're right. I didn't mean to—" He squeezed his eyes shut for a long moment, then awkwardly met her gaze, tears now pooling in his brown eyes. "I'm sorry. I'm trying to be a better person. I'm trying. I really am."

She hurried toward Ronan and, still clutching her father's letter, embraced him. As she pulled away, she forged a smile, if only to ensure him that she understood. She tapped at his chin. "It takes a real gentleman to apologize. Thank you."

Ronan nodded, but wouldn't meet her gaze as he scrambled away. Darting around Matthew, Ronan hurried up the stairs and out of sight.

She sighed and met Matthew's stare, cradling her father's letter against her chest.

Matthew's gaze snapped to the letter she held. His square jaw tightened as he stepped back and back. Swinging away, he grabbed up his coat from the banister and jogged up the stairs, taking two steps at a time, and disappeared.

She swallowed against the tightness in her throat.

Oh, now that wasn't fair.

For, now he appeared to be angry with *her*.

Still clutching the parchment, she hurried up the long staircase after him. "Matthew?"

Peering into every open door she passed, she eventually paused before what appeared to be his bedchamber. She blinked at what she saw within.

Matthew had stripped to mere trousers, leaving his

clothing in a bundled pile on the floor a few feet from his bed.

She lingered in the doorway. "Matthew?"

He lowered himself to the floor and, to her astonishment, set both hands flat on the floor, with his long legs outstretched, and proceeded to lift and lower his entire body. Every muscle in his back and his arms tightened and flexed as he kept lifting and lowering, lifting and lowering without pause.

She stepped in, closing the bedchamber door behind herself to allow privacy. "What are you doing?"

He didn't pause. "I'm ensuring I don't hit any more walls. Given that it upsets you." Perspiration beaded his forehead as he focused on the floor beneath him, pumping his arms up and down.

Sensing he wasn't about to stop, Bernadette lowered herself to the floor beside him. "Matthew, please."

He paused and glanced over at her, holding himself in midair. Pushing himself up and back, he landed on the floor across from her with a thud, sitting cross-legged beside her. He searched her face, but said nothing.

"Why are you angry?" She tried to keep her voice steady.

He leaned back. "Because I'm confused."

"About what?"

"Do you plan on keeping it? And if so, why?"

She blinked. "Keeping what?"

He gestured rigidly toward the letter. "What he wrote to you. You've been cradling that goddamn letter from start to finish."

That was why he was angry. He thought she was cradling a letter from Jacob. Even after what had happened. "Oh, Matthew." She shook her head and held it out. "'Tis from my father. He didn't have my new address. He was therefore forced to send it to the Astors. Jacob was delivering it. I'm afraid I must leave New York. I must go to him."

Matthew paused. He quickly leaned back in, taking the unfolded parchment, his rugged features now anguished and soft. "Now I feel like a dolt. I didn't mean to accuse you of…" He sighed, set aside the letter, reached out and dragged her over to him, shifting against the floor they still sat on.

Bernadette buried her face against the warmth of his chest.

His lips trailed from the top of her head to her forehead. He paused. Releasing her, he grabbed her face so as to better look at her. "Do you know how damn hard it was to watch that? To remain calm? To doubt what you would say or what you would do?"

Tears blinded her, feeling and seeing the emotional intensity in his face and in those large hands that held her rigidly in place. And she knew what *she* needed to do.

She grabbed his hands and dragged him and herself up off the floor. Angling him toward herself, she let out a shaky breath and then, as Jacob had done, lowered herself onto her knees, her gown bundling around her. "If you must know, Matthew, that should have been *me* kneeling before *you*. As I am now. I should have done it that day on the ice when you kept me from falling and the world stood still. For that is when I knew I was yours and would forever be yours."

He stared down at her, his bare chest rising and falling in uneven takes. "What are you saying?"

Through tears that were now overwhelming her at realizing just how momentous this moment truly was for her, given she never thought she would ever love or find a man like him, she grabbed his hands and choked out, "Marry me, Mr. Matthew Joseph Milton. For I love you."

"Bernadette." He stumbled down to his knees, joining her back on the floor and grabbed her face with both hands again.

His mouth hovered close. "Bernadette. Surely you already know how I feel."

A sob escaped her at knowing that, by seizing her chance, she had seized him.

He leaned in and brushed his lips against hers. Gently, he parted her lips by sliding his tongue into her mouth, silently announcing that he was indeed forever hers.

His hold tightened as his hot tongue now fully roamed hers. He molded and remolded his mouth against hers, his fingers digging harder into her.

She melted. And she not only melted but almost slumped against him in agonizing bliss she'd never felt in all her life. Wrapping her arms around his broad shoulders, she reveled in the heat of his mouth and the dominance of that hot tongue that raked her teeth and the inside of her own mouth.

They kissed and kissed and kissed and kissed.

It was like kissing him for the first time.

His large hands rounded from her waist to her backside, his palms roving up her back and into her hair and back down again.

He jerked her toward him. Releasing her mouth, he jumped to his feet, bent and swung her up and into his arms with a tilt and a sweep.

She clung to him as he veered straight toward the mahogany four-poster covered with white linens and pillows.

He paused and captured her mouth again, tightening his hold on her and crushing her body against his chest. Even though that crushing hold pinched her dangling legs against his muscled arms, she didn't mind at all.

He set her gently atop the mattress. Holding her gaze, he stepped back and stripped the last two pieces of clothing from his half-nude body—his trousers and the undergarments beneath them. He now stood gloriously naked.

She sank back against the mattress, feeling rather faint in between ragged breaths she couldn't seem to take. From that broad chest and that scar she remembered all too well, to his narrow waist, to—

Climbing onto the bed with her, he grasped her ankles, tossing off one slipper then the other. Shoving his hands up the length of her stockinged legs, he dragged her gown, along with all of her petticoats and chemise, up, up to her waist, watching himself do it.

She had never felt more aware of him or of them.

He pushed all the material to the side of her waist, completely exposing her lower half and climbed on top of her, pressing her into the mattress with his own naked body. "Bernadette," he murmured from above. He smoothed away her hair from her forehead with both hands. "I've loved you ever since you kissed me in front of that bastard Royce and saw past every single broken window of my life."

This glorious man had loved her all along.

He searched her face and ground his erection against her exposed lower half. "I want to change everything between us. Let me."

"How?"

Spitting into his hand twice, he leaned away and lubricated his rigid length well, holding her gaze. He lowered himself back onto her and, still holding her gaze, pressed the tip of his length against her bum. "I want this."

Her eyes widened as he rigidly held the wet tip of his erection against her, waiting for permission. She'd never let any man penetrate her there.

She swallowed, still holding his gaze.

Matthew leaned down and licked her mouth, then kissed it, making her fade with the eroticism of it. "Hurting you is the last thing I'd ever want to do. If it hurts, I'll stop."

Her breaths escaped in shallow takes. He wanted it and so she wanted it. She wanted to give this incredible man something no man had ever taken from her. She slid her hands across his shoulders, savoring him against her fingers. "Yes. Simply know that I have never…" She couldn't say it.

His jaw tightened. "And that is why I want it." Wetting and rewetting his hand with the moisture of his mouth, he covered the tip of his length until it was fully slick and, capturing her gaze from above, pressed gently against the opening no man had ever touched.

She could feel his wet length slowly sliding in. Though it felt uncomfortable, it didn't hurt given that rigid length was wet and going in very, very slowly.

As he edged in deeper, his hand slid from his cock to her wet folds. He spread them and commenced fingering her nub, intent on pleasuring her as he pushed deeper into her. She closed her eyes, giving in to the tight, stretching sensation of her backside being entered and being fingered at the same time. It was a twisting of pleasure and pain that wildly heightened with each breath she took.

It was incredible.

He pushed all the way in with a groan, fingering her faster. "You are now my virgin. Mine."

She gasped, unable to think as he slowly stroked into her bum and fingered her at the same time, using equal rhythm for both. She felt as if both strokes would be her undoing. Her pleasure and climax were already so close at hand even though he'd barely started.

She gripped his smooth, muscled shoulders and slid her hands down, down to his naked waist, digging her nails into him.

He groaned and groaned again, stroking his length into her backside more and more.

Those constant strokes and incessant fingering finally made her burst. She cried out in awed anguish, bucking beneath him and the pressure that made her writhe. She extended her throat and body in an effort to feel every last inch of his length inside her, not wanting it to end.

He slid out completely, releasing her, and with a breath, penetrated the wetness leading to her womb. He savagely held on to her, pressing her hard into the mattress, and pounded into her relentlessly. He dug his teeth deep into her shoulder and with one last thrust, stilled, groaning out his climax as his seed filled her. He clamped his teeth into her shoulder harder.

The sting of his teeth made her wince before it lulled as he loosened his bite. She tightened her hold on him.

He kissed her shoulder twice where he had bitten into it. "Sorry. I didn't mean to bite so hard."

She smiled. "I didn't mind."

His chest heaved against hers as he rolled them both over on the mattress. He tucked her against his chest, settling on his back. He drew in a breath, his fingers digging into her. "I owe everything that I have to you. Even the air I'm breathing."

She nestled her head against that solid, warm chest. "Cease."

He kissed the top of her head several times. "Are you sore? I tried not to…overdo it."

She choked on a rather awkward laugh. "I will not lie. I feel like any virgin would after her first encounter."

He tightened his hold. "Did you enjoy it?"

Why did she feel so awkward talking about it? "I… Yes. I will admit I did."

"Good."

She smiled and traced a finger from his nipple down toward one of his scars, happy to know he was no longer a part of that rough life on the street and living in bare rooms with broken windows. She shifted herself against him so as to better glance up at him.

His features were relaxed, though in deep thought. He stared up at the upholstered canopy of the bed.

"What are you thinking about?" she asked.

"You." His brows came together. "I never answered. Yes. Yes, I will marry you."

Her heart squeezed knowing that marrying this man would be marrying into a lifetime of everything she had ever wanted. It was hard to believe she ever could have doubted that the promise of matrimony could bring her such happiness. But then again, Matthew himself was hard to believe. "To be your wife will be the greatest honor I will ever know as a person and as a woman. I want you to know that."

He glanced down at her, capturing her gaze. "I never thought I'd hear you say that." He squeezed her against himself, kissing her forehead. "So much for our courtship."

She let out a laugh. "It was glorious while it lasted."

Grabbing her face, he kissed her on the lips several times. "I want five children. Maybe six if we get around to it. Are you up for it?"

Bernadette's lips parted, realizing she had yet to share that particular detail about herself. "Matthew. I…" Lowering her gaze to the scar on his chest, tears stung her eyes. Fighting against the burn, a sob escaped her. "I'm so sorry."

He stiffened. Grasped her chin, he jerked it toward her. "What? Why are you crying?"

She sniffed, annoyed with herself for having no strength. "I am incapable of having children, Matthew. My husband and I tried for twelve years. I'm sorry. I should have told you."

"I didn't realize that…" He grew quiet.

When he still said nothing, she choked out, "Say something. Say what you really feel. Please. I need to hear it."

He released her chin and kissed her hand hard, digging his lips into her skin. "It doesn't matter how I feel," he murmured against her hand, even though she sensed it meant *everything* to him.

Her lips trembled as she fought against sobbing again. "A man who hosts charity events for children and becomes the guardian to a boy that isn't his own clearly longs to be a father."

He shook his head. "Stop. No. It doesn't matter."

He swiped away the tears running down her cheeks with his thumb and softly said, "Don't cry, luv. I already have everything I could ever want. Ronan needs us. Other children need us. There are so many orphans, we shouldn't be selfish and think our love ends with us. And what of this thing you call hope? We have time to try."

Squeezing her eyes shut, she savagely clung to him and those beautiful words she hoped were, in fact… true.

"Bernadette," he whispered.

"Yes?"

"I love you."

A choked sob escaped her. "And I love you."

He kissed her forehead. "We'll marry at once and go straight from here to London. It's important you see your father. I'll have Kerner take over the paper while I'm gone. That way, you and I can arrive before your father, not in shame, but as husband and wife."

She nodded against him and prayed that whatever was left of the father she once knew—the one who would lovingly set her upon his knee and kiss her forehead—would accept them both.

CHAPTER TWENTY-SEVEN

A wife will say that her husband forgets to honor and cherish her, to which the husband says, he did not forget, she merely forgot to obey. With this sort of rancid perception, gentlemen, 'tis no wonder the world is in the state it is in. Honor and cherish not only your wives but your children.

—*The Truth Teller, a New York Newspaper for Gentlemen*

BY THE END OF THE TWO weeks, by special license, Matthew had taken Bernadette Marie as his wife. He knew without any doubt—for, his heart and soul whispered of it—that she would, indeed, be carrying his child, and soon.

As they journeyed from New York to Liverpool and into London, in between stolen moments away from Ronan, who was excitedly making the journey with them, Matthew made love to his Bernadette, spilling his seed into her with a passion and a purpose he'd never known as a man. He wanted to prove to her that he could make all of her dreams come true. Even that of being a mother. It was his hope that by the time they left England, she would be carrying the first of his five children.

London, England—Park Lane

THE FOOTMAN GESTURED TOWARD the open doors of the library beyond. Matthew reached out and grabbed his wife's ungloved hand, squeezing it. Ronan rounded to the other side of Bernadette and also took her hand, lending equal support that they were all a family. No matter what the old man did or said.

Drawing in a steadying breath, Matthew let it out, knowing that having a one-eyed Irishman for a son-in-law wasn't every aristocrat father's dream come true. Together, they entered through the double doors of the cavernous room lined with endless books that swept floor to ceiling, from corner to corner.

Matthew's brows rose. He'd never seen so many god-damn books in his life.

Bernadette leaned in and whispered, "I used to build pirate ships out of these books when I was a girl. And here I am with my own Pirate King." She nudged him.

His chest tightened as he scanned the brightly lit room, imagining his Bernadette scampering around, with braids swaying as she piled up those books with fiery determination and a glint in her eye.

As they came to the other end of the room, his gaze settled on an old man with snowy white hair. *Lord Westrop.* The man sat in a large, leather wing-tipped chair dressed in a tawny Turkish robe, those slippered feet propped atop a plush ottoman.

Eerily, the man reminded him of…his father. His father used to sit like that, with feet always propped on something.

Upon seeing them, Lord Westrop's eyes widened.

Matthew could see the old man sinking back against that chair. Those dark eyes darted from Matthew to Bernadette and settled on Ronan.

Fortunately the man didn't bolt out of the room. Although…given the man's age, Matthew doubted he could.

They paused before him, releasing hands.

Matthew inclined his head. "My lord."

The man's veined hand trembled as he set it onto the armrest of his chair. Glancing from him to Ronan, he eventually asked, "Which one did she marry? Which one is Mr. Milton?"

Bernadette choked. "Papa. Do be serious."

Matthew cleared his throat. "I am her husband. Not the other one."

Ronan smirked, leaned forward and added, "Bernadette ain't my type. Too much of a lady."

Bernadette smacked the boy's arm.

Lord Westrop's eyes stoically swept the length of Matthew before landing upon his face. "I see."

Matthew felt like a lame horse begging to be purchased. "It's an honor to at long last meet you, my lord."

Lord Westrop stared. "What happened to your eye? It looks clouded."

Apparently, the man shared his daughter's tongue in all things blunt. "I lost sight in it many years ago."

"How?" the old man pressed.

Matthew's jaw tightened.

"Papa," Bernadette gently scolded. "Have more tact. You and he met all but a moment ago."

Ronan reached up and hooked an arm around Matthew. In a strained tone, Ronan said, "He lost it because of me. He rescued me when I was six."

Matthew wrapped his own arm around the boy's shoulders. He tightened his hold. "You know damn well it wasn't because of you, Ronan. I could have handled the situation differently, but I stupidly chose to fight."

Silence hummed.

Lord Westrop shifted in his chair. "Bernadette. You didn't even greet me. Give your old father a kiss on the cheek."

She hesitated. "Forgive me. I didn't know if you would have wanted to be greeted."

The old man grunted. "Why would I have called you all the way out to London not to greet you? Now, come."

She smiled brokenly and hurried toward him. Leaning down, she kissed his weathered cheek. "'Tis a blessing you are in such good health and in good spirit."

Lord Westrop grabbed her hand and patted it. "In good enough health and spirit to survive this, I assure you. A letter was not the way to go about announcing your marriage." He sighed. "I would like to speak to Mr. Milton alone. If I may."

Holding Matthew's gaze, and clearly ready to fight

for him, Bernadette confided, "Only if my husband wishes it."

Matthew smirked, endlessly touched. "I promise not to pull out the pistols." He paused and tauntingly patted his waist for her, which hadn't seen a leather belt or weapons since he left Five Points.

She tsked and shook her head, grabbing Ronan's arm. "Come, Ronan. Would you like to see the stables?"

Ronan set his shoulders. "If I can take a carriage out and ride it across Town, yes."

A laugh escaped her. She nudged him. "Let us think on that, shall we? Now, come."

Together, they walked across the library and out.

Matthew stood alone before Lord Westrop. He set his hands behind his back, and knew it was best they get to the point. "There is no need to pretend that you're pleased with this marriage, my lord. I'm not by any means every father's choice in man, be he an aristo or a butcher. Even I know that. But you might like to know that she and I are happy. Gloriously happy, in fact. She is an incredible woman and I'm blessed to call her my own."

Lord Westrop's features tightened. "Her mother and I were happy. It was an arranged marriage, mind you, and I was much, much older than the woman, but we were happy. I...I tried to make Bernadette happy, thinking I knew what was best for her. At the time, I really didn't think her happiness could be found in a young man. Young men these days are...overly ambitious and have a tendency not to take their duties of matrimony seriously. They give in to their passions and bed women just because they can and break their wives all in one go. And I didn't want that for her. William, her first husband, was a good man. He adored Bernadette. And that was what I wanted for her. But in the end, I only made the poor creature miserable. 'Tis something I still live with every day."

It appeared this man understood how he had wronged his Bernadette. And he supposed that was all that mattered. "Have you told her any of this?"

Lord Westrop shook his head. "I live in shame enough."

Matthew stepped toward him. "I think it time you give peace not only to yourself, but to her. I know without any doubt that she would want to hear this from you."

"In time…in time I will tell her. When I am ready." Lowering his gaze to his lap, he adjusted his robe over himself. "I have but one request before I give this marriage my blessing."

Matthew lowered his chin, astounded they had already veered past any lectures. "But of course. What is it?"

"I ask that you, she and this boy stay in London." Lord Westrop cleared his throat. "I wish to be present for the coming of my first grandchild. I have waited many, many years for it."

Matthew drew in a shaky breath and let it out. The staying in London bit he could get past, given Coleman and Georgia had both settled into new lives. Coleman as Atwood and Georgia as duchess. He rather liked the idea of being around his friends. The newspaper was the one and only thing that truly held him in New York, and that, he realized, he could turn over to Kerner. Even though it was his father's legacy, and it would be difficult to let go, Kerner loved the publication and Matthew knew it would be safe in his hands.

But this whole business of children...

He swallowed hard and tried to keep his voice from quaking. "If Bernadette wishes to stay, we will." He couldn't bring himself to say much else.

"Good." Lord Westrop captured his gaze, those dark eyes unexpectedly brightening. After a long moment of silence, he asked, "Do you fence at all? You appear to be the type."

Matthew's brows rose. "Fence?"

"Yes. As in swords."

A gruff laugh escaped Matthew. "Is this your way of announcing a duel?"

Lord Westrop snorted. "Quite the opposite." The old man slowly stood, grabbing the cane set against his chair. "I used to fence in my younger years. And was rather good at it. I wouldn't mind another go before I find myself unable to walk. There is a fencing academy just down the way—Angelo's. I used to fence there all the time when my wife was still alive. I stopped going when she passed. I felt my time was better spent with Bernadette." He nodded and eyed him. "Perhaps we could tap the swords a bit?"

Another gruff laugh escaped Matthew. "I really don't think Bernadette would approve of us—"

"This is between us men." Lord Westrop pointed the cane at him. "She doesn't need to know. The devil that she is, she never tells me anything she does until *after* she does it. You, being a good example of that. She and you owe me this."

Matthew inclined his head, not about to argue with an old man. "We'll tap the swords anytime you're ready, my lord."

"Good. That is exactly the sort of cooperation I want out of a son-in-law. Now. If you don't mind, I intend on finding that daughter of mine. She said something about the stables."

Lord Westrop marched his way out with the cane.

When the man was gone, Matthew swiped his face and for the first time since becoming a husband to his Bernadette, he doubted if, in fact, he would ever be a father to a child of his own. A part of him felt guilty as hell even thinking it, as though he was betraying Bernadette by already giving up hope, when it had been only about two months of trying.

RONAN PATTED ALL of the horses, one by one, going down each and every stall. "How is it one old man needs all of these horses?"

Bernadette sighed. "'Tis the curse of the aristocracy. One horse is never enough."

Someone grunted from behind her. "I dare say, who ever knew a man could feel so insulted before his own horses?"

Bernadette blinked and swung toward her father, who stood at the entrance in his robe, hay scattered at his slippered feet. "Papa. What are you doing out here? You shouldn't be wandering outside the house in your robe."

"I'm an old man," he tossed out. "No one cares what the devil I do anymore."

Ronan hesitated. "Should I leave?"

Lord Westrop pointed the cane at him. "No. In fact, once I up and dress, you can drive me about Town in my chaise. The air is good and the weather dry. What say you?"

Ronan's eyes widened. "You'd let me drive?"

Bernadette's own eyes widened. "Papa. He has never driven a chaise before."

"Eh." Lord Westrop waved her off. "I'll teach him. 'Tis a pull of reins here and there. Mr. Sullivan, go hunt down one of my coachmen. Have him show you where everything is."

Ronan let out a whoop and sprinted past, skidding through the hay and out of the stables.

Bernadette rolled her eyes, gathered her skirts to keep them from dragging against the dirt-pounded floor and made her way toward her father. "Do be careful driving. He is only fifteen."

"I was ten when I learned to drive a chaise."

Her brows rose. "Ten? I didn't know that."

He puffed out a breath and after a long moment said, "There is a lot you don't know about me, my dear." He reached out and grabbed her arm, shaking it. "I will make this brief, for I promised that boy a ride through Town, but I came to say three things. One, that husband of yours clearly adores you. As such, I have no choice but to accept him. Two, I hope you will remain

in London. And three—" His brows came together as
he searched her face. "If I had one of your dolls, I would
use it to ask that you forgive me. For everything."

"Oh, Papa." Bernadette leaned in, setting her hands
gently on those shaven cheeks that had been etched
with too many woes in life. Many more beyond her
own, that she knew. All she had ever wanted was to
be loved by him.

She had known of his love when she was a girl, and
adored him and that love above all else, but the older
she got, the less he knew how to communicate with her
and the more awkward it became. When she was about
five, shortly after her mama had passed, he used to toss
out the governess for three hours every afternoon and
sit on the floor and play dolls with her. They were his
means of communication, her dolls. For he didn't know
how else to communicate with her.

He would assume a silly high-pitched voice to speak
through the dolls, saying things such as, "I have a bit
of gossip. Though you might not like it."

She thought it great fun and played along, by wagging her own doll at him and saying, "What sort of
gossip?"

He would wag his doll back and say, "Lord Westrop,
droll man that he is, has decided to hire a new governess. A better one. For less money. For we have very
little of it, sadly. You won't mind, will you?"

Depending on what he said, she might throw her
doll at him. The dolls were how they always settled
all of their disputes.

Obviously, as she grew older, it was outright demented to use dolls to speak with each other. This method therefore ceased when she was eleven. And from thereon out, with no other means of communication, it was as though their relationship had ceased.

But this…this acknowledgment of what had once been, was enough to make her feel she could move on. "If I had my doll," she whispered, "I would use her to say, 'I forgive you, Papa.'"

Tears appeared in his eyes. He nodded against her hands, sniffed hard and stepped away, ensuring his face was turned.

He gestured with his cane. "I should dress. I don't want to keep the boy waiting." He strode out, each step thudding in time with his cane.

Bernadette could do nothing but stare after him. Without any doubt, she knew Matthew, her beloved Matthew, had something, perhaps everything, to do with what had just happened.

WHILST MATTHEW VISITED with Lord Atwood, who had astoundingly up and married, Bernadette took the carriage across town and called upon her own dear friend Georgia, who was officially *Lady* Yardley, and had been for almost a year.

Imagine her astonishment when the redhead waddled across the parlor with an oversized stomach no gown could ever hide.

Bernadette's lips parted. She rose to her feet. "Georgia! Heavens above. I didn't know you were…"

"With child?" Georgia tossed back. She sighed and eased herself into a chair. "'Tis tradition never to say a word until after the child comes. Even if it's obvious." She rubbed her large belly and slowly grinned, the edges of those green eyes crinkling. "Which it is. This here babe ought to be due any moment. Robinson has been asking me every two blinks if I'm feeling any twinges."

Bernadette hurried over to Georgia, grabbed that freckled face and kissed her forehead twice. "Many blessings and more."

Georgia reached up, grabbed her hands and squeezed them. "I hear you and Matthew are married."

"I most certainly am." Bernadette gently grazed a hand across Georgia's belly, knowing there was a little babe inside and tried not to be sad that she and Matthew would most likely never have this.

Georgia smiled. "I imagine you'll be next. If you aren't already, that is."

Bernadette drew away her hand, tears now burning her eyes. She felt selfish ruining this moment for Georgia and tried not to cry as she pinched her lips.

Georgia's smile faded. "What is it?"

Bernadette shook her head and turned away, swiping away tears that had stupidly run down her cheeks. "We have been trying. So much so, I am exhausting him and he is exhausting me. I was never able to sire an heir for my first husband and being that I am but a few years from forty, I am beginning to accept that no child will ever find its way into my life. Not into my belly, at least."

"Bernadette," Georgia softly said. "Come. Come here."

Slowly facing her, Bernadette sniffed and took her friend's outstretched hand.

Georgia shook it. "Did I ever tell you that I had a dream about you and Matthew? You had a boy and named him Andrew. He was beautiful."

Bernadette sobbed, unable to see anymore and squeezed that dear hand with as much love as she could. "Tell me what he looked like."

"He had black hair, like yours. Eyes as black as any night. He was round and pudgy and all things perfect."

Another sob escaped her. "And I named him Andrew."

"That you did. Andrew Joseph Milton."

"Oh, Georgia." Her breaths were ragged. "I shouldn't be asking for more than I already have. Matthew and I...we plan to take in orphans soon. Five, actually."

"You do that. Until Andrew comes."

Bernadette grabbed hold of Georgia's face and kissed her forehead again and again. "I will do that. Until Andrew comes."

EPILOGUE

A year later
Port Royal

THERE WAS NO DOUBT IN Matthew's mind that, as he watched his Bernadette gleefully bustle through the sand and into clear blue water with her skirts hitched to her knees, alongside their children, that his family was in all ways perfect.

"Papa." Annabelle poked him with a determined little finger, her blue eyes darting up toward his face. "You aren't helping."

Matthew grinned and helped scoop up sand and pile it for her. "Yes, Captain." They called her Captain because she enjoyed giving orders ever since they took her in.

All six of their children, whom they had taken in from the Five Points, varied in age, shape and size— Ronan, being now sixteen, Charles being eight, Annabelle being four, Elizabeth being ten, John being six and Marie being twelve. With *The Truth Teller* no longer on his hands, and the mayor keeping the council busy with Five Points business, he could keep himself occupied with more important things. Such as being a husband and a father.

Life was good. A man couldn't ask for anything more than beach, sun and family.

Ronan fell down into the sand and yelled out to everyone around him, "Who wants to bury this here treasure? Bring all hands on deck!"

John, Charles, Elizabeth and Marie all shouted in unison, "Me!" And together, they darted over and started doing exactly that.

"Not the face," Ronan warned. "Not the face!"

"Matthew!" Bernadette called out as waves slowly rolled against her muslin skirts, splashing water up and around her. "Might you join me?"

He lifted a brow and gestured toward Annabelle. "Can't you see the Captain here is keeping me hostage?"

"Bring the Captain along."

"Yes, Mrs. Captain." Matthew jumped onto his bare feet and grabbed up Annabelle, yanking her up and into his arms.

"Did I say we were done?" Annabelle tossed up at him, clearly not pleased.

He leaned in and whispered, "The pirates are coming. So we have to make a run for it." With that, he dashed with her, giggling and bouncing along in his arms, toward Bernadette. Arriving at the edge of the water, he plunked down Annabelle and called out, "Abandon ship!"

Annabelle giggled again and darted around him.

Her bare feet sprinted toward Ronan, who was being buried, kicking up sand and her skirts. "I want to bury him, too."

Pleased to have a moment alone with his wife, Matthew grabbed hold of Bernadette's waist and dragged her over. "Are you enjoying all things known as privateering?"

"More than you will ever know." She searched his face for a long moment, her dark eyes bright. "He is coming."

Matthew paused. "Who is coming?"

"Andrew."

Matthew stared down at her, his stomach almost flipping. "You mean...Andrew, Andrew?"

She grinned and nodded. "Andrew, Andrew. I wanted to wait until I was certain. Remember how ill I was on the ship? Apparently it wasn't sickness of the sea. We are going to have our own. Just as Georgia had predicted."

His eyes widened. He was going to be a father. *Again.* Grabbing her face, he kissed her hard. Releasing her, he dragged himself down the length of her and fell upon his knees into the sand and water, drenching his trousers and linen shirt.

He rubbed his hand against that belly, which had yet to grow, and kissed it several times. He glanced up at her. "And what if it's a girl?"

"If it is a girl, we will have to call her Andrewlina." Her tone indicated she was rather serious.

He snorted. "Don't be ridiculous."

She stared down at him. "Georgia gave us this baby,

Matthew. We honor that by having Andrew *somewhere* in his or her name."

He laughed and put up both hands, rising. "I'm not about to argue with the woman I love. If it's a girl, Andrewlina Milton it is."

* * * * *

Coleman's story is next! Look for
FOREVER A LORD, coming soon
from Delilah Marvelle and HQN Books.

AUTHOR'S NOTE

THE TRUTH TELLER was a real newspaper with a very unique history. On April 2, 1825, *The Truth Teller* debuted with its first printing. It was published every Saturday out of Office No. 95 Maiden-Lane. It was New York City's first Irish-Catholic paper and was created by a gentleman whose motto was Truth Is Powerful and Will Prevail. With a motto and a message like that, I knew I *had* to dig in and find a story to match its passion and flavor.

As I continued to research the paper's history, I was fortunate enough to dig up the actual paper from the archives of the New York City Library. Reading through years' and years' worth of eye-squinting pages of microfiche, I was astounded by its level of intelligence and its political and social stances pertaining to New York City, Ireland and England. It was breathtaking to actually see history through the eyes of a real New Yorker back in the day and I tried to infuse that into the pages of my book. A very unique aspect of *The Truth Teller* was that it also featured notices pertaining to missing people. Sections upon sections were dedicated to it, whispering of stories that the newspaper and its owner thought important.

Scanning through those pages revealed a rich history. Everything was in between those pages, from prices of food to cigars (yes, those nine-cent cigars the mayor smoked) and everything in between. It helped me piece together real information that applied to the world of my characters living in New York City back in 1830.

Though I stretched and rearranged who owned the actual newspaper (because Matthew and his father most certainly didn't, as they are fictitious characters), the quotes at the beginning of each chapter were snagged straight out of the paper itself. There is a character and a flavor that spoke to me that I wanted to share. Those words would have otherwise been buried in history, since the only known copies of *The Truth Teller* are sitting in the archives of the New York City Library. Its last printing, before the newspaper folded, was in May 26, 1855.

I wanted to add that the history pertaining to Sing Sing Prison is real. From the warden's name to the lashings and the code of silence. The only thing that wouldn't have been allowed is actual visitors. I was astounded to discover that striped uniforms were, in fact, being used back in 1830. For some reason, I always thought that was a 1900s thing. Sadly, prisoners died from severe lashings on a regular basis, and there were other far more gruesome forms of punishment in place, as well. Murderers and mere pickpockets were treated the same. Without anyone watching over the guards, I imagine it was more gruesome than what I had touched on.

For those of you who are curious to know where certain New York City streets have disappeared to, the original streets that made up the Five Points itself back in the 1800s were: Mulberry, Anthony, Orange, Cross and Little Water. Today Orange Street is known as Baxter Street, Anthony Street is Worth Street and Cross Street is Park Street. Little Water no longer exists and Mulberry is the only street that remains from the original Five Points. All the places and streets mentioned in this book, including The Diving Bell, existed.

As you might have guessed, I went through countless newspapers, photos, paintings, books, as well as dozens of maps portraying New York City between the years of 1800–1833. It was the closest I was ever going to get to touching New York City back in the day and I hope you felt like you touched it, too.

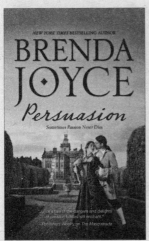

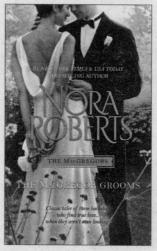

REQUEST YOUR FREE BOOKS!

2 FREE NOVELS
FROM THE ROMANCE COLLECTION
PLUS 2 FREE GIFTS!

YES! Please send me 2 FREE novels from the Romance Collection and my 2 FREE gifts (gifts are worth about $10). After receiving them, if I don't wish to receive any more books, I can return the shipping statement marked "cancel." If I don't cancel, I will receive 4 brand-new novels every month and be billed just $5.99 per book in the U.S. or $6.49 per book in Canada. That's a saving of at least 25% off the cover price. It's quite a bargain! Shipping and handling is just 50¢ per book in the U.S. and 75¢ per book in Canada.* I understand that accepting the 2 free books and gifts places me under no obligation to buy anything. I can always return a shipment and cancel at any time. Even if I never buy another book, the two free books and gifts are mine to keep forever.

194/394 MDN FELQ

Name _____
(PLEASE PRINT)

Address _____ Apt. # _____

City _____ State/Prov. _____ Zip/Postal Code _____

Signature (if under 18, a parent or guardian must sign) _____

Mail to the **Reader Service:**
IN U.S.A.: P.O. Box 1867, Buffalo, NY 14240-1867
IN CANADA: P.O. Box 609, Fort Erie, Ontario L2A 5X3

Not valid for current subscribers to the Romance Collection
or the Romance/Suspense Collection.

Want to try two free books from another line?
Call 1-800-873-8635 or visit www.ReaderService.com.

* Terms and prices subject to change without notice. Prices do not include applicable taxes. Sales tax applicable in N.Y. Canadian residents will be charged applicable taxes. Offer not valid in Quebec. This offer is limited to one order per household. All orders subject to credit approval. Credit or debit balances in a customer's account(s) may be offset by any other outstanding balance owed by or to the customer. Please allow 4 to 6 weeks for delivery. Offer available while quantities last.

Your Privacy—The Reader Service is committed to protecting your privacy. Our Privacy Policy is available online at www.ReaderService.com or upon request from the Reader Service.

We make a portion of our mailing list available to reputable third parties that offer products we believe may interest you. If you prefer that we not exchange your name with third parties, or if you wish to clarify or modify your communication preferences, please visit us at www.ReaderService.com/consumerchoice or write to us at Reader Service Preference Service, P.O. Box 9062, Buffalo, NY 14269. Include your complete name and address.

ROM11

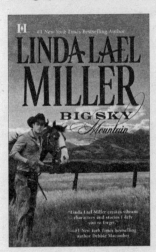

DELILAH MARVELLE

77636 FOREVER AND A DAY	___ $7.99 U.S.	___ $9.99 CAN.
77554 THE PERFECT SCANDAL	___ $7.99 U.S.	___ $9.99 CAN.
77545 ONCE UPON A SCANDAL	___ $7.99 U.S.	___ $9.99 CAN.
77537 PRELUDE TO A SCANDAL	___ $7.99 U.S.	___ $9.99 CAN.

(limited quantities available)

TOTAL AMOUNT	$ _____
POSTAGE & HANDLING	$ _____
($1.00 FOR 1 BOOK, 50¢ for each additional)	
APPLICABLE TAXES*	$ _____
TOTAL PAYABLE	$ _____

(check or money order—please do not send cash)

To order, complete this form and send it, along with a check or money order for the total above, payable to HQN Books, to: **In the U.S.:** 3010 Walden Avenue, P.O. Box 9077, Buffalo, NY 14269-9077; **In Canada:** P.O. Box 636, Fort Erie, Ontario, L2A 5X3.

Name: _____

Address: _____ City: _____

State/Prov.: _____ Zip/Postal Code: _____

Account Number (if applicable): _____

075 CSAS

*New York residents remit applicable sales taxes.
*Canadian residents remit applicable GST and provincial taxes.

HARLEQUIN® HQN™
™www.Harlequin.com

PHDM0812BL